*A real lady will
never kiss and tell...*

Sunrise
with a
Notorious
Lord

A LORDS OF VICE
NOVEL

Alexandra Hawkins

USA Today bestselling author of *After Dark with a Scoundrel*

Don't miss these scandalous
Lords of Vice novels by
ALEXANDRA HAWKINS

AFTER DARK WITH A SCOUNDREL

ALL NIGHT WITH A ROGUE

TILL DAWN WITH THE DEVIL

Available from St. Martin's Paperbacks

SheLovesHotReads.com
Original Stories, Interviews,
Exclusive Content,
and Much More!

"Perfect explosion of emotional fireworks blasted off the pages and set the rest of the tone for the book."
—*Romantic Crush Junkies* (4.5 quills)

"Poignant, sweetly romantic, and sexy as can be."
—*Reader to Reader*

Till Dawn with the Devil
"*Till Dawn with the Devil*'s romance is first-rate with unusual characters and an underlying mystery that will intrigue readers." —Robin Lee, *Romance Reviews Today*

"A terrific second book in this series. I had it read in a day and then bemoaned the fact it was over."
—*The Good, The Bad, and The Unread* (A+)

"You will devour every sexy and intriguing morsel of this divine read." —*Romantic Crush Junkies* (4 stars)

"Hawkins cements her reputation for bringing compelling, unique, and lush romances to fans eager for fresh storytelling." —*Romantic Times BOOKreviews* (4 stars)

"Delightful and enjoyed every delicious minute of the book." —*Single Titles* (5 stars)

"You will devour every sexy and intriguing morsel of this divine read." —*Romantic Crush Junkies* (4½ quills)

"An absolutely tantalizing read!"
—*Huntress Reviews* (5 stars)

"Her characters are vibrant, sincere, and will surely steal your heart." —*The Romance Dish* (4½ stars)

"Alexandra Hawkins is making a splash in historical romance and fans of the genre who haven't read the Lords of Vice series should sit up and take notice."
—*The Season*

"Promises an intoxicating journey, and delivers with an exciting series of twists and turns that leave the reader disoriented and begging for more." —*Fresh Fiction*

"Alexandra Hawkins did a splendid job of weaving believable characters, palpable attraction, and a soundly satisfying plotline that will leave you *panting* for more!" —*Not Another Romance Blog* (5 red roses)

All Night with a Rogue
"Sizzling, smart, and sophisticated."
—*New York Times* bestselling author Gaelen Foley

"Wickedly sensual and entertaining! Alexandra Hawkins is an exceptional talent."
—*New York Times* bestselling author Lorraine Heath

"A romantic and erotic tale of social intrigue vs. steadfast hearts. This first story in the Lords of Vice series is hot enough to curl your toes!"
—*New York Times* bestselling author Celeste Bradley

"Alexandra Hawkins does the Regency era as no other!"
—*Huntress Book Reviews* (4 stars)

St. Martin's Paperbacks Titles by

Alexandra Hawkins

After Dark with a Scoundrel

All Night with a Rogue

Till Dawn with the Devil

Sunrise
with a
Notorious
Lord

Alexandra Hawkins

St. Martin's Paperbacks

This is a work of fiction. All of the characters, organizations, and events portrayed in this novel are either products of the author's imagination or are used fictitiously.

SUNRISE WITH A NOTORIOUS LORD

Copyright © 2012 by Alexandra Hawkins.

All rights reserved.

For information address St. Martin's Press, 175 Fifth Avenue, New York, NY 10010.

ISBN: 978-1-250-00136-8

Printed in the United States of America

St. Martin's Paperbacks edition / January 2012

St. Martin's Paperbacks are published by St. Martin's Press, 175 Fifth Avenue, New York, NY 10010.

10 9 8 7 6 5 4 3 2 1

Vices are often habits rather than passions.
–Antoine de Rivarol

Chapter One

January 28, 1823

"Never has God created a more devious creature," Christopher Avery Courtland, Earl of Vanewright, declared as he walked the vale of Blackmoor one early morning in January with his friends, the Marquess of Sainthill and the Duke of Huntsley, as they hunted hare. Cold and hungry, the earl, who was often acknowledged by the abbreviated version of his title, wished they had taken their horses on the trail hunt.

Squinting at the pack of baying harriers on the horizon, the duke spared a glance at Vane. "What are you muttering on about?"

Huntsley, or simply Hunter to his friends, was aptly named. He excelled at sports whether they involved pursuing game on the frost-crusted low-lying meadow or more challenging quarry, the ladies of the *ton*. Perhaps it was because his days as a free man were numbered. Though he rarely spoke of it unless he was deeply in his cups, his wily grandmother had betrothed her twelve-year-old grandson to a young girl barely out of her swaddling clothes to increase the family's landholdings.

Now that his own mother, the Marchioness of Netherley, had decided it was time for her surviving son to marry, Vane had nothing but sympathy for his friend.

Simon Wyndham Jefferes, Marquess of Sainthill, or Saint, on the other hand, did not possess the temperament or patience that his nickname implied. Having severed his ties to his family in his youth, the twenty-nine-year-old marquess lived only for himself. It was an enviable position, to be certain, when Vane could not seem to prevent his own family from meddling in his life.

"Likely his new mistress," Saint said, the butt of his double-barreled gun nestled in the crook of his arm.

"No, have you not been paying attention for the past hour? I am speaking of my mother," Vane said, scowling at Saint. "She is determined to ruin my stay in London this season. I feel it like a damp chill in my bones."

Hunter looked askance at Saint. "Care to wager on it?"

Saint's gaze sharpened with interest. "Will a hundred pounds suffice?"

"Two hundred," Hunter countered.

Irritated—it was on the tip of his tongue to increase the wager to five hundred pounds—Vane kicked Saint in the calf, causing him to stumble. Hunter, regrettably, was too far away to punch. "Have some respect, gents! This is my cursed future both of you are discussing with such disrespect. Not that either one of you seems to care. If my mother gets her way, I shall be wed by summer."

Hunter dismissed Vane's accusation with a casual wave of his hand. "Your charming seventy-two-year-old mother has been determined to see you leg-shackled for the past two years. Nothing has come of it."

"You have deftly avoided all her elegant snares," Saint pointed out. "You will best your dear mother again." To Hunter, he added, "And I am willing to wager three hundred pounds on our dear friend's victory."

Hunter's brows came together as he mulled over Saint's terms. "A reckless wager, to be certain. However, I'll accept." He sent Vane an apologetic look. "No disrespect to you, of course."

"Of course." Vane took no offense at the wager. The Lords of Vice—as he and his six friends had been dubbed by the *ton*—thrived on outrageous bets and impossible odds.

Hunter must have been feeling slightly guilty for not siding with his friend. His gait slowed as he added, "Cynical as I may be of Lady Netherley's triumph, it would be rude not to offer the dear woman my support."

Vane gave the two men a morose glance. "Both of you are underestimating my mother. Two failed seasons in London have made her desperate. As far as she is concerned, I am as unmarriageable as a toothless spinster without a penny to her name."

Hunter and Saint chuckled at Vane's absurd comparison.

"Never yield to a woman, my friend," Hunter advised. "It's an indisputable fact that they are ruthless if they believe they have the upper hand."

Chapter Two

"Delia!"

Thoroughly exasperated at her sister's ability to disappear at a moment's notice, Isabel Thorne stood stiffly at the bottom of the narrow staircase as she awaited a response.

A lady never has to raise her voice to oversee the household.

Isabel mentally winced as one of her mother's pithy little sayings grated on her already frayed nerves. Had Sybil not retired early to her bedchamber to sleep off the tea she laced liberally with laudanum and brandy every afternoon, Isabel was certain she would have been scolded for her rudeness.

She forced a smile into place when their housekeeper's face appeared over the polished wooden balustrade on the second landing. "I have looked high and low, Miss Thorne. There is just no sign of her."

"Thank you, Mrs. Dalman. You may return to your duties," Isabel said, her eyes narrowing as she contemplated where her sister might have wandered in an attempt to avoid the chores given to her. "Delia, you cannot keep running off when it pleases you. This household is showing signs of neglect, and we cannot afford to hire more servants."

Of course no one was listening to Isabel's quiet complaints.

With a sigh escaping her lips, she pivoted and strode toward the back of the house. There was the informal parlor to check, and the kitchen. Delia might have even escaped the house to flirt with one of the many gentlemen who seemed to show up at all hours of the day to court her.

Even though Delia accepted their small tokens of esteem and fluttered about prettily under their fervent regard, Isabel could have told all of them that they were wasting their time. Much like their mother, Delia had a high opinion of herself. As the granddaughter of Viscount Botly, her sister thought she could do better than a hardworking farmer or tradesman when it came to finding a husband.

Delia was certainly beautiful enough to aspire higher.

"Isabel," Mrs. Willow said, stepping out from the study. "There you are. I was just about to go upstairs and check on your mother."

The thirty-nine-year-old woman was a blessing. Widowed nine years earlier, she was a close friend of the Thorne family. When Isabel had difficulties handling her mother's bouts of melancholy, Mrs. Willow had always been on hand to assist the young girls.

Isabel smoothed an errant tendril of hair back into

place. "There is no need. Sybil retired with her tea. With luck, she will sleep the entire afternoon. Have you seen Delia? A thousand things need to be done, so naturally my sister has gone into hiding."

"Have patience, Isabel," the older woman instructed. "Delia is young. She will find a good man, marry him, and give up her flighty ways."

She did not share Mrs. Willow's faith in Delia. Her sister's volatile moods and vanity reminded her too much of their mother. Sybil was a forty-three-year-old widow with two grown daughters and a dwindling annual income. If her responsibilities had not curbed her reckless nature, what hope did Delia have?

"I almost forgot." Mrs. Willow offered the letter in her hand to Isabel. "This arrived for you. I was going to put it on your father's desk, but I was worried it might get overlooked."

Puzzled that anyone would be writing her, Isabel accepted the letter with a slight frown. "I wonder who . . . why, it is from Lady Netherley!"

It was toward the end of summer that Isabel and Delia had had the pleasure of being introduced to the elderly Marchioness of Netherley. Distinguished visitors such as the marchioness were rare in Cotersage, so word quickly spread throughout the tiny village that Mrs. Whitechurch's cousin was spending the fortnight at her house.

When her mother had learned of the noblewoman's visit, she'd naturally insisted that the three of them call on their good neighbor. Sybil had argued that Lady Netherley would be insulted if she was not properly introduced to Viscount Botly's granddaughters. She was quite happy to ignore the unpleasant detail that their grandfather had disowned his only daughter for marrying a commoner. As far as he was concerned, his granddaughters did not exist.

It also had not boded well that their initial visit with their neighbor and Lady Netherley had been an appalling disaster. Agitated and most likely drunk, their mother had managed to insult Mrs. Whitechurch within minutes of their arrival. The conversation had been stilted and the visit blessedly brief. On the drive home, Sybil had railed at the injustice of it all. She told her daughters that their neighbor was envious of their beauty so she had deliberately portrayed the Thorne women in the worst light to the visiting marchioness.

Needless to say, Isabel was quite surprised when Mrs. Willow approached her days later with an invitation from Mrs. Whitechurch for a second visit. The good woman had claimed that Lady Netherley had enjoyed meeting her and Delia. It was also politely suggested that their mother should refrain from joining her daughters. When Sybil learned of the invitation, she reacted in her typical manner by throwing a tantrum and sulking. However, even she could not deny that a connection to Lady Netherley could open doors for her unmarried daughters. She did not try to discourage their visits.

During the fortnight of the marchioness's stay at Cotersage, she and Delia called on the Whitechurch residence five times.

"Well, girl, are you going to just stand there woolgathering or are you going to open the letter?" Mrs. Willow teased.

Isabel smiled mischievously, sensing that Mrs. Willow was just as curious as she about the contents of the missive. "Later. First, I must find Delia. She will want to hear what Lady Netherley has to say, too."

Knowing it was useless to press Isabel further, the older woman hugged her. "Off with you then. You might want to try the back of the house near the gardens. I've caught Delia fluttering about the hedges with the rest of the butterflies."

Isabel was still smiling as she passed through the kitchen, sparing a moment to chat with the cook about their dinner before she stepped outdoors.

It was a brisk sunny day. Wishing she had thought to collect a shawl, Isabel wrapped her arms around her chest and started for the hedges Mrs. Willow had mentioned. There were a dozen places Delia could have picked to avoid her household chores, and if Isabel had her way, she intended to add a few more tasks to her sister's list as punishment.

Before Isabel had walked halfway across the weed-choked yard, she heard a soft giggle coming from one of the outbuildings. Changing directions, she marched over to the building, noting absently that it needed a new coat of paint. As she opened her mouth and prepared to blister Delia's ears for her laziness, Isabel skidded to a halt at the sight of her sister in the arms of Mr. Ruddel.

Her Mr. Ruddel.

Well, not hers exactly, she silently amended. Isabel considered the thirty-one-year-old gentleman a good friend. A respectable three inches taller than her own willowy five-foot-seven-inch stature, the handsome, softly spoken blond stranger had come into her life quite by chance eighteen months earlier when a mutual friend brought about an introduction because of their shared interests.

Like her father, Mr. Ruddel was an inventor and natural philosopher. Over the course of their acquaintance, she had sought his opinion on numerous occasions as she quietly sold off her father's papers to keep the creditors at bay. Mr. Ruddel had offered her friendship, and had seemed to be on the verge of offering more if his somewhat chaste kisses had been any indication.

There was nothing chaste about the kiss he was sharing with her sister.

Isabel's right brow arched as the gentleman, overwhelmed with passion, cupped Delia's backside in his hands.

Oh, for heaven's sake, enough is enough!

"Pardon me," she said, despising the waspish quality in her voice. "I was not aware that we had a guest, sister."

Mr. Ruddel practically shoved Delia away from him. Isabel might have laughed if her throat hadn't constricted with unexpected anguish.

"Oh, my, *Isabel!*" he said, taking out a folded handkerchief and dabbing the wetness from his mouth. Mr. Ruddel looked profoundly embarrassed to have been caught in a torrid embrace. "I can explain."

Delia, on the other hand, was staring at Isabel with smug satisfaction on her beautiful face. Her sister had known that Isabel was rather fond of Mr. Ruddel. It was as if Delia had deliberately set out to ruin her happiness.

"That will not be necessary," she said coldly. "Delia, Mrs. Dalman is waiting for you indoors. She will give you a list of tasks."

Her sister's lower lip jutted out mutinously. "But I do not want—"

"Your wants are of little concern, Delia. Go. Now!"

It was a silent battle of wills as the two sisters locked gazes. Isabel was not a person who condoned violence, but if Delia thought to defy her, she would not be accountable for her actions.

Mr. Ruddel took a wary step toward her. "Isabel . . . Delia . . . please, I feel responsible for this."

"You are, sir," Isabel snapped, leaving the stunned man sputtering in wordless outrage. "However, not in the manner in which you believe. If you wish to make amends, you may do so by taking your leave."

From the corner of her eye, she observed that the man had sent Delia a beseeching look. She could have told him that her sister only looked after her own interests.

"Perhaps you are right, my dear," he said, when Delia remained silent. "I will call on you another day."

"Do not rush back on my account, sir," Isabel said in chilling tones. "I have neglected my work of late and cannot promise to be home."

To you.

Mr. Ruddel hastily bowed, and backed away. "I shall return when cooler heads prevail. Good day, ladies."

Delia broke eye contract, and bent over to pick up a stick. Both women watched Mr. Ruddel's harried stride as he disappeared around the corner of the cottage. "You frightened poor Malcolm. What do you intend to do if he calls on us again—wave our father's old pistol under his nose to protect my honor?" she teased.

Isabel blinked, fighting back the sting of tears now that Mr. Ruddel was gone. She would not cry in front of Delia. "You have no honor, sister," she said bluntly, causing her sister to gasp. "And that will be your downfall. Now be useful and go help Mrs. Dalman."

"You are just being hateful because you are jealous that Malcolm would rather kiss me than you!" Delia cried before she dashed off toward the house.

With unshed tears blinding her, Isabel ran in the opposite direction. She kept running until the sharp pain in her side caused her to stop near an unused shed. Leaning against the wall, Isabel finally allowed her tears to fall.

Oh, she knew she was making a fool of herself over Mr. Ruddel. He had just been so helpful and kind and she had been so lonely. Delia was right. Isabel had been hateful to her because she *had* been jealous. And why not? Everyone paid attention to Delia while Isabel seemed to blend into the wallpaper. She was considered the good daughter, the responsible one.

For once in her life, she would not mind being the one who tossed caution in the wind. Unfortunately, recklessness did not pay the creditors or keep the household running.

Isabel wallowed in self-pity for several minutes, an indulgence she rarely afforded herself. It wasn't until she started to retrieve her handkerchief that she recalled Lady Netherley's letter. Using the back of her hand to wipe away her tears, Isabel took a fortifying breath and broke the wax seal on the letter.

"Dear Miss Thorne," she read aloud. "I trust my letter finds you in good spirits. I have thought of you and your sister often these passing months." Her gaze skimmed over the flattery and usual pleasantries about health and weather. Then Lady Netherley got down to business. "I have a proposition for you, Miss Thorne, and I do not make this offer lightly since this is a matter of utmost importance to me. I hope I can trust you to be discreet. This involves my son and your sister, Delia . . ."

In disbelief, Isabel read the marchioness's letter three times before she could put it down. She carefully folded the paper and tucked it into the top portion of her bodice. Although she was chilled to the bone, she crossed her arms and stared off into the distance at the apple orchard as she contemplated Lady Netherley's outrageous invitation.

Was she daring enough to accept?

Chapter Three

May 3, 1823, London

"Which do you prefer?"

With a faint smile on his lips, Vane admired the half-naked backside of his current mistress as the seamstress held a swath of yellow fabric under her chin. The yellow print was as charmingly cheerful as Miss Bridget Corsar, but the color did not complement her reddish orange tresses, which seemed to defy any attempts to tame them.

Miss Bridget Corsar was an agreeable mistress.

It was a real pity that he intended to give her up this afternoon.

Vane opened his mouth to offer his opinion on the yellow print.

"Oh, why am I asking *you*?" she said, admiring her reflection in the mirror. "If you had your way, I would greet you wearing only a sheet."

The narrow-faced seamstress glanced sharply at him.

Vane straightened as her somber dark gaze silently took his measure and seemed intrigued by what she saw. Clearing his throat, he resisted the urge to cover himself as the woman's gaze slid to the front of his trousers. God's blood, the woman was old enough to be his mother, he thought.

Bridget's laughter filled the tiny private dressing room. "So pleasing to the eye, is he not?" she asked the seamstress as she looked over her left shoulder to admire her lover.

Her prize. The calculation in her pretty eyes was one of a dozen reasons why he had to get rid of her. He just prayed the small fortune he intended to spend on her new wardrobe would appease her womanly pride after his abrupt dismissal.

Blissfully ignorant of Vane's plans for their afternoon, she confided to the seamstress, "And you should see him without his fine clothes—"

"Bridget, enough." A bold and sensual creature, Vane would not have been astonished if Bridget asked him to undress for the other woman. He gave the seamstress an apologetic smile. "You are embarrassing Mrs.—"

What the devil was the woman's name?

"Mrs. Gilbert, milord," the seamstress hastily interjected. "And there is no need to worry about upsetting me. I have worked as a seamstress for thirty-eight years and have witnessed all manner of worldly things." She nodded at Vane before her attention returned to Bridget, who stood in front of the mirror dressed only in her chemise and stays. "Pardon me for saying so, Miss Corsar. As pretty as this print is, it is not for you. Your coloring is all wrong for it."

Bridget did not protest as Mrs. Gilbert gently tugged and gathered up the fabric in her arms. With her gaze locked on Vane's face, there was mischief and hunger in his mistress's vibrant blue eyes. He was well acquainted with that particular look. His body warmed in anticipation of the energetic and satisfying afternoon she was promising with her expression.

It was a shame he was giving her up. He crossed the room, his intent gaze fixed on his willing quarry.

Slightly overwhelmed by the undisguised lust she glimpsed in the couple's faces, Mrs. Gilbert hugged the yards of yellow cloth to her chest. "I-I have several unfinished dresses. Perhaps Miss Corsar would like to view them."

She swiftly headed for the closed curtain, sparing man and woman one final glance. "Much later," she muttered, before she parted the cloth partition and disappeared through the narrow opening.

"No."

Delia chased after Isabel as she stepped across the threshold of one of the many establishments they had patronized this afternoon. Both ladies nodded to gentlemen who paused to hold the door for them. "Can we not even discuss it?"

"There is little point."

"Oh, you are being unreasonable."

"No, Delia, I am being practical. Someone has to be."

"But Lady Netherley—"

Isabel gave Delia a quelling look. "Hush! Until I have the opportunity to speak with the marchioness, I think it prudent that we refrain from mentioning our connection to her."

"Why would Lady Neth"—Delia halted at Isabel's

thunderous expression—"our dear friend worry over such matters when she is the reason why we are in town at all?"

"It is complicated."

Isabel frowned as she thought about the desperation that had driven her to accept Lady Netherley's generous offer. Of the sacrifices she had made to raise the funds needed for the journey, and the arrangements she had made with Mrs. Willow to look after their mother. Isabel's feelings were still raw from the horrid arguments she and her mother had had about the trip to London. Although her mother was unaware of Lady Netherley's invitation, the notion of escaping Cotersage for London was too appealing to the older woman. Isabel ordered Mrs. Willow to use any means available to keep Mrs. Thorne from following her daughters, including tying her to the bed!

"It would be unwise for us to presume our good friend's invitation to join her in London was anything more than civility."

Now it was Delia's turn to frown. "It was more than civility and you know it. One day, I overheard you and Mrs. Willow debating on how the funds should be spent."

"I have told you more than once that listening at closed doors is an improper pastime for a lady."

"Well, it is your fault. You never tell me anything!"

"And why should I bother when you have no patience to listen." *Or help me,* Isabel added silently. She gestured blindly at the table they had approached. "What is your opinion?"

"My opinion?" Delia echoed in disbelief. "Now you

want my opinion. Well, I will tell you exactly what I think—"

Both Isabel and her sister started at the low masculine growl that emanated from behind them. In unison, the women turned their heads and stared at the closed curtain.

"Oh, you wicked man!" a feminine voice murmured. A few seconds later, her peal of sensual laughter caused most of the patrons in the store to pause and glance curiously in the direction of the room.

"Care to speculate on the mischief being carried out in that private room?" Delia whispered, her voice tight with suppressed laughter.

"No, I do not," Isabel said crisply. She took her sister by the elbow and steered her away from the curtain. "And neither should you. Come along, Delia. We have our own business to attend to."

Isabel turned her back on the closed curtain, dismissing the unknown couple to concentrate on her tasks.

It appeared Bridget had no intention of waiting for a more discreet setting. With his arms full of a half-naked woman, Vane's gaze shifted from the plump mounds of Bridget's breasts to the closed curtain. It was a pity he was giving up this affectionate woman, because discretion was something he rarely practiced.

"Bridget, my pretty girl," he drawled, groaning when her clever hand gave his half-aroused cock—thankfully still tucked in his unbuttoned trousers—a playful squeeze. "Mrs. Gilbert should be returning soon and I, for one, do not relish her discovering me bare-arsed."

She bit his earlobe in retaliation when Vane brushed away her hands and attempted to fasten his trousers. "I do not recall you being so shy at Lady S—"

"Enough," he ordered, his unruly body not needing any encouragement. Elderly Lady Steele would have been outraged had she learned of the liberties he and Bridget had engaged in upon her chaste bed, which was precisely the reason why they had chosen her bed-chamber for their tryst. Vane clasped her by the shoulders and spun her around to face the mirror. "Now behave yourself and go tidy your hair."

The impossible task should keep his soon-to-be-former mistress occupied until the seamstress's return.

Bridget's eyes narrowed as she watched him tuck in his shirt. "You wouldn't dare."

Momentarily distracted by the disheveled state of his clothing, he murmured, "Dare what, my dear?"

Bridget pivoted and planted her fists on her hips. "You are breaking with me." Her fingers splayed open as she gestured at their sparse surroundings. "Here . . . in a dressmaker's shop of all places!"

Vane took a step backward. "A few minutes ago, you thought it was a grand place to fondle my cock."

She tossed her head back and sneered at him. "Bastard!"

"Can you insult me later when we have the luxury of privacy?" Vane pleaded, sending a meaningful glance at the curtain. "Besides, I had no intention of breaking with you at the dressmaker's. What sort of gent do you think I am?"

His question gave her pause. It was fortunate since

Bridget was eyeing the chair with enthusiasm. Her lower lip trembled. "Then, this new wardrobe is not my congé?"

Vane hesitated, feeling like he was about to walk into a trap of his own making. He never enjoyed breaking with a mistress. The final encounters tended to be emotional and occasionally violent. His friend Frost was aptly named, since he was never troubled by a messy parting. Saint could also be rather cold-blooded when it came to dismissing lovers. Vane wished he weren't so damn tenderhearted. It always got him in trouble.

"Bridget," he began, suddenly feeling older than his eight-and-twenty years. If he told her the true reason why he was giving her up, the woman before him would likely want to spill his blood.

As the realization that she was indeed being discarded sank in, her lovely blue eyes hardened. "Very well." While Vane was not the first protector to abandon her, she still had her pride to assuage. It was rather petty of her, but she was prepared to make Vane suffer. "You may wait beyond the curtain while Mrs. Gilbert attends me."

Vane practically jumped out of his skin when he became aware that the seamstress was standing behind him. "Mrs. Gilbert, I do beg your pardon." He wondered how much of their discussion had been overheard.

"My pardon isn't the one you'll be needing, milord," the older woman muttered, stepping around him. "I think you will find these colors more to your liking, miss."

"Thank you, Mrs. Gilbert," Bridget said, greeting the unfinished dresses with false enthusiasm. Without glancing at Vane, she said, "You may leave us, Lord Vanewright."

Although this had been his intention all along, Vane felt like a cowardly worm. "Bridget, be reasonable."

"The only thing I require is your assurance that you will pay the dressmaker's bill," Bridget said coldly, her tone implying that she expected him to ignore it.

"Careful, Miss Corsar," Vane said, his countenance darkening with indignation. "Lest others might think you are impugning my honor."

"I'll leave that to you, Lord Vanewright." Bridget's hand shook with fury and her daring as she caressed the green cloth folded over the seamstress's arm. A few malicious rumors about her poor health or lack of inventiveness in the bedchamber, and Vane could potentially ruin her chances of securing a new protector. Still, she could not seem to control her tongue. "Pray leave us, my lord. Find your amusements elsewhere."

Bridget's parting insult might have been well deserved, but it still pricked his temper. "I shall, indeed, Miss Corsar. Amiable companions are as plentiful as pins in a dressmaker's shop. I wager I will not have to wander far to find one."

Chapter Four

Vane's parting words to Bridget had been spoken in anger.

Vane had no intention of securing another mistress this season.

With his mother continuously harping that he should cease his frivolous dalliances and find a genteel lady to take as his wife, it might bode well to give up females while his family resided in London.

Vane could almost hear his friends' snorts of disbelief and unabashed laughter at such a ridiculous notion. Each season, there was always a pretty lady or two who caught his eye. His liaisons were casual, flirtatious, and blessedly short-lived. When one of his lovers began hinting about marriage or arrangements that required solicitors and annual annuities, the back of his neck began to itch, an irksome sign that it was time to break with the lady.

Absently Vane slid his hand to the nape of his neck and scratched just below his hairline, convinced the unpleasant parting with the vivacious Bridget Corsar had been inevitable.

"No, not that one," a crisp authoritative feminine voice instructed, distracting Vane from his gloomy thoughts. "Let us take a closer look at the blue."

Vane grinned. How fortuitous that attractive females were indeed as plentiful as pins in a dressmaker's shop!

Intrigued, he abandoned his post near the curtain and strolled to one of the tables. To his right, two beautiful golden-haired Venuses were admiring the evening dress a female shop clerk had displayed on a bare wooden table.

"Too staid," the taller of the twosome declared. "The bodice is clearly designed for a mature lady. Isabel, perhaps you might want to consider this dress for yourself?"

Turning away, Vane masked his soft laugh by coughing into his hand. The younger one, and most likely the other woman's sister, had unsheathed her sharp claws. He circled around the table piled with bolts of colorful cloth so he could discreetly observe the battle of wills.

"Delia, since this is our first visit to London, I recommend prudence for our introduction into polite society. After all, do you want to be mistaken for a demirep?"

As Vane caressed the satin cloth on the table, he was unable to conceal his amusement. Even if she had been dressed provocatively, no one would have mistaken Isabel for a courtesan. Oh, she certainly caught a man's eye with a stature that rivaled her taller younger sister. Such long limbs were meant to be wrapped around a man's hips. Preferably his. Vane shook his head at the unbidden thought. It was a damn pity he was giving up his wild ways this season.

From his limited view, only Isabel's profile was visible, with most of her golden hair tucked under her simple bonnet. Her face seemed pleasing enough. It was not the lack of adornment that dispelled the suggestion that she could be in the market for a new protector. No, it was her mannerisms and speech, which marked her as a lady. Her no-nonsense approach with her sister reminded Vane of his older sister, Susan.

The younger woman, he mused silently, had the look and temperament of a courtesan. Unlike her older sister, Delia dressed to catch a man's gaze and wanted him to admire her sleek body. Her hair, a lighter hue than her sister's, had been curled into dozens of ringlets. Vane suspected if he approached the ladies and invited them to join him for pastries at Gunter's, Delia would accept without thinking of the risks to her reputation while Isabel might slap his face for his boldness.

For a gentleman who was too accustomed to willing females, getting slapped by the intriguing Isabel held more appeal. Unwittingly, she was presenting him with a challenge.

As Vane silently mulled over his tactical approach, the shop clerk offered another unfinished dress for the ladies' inspection.

"Oh, Isabel." Delia cooed as the vibrant poppy-colored evening dress was laid over the insipid blue both ladies had rejected. "I adore the lace and wadded hem," she said, stroking the stomacher made up of double rows of gold lace. "We *must* purchase it."

Vane watched as Isabel nibbled her lower lip. Unlike her sister, she did not reach out to touch the elegant evening dress, but he saw the flicker of yearning in her expression.

"How much?" Isabel murmured, glancing about to make certain no one had heard her vulgar question.

"Really, Isabel," Delia huffed. "Mama would be disappointed to hear you speak like a tradesman."

Isabel held up her hand and silenced her sister's tirade.

Quite unexpectedly, she looked away from the table and her gaze locked with his. Although he did not visibly react, he felt the impact of the connection as if the lady had indeed slapped him. There was no coyness or surprise in Isabel's frank perusal. It was as if she had been aware of his presence all along.

Before he could collect his thoughts, she severed the invisible current of energy between them by abruptly shifting her attention to the shop clerk as the woman quietly responded to Isabel's query.

"May I have a private word with my sister?"

The woman nodded and quickly withdrew. She was probably relieved that she would not be drawn into the simmering argument between the two ladies.

Delia touched the poppy-colored skirt in a possessive fashion. "We should purchase the dress."

"Delia." Isabel sighed. "We could purchase two evening dresses for the price of this one."

"Do not try to tell me that you do not covet it," her sister said, seizing Isabel by the wrist and encouraging her to feel the quality of the cloth. "Does it not feel glorious? A lady would look like a queen in such a dress."

Isabel's frown softened into something akin to wistfulness as her fingers traced the gold lace patterns at the bottom of the skirt. In that moment, Vane decided that he was going to buy her the dress. Her sister was correct. Isabel would look as regal as any queen if she entered a ballroom wearing the poppy-and-gold evening dress.

The regret in her eyes did not prevent Isabel from shaking her head. "To own such a dress . . . it is a grand dream, but it isn't practical. Not when we have other expenses."

Vane had heard enough. He had entered the dressmaker's shop with the intention of purchasing a new wardrobe for his former mistress to ease his guilt over his unwarranted dismissal. One more dress would not beggar him. As the Earl of Vanewright, he had plenty of wealth at his disposal. He was also the Marquess of Netherley's heir. To gain their favor, he would have happily purchased Isabel and her sister a dozen dresses.

Although he was still pondering the many virtues of abstaining from the pleasures of the flesh this season, there was no harm in a casual flirtation with the pretty sisters. A smile from the too serious Isabel would be worth the cost of the dress. He moved away from the table and took a step toward the quietly quarreling women.

From his left, a lanky youth bumped into him.

Vane grunted softly as the corner of the table dug into his hip. To balance himself, he caught the lad by the arm.

"Begging yer pardon, milord," the youth mumbled, and tugged on his cap. He stepped out of reach and gave Vane a self-deprecating grin. "Clumsy as a three-legged lamb, I am."

The young man had taken three steps when Vane realized the snuffbox he kept in the inner pocket of his waistcoat was missing. He groaned, annoyed at himself for being so careless. "You!" He pointed an accusing finger at the retreating youth. "Give me back my property!"

His accusation caught the attention of everyone in the shop, including the young pickpocket who had halted at Vane's booming command. The thought of being transported or hanged for his theft prompted the lad into action. He jumped over the table in his path, shoving bolts of cloth and frippery to the floor.

Several ladies cried in surprise and dismay as Vane dashed after his nimble quarry. Though he rarely used snuff, the jewel-encrusted box was valuable—and he refused to be bested by a petty criminal.

The pickpocket ran a reckless course to the door, shoving aside anything and anyone that got in his way. Glancing over his shoulder at Vane, he did not see that a new obstacle had presented itself.

Isabel.

The young woman had stepped into the pathway of the fleeing youth. Delia cried out her sister's name as the pickpocket collided with Isabel and the pair fell to the floor in a tangle of limbs and fabric.

Isabel appeared momentarily dazed by the impact. It was not until the lad tried to crawl away that she seized him by the ankle. Her other hand clamped onto his arm.

Of all the mad things to do!

Fortunately, Isabel was no match for the desperate pickpocket. He freed himself with a forceful kick and staggered to his feet. He was out the door before anyone could stop him. Vane pursued the lad through the open doorway, prepared to chase him to the outskirts of town. His head snapped right and then left as he searched the crowded walkway and street for his quarry. The youth had simply vanished.

Damn . . . damn . . . damn!

Vane stomped back into the dressmaker's shop, furious. The sight of Isabel sitting on the floor surrounded by her sister and several well-meaning albeit useless bystanders made him want to snarl at someone.

With her straw bonnet askew and her hands clasped together, Isabel gave him a hesitant smile. "Good sir, the pickpocket might have escaped you, but he was denied his prize."

Her clasped hands parted, revealing his jeweled snuffbox.

The people around them cheered and applauded Isabel for her heroics as Vane scowled down at the snuffbox cupped in her gloved hands. Even though he had been denied the pleasure of throttling the clever pickpocket, the foolishly brave lady sitting on the floor would not escape his fury.

Chapter Five

"Never have I witnessed such a daft spectacle in my life!"

Isabel's smile faded at the furious declaration. If she had expected to be praised for her courage, the enraged gentleman towering over her was about to amend her expectations. Granted, she had never done anything so brazen in her young life, but she had come to London for new opportunities and a little adventure, had she not?

"You should be commending Isabel for her bravery, sir!" Delia rose from her crouched position to full height. "After all, she did manage to retrieve your expensive trinket from the pickpocket."

"Isabel," the gentleman said, enunciating each syllable of her name as if he were uttering a curse, "has less sense than an addled child rushing toward danger instead of away from it." He jammed his fists into his hips and glared at her. "I would have caught the lad if you had not stumbled into his path and ruined everything!"

Isabel did not care if she was being chastised by the

king himself. No one spoke to her in such an insulting manner. "*I* ruined everything? *I* did?"

His smile was humorless and full of masculine smugness. "Yes!"

With a growl of outrage, Isabel flung the snuffbox at the condescending man's head.

His hand shot up and he effortlessly snatched the box from the air. He did not seem particularly surprised that he had driven her to violence. Perhaps this was a common occurrence for him. It was the unintelligible murmurs of appreciation regarding his quick reflexes that provoked her ire.

"Of all the insufferable, erroneous accusations—I was not rescuing your blasted snuffbox, you stupid man! I was attempting to protect my sister, who was dashing for the door."

The unspoken suggestion of cowardice stirred her sister into defending her actions. "I was not running for the door. I was merely—"

Isabel strove for patience. "Not now, Delia. It is apparent to this *gentleman*," she said, fluttering her hand in his general direction, "that any attempt in retrieving his property, whether it was intentional or by chance, was unwarranted."

More amused than insulted by her disrespectful tone, he said, "I have been remiss in formalities. Christopher Avery Courtland, Earl of Vanewright. At your service, Lady—"

If he thought to impress her with his title and then vanquish her anger with flattery, the earl was mistaken. Chillingly polite, she said, "Miss Isabel Thorne. This is my sister, Delia." Feeling silly that she was conversing with a complete stranger while she sat on the floor of a dressmaker's shop, Isabel braced her hand on the floor so she could climb to her feet. "Now that you have your precious snuffbox, Lord Vanewright, my sister and I will be on our way."

Delia made a soft sound of disappointment. "But what of the dress, and the other—"

"Leave it for another day," Isabel said through clenched teeth. "I have suffered enough excitement for—" She gasped and reached for her ankle.

The amusement fled from the earl's handsome face. "You're hurt. You should have said something immediately instead of flirting with me."

Lord Vanewright was so serious in his delivery, Isabel thought he was serious. "F-flirting? I did no such thing!" she stammered, bowing her head so no one could see how mortified she was. "Good grief, I threw your snuffbox at your head!"

The earl crouched down at her feet. "You have better aim than most women." When her gaze snapped up to his in surprise, he winked at her. "Now let's see to your ankle."

Isabel slapped his hand away. "Mind your own ankle." She gave her sister a beseeching look. "Delia, find someone to hail a hackney coach so we can depart for home."

"Miss Thorne, I must respectfully overrule your order." Before she could argue, he silenced her with a gesture and gave her a smile that was designed to charm her. "A hackney coach? That will not do for the lady to whom I am indebted." He pointed to the clerk who had been helping them earlier. "Would you be so kind as to bring me a length of cloth to bind Miss Thorne's ankle. A little padding will make her journey home more comfortable."

"Aye, milord."

Isabel grimaced more from humiliation than pain. There were too many patrons crowding around her, and the air was stifling. She was also very aware of the impropriety of having Lord Vanewright kneeling at her feet. "Will you cease fondling my ankle? You are only making it hurt."

"Fondling, eh?" He shook his head and struggled not to smile. Although it had not been her intention, she had managed to amuse him again. "Usually when I—"

The earl suddenly cleared his throat and studied her ankle with keen interest. Clearly his words were as improper as his actions. When the clerk returned with the cloth he had asked for, Lord Vanewright did not bother hiding his relief.

Ignoring her protests, the earl unlaced and removed her shoe. His head bowed over his task, Isabel took advantage of his distracted pose and studied the man touching her as intimately as her personal maid.

At first glance, she had dubbed him handsome, and a closer scrutiny had not altered her opinion. Broad, muscular shoulders and arms filled out his frock coat. She inhaled sharply as his fingers found a tender spot. Straightaway, his blue-green gaze locked on to hers.

"How badly does it hurt?"

"You merely startled me," she said, uncomfortable that she was the center of attention.

The earl gave her an exasperated look and braced his forearm on his thigh. "I am tempted to call you a liar, but I will concede you may be suffering from something far worse."

Isabel tilted her head to the side. "And what is that?"

"Excellent manners." He shuddered in an exaggerated manner, and several of the nearby ladies tittered.

Even Isabel could not prevent herself from smiling. "I presume you, on the other hand, are not troubled with such an affliction."

"Only if it is unavoidable," he quipped, his expression sobering when his attention returned to her bruised ankle.

"And what of your wife? What does she say about your atrocious manners?"

Isabel found herself the focus of those incredible blue-green eyes again.

"Wife? Oh, I haven't one. No intelligent lady will have me." The incorrigible earl winked at Delia, and she rewarded him with a brilliant smile. "I confess, I am a great disappointment to my mother."

"As well you should be," Isabel replied, lightly scolding the earl for his prideful boast. "You do not appear to be the least repentant for your misdeeds."

He finished binding her ankle and appeared pleased with his efforts. "And why should I be? I would not have been introduced to you and your lovely sister were I a respectable gentleman."

As if determined to torment her, the earl tickled the

bottom of her foot, causing a ridiculous bark of laughter to erupt from her throat.

Mortified, she exclaimed, "Stop that!" Isabel sent her sister an appealing look. "Help me stand and we can get on our way."

"Allow me." Despite his pugilist build, Lord Vanewright possessed agility and grace unexpected for his stature. He climbed to his feet and extended his hand. "I will see you and your sister home."

"Lord Vanewright—"

"No trouble at all," he said, taking her hand and pulling her to her feet. When Isabel winced at the sharp twinge in her ankle, the earl swept her up into his arms.

"See here, Lord Vanewright!" Isabel was so distressed by her predicament, her entire body shook with outrage.

"Light as a feather," he assured her and their audience as he carried her toward the door.

Isabel seethed since Delia was not being helpful at all. "Now who is the liar?" she muttered under her breath.

Vane thought nothing short of a swift uppercut to the delightfully haughty chin would get Miss Thorne into his coach. First he tried charm, and when that failed he resorted to bullying. He had never encountered a lady so reluctant to remain in his company. If not for Miss Delia's cheery albeit mercenary interest, he might have thought something was lacking in his morning ablutions.

"It is very gallant of you to see my sister and me home," Delia said with a natural exuberance that Vane found disarming.

"Yes, very gallant," Isabel echoed drily as she stared out the window.

Enjoying himself, Vane smiled indulgently at the two ladies seated across from him. For a gentleman who was swearing off female companions this season, he had stumbled upon two enticing replacements for Miss Corsar, though he had learned from past experiences that seducing sisters never ended well for him.

"Will you be remaining in London?"

"Delia," Isabel scolded, sparing her sister a censuring look. "Lord Vanewright's affairs are none of our concern." The second she uttered the word *affairs,* however, it was apparent poor Isabel regretted it. Her cheeks bloomed like a summer rose garden. "Do not feel obliged to answer my sister's questions, my lord. She does not mean to be impertinent."

If he had been kinder, he might have taken pity on the lady's discomfort and assured her that he was not offended by Delia's curiosity. Despite his upbringing, however, he was no gentleman where ladies were concerned. Some viewed him and his fellow Lords of Vice as notorious scoundrels. Besides, he was having too much fun poking holes into fair Isabel's composure.

"Was she being impertinent?" He looked askance at Delia, which caused the woman to collapse in a fit of giggles at his feigned innocence. Yes, he truly liked the younger woman. He also had no doubt that her older sister was a veritable lioness when it came to protecting the delectable Delia from improper gentlemen.

Isabel did not rise to his subtle baiting. Instead she grimaced and edged closer to the window. Vane scowled as his gaze dropped to her swollen ankle, respectably covered by her skirt. He had forgotten about her discomfort. The workmanship and design of his coach might have been superior to an old hackney coach, but it could not prevent her from being jostled about.

"Your ankle is paining you."

"I am fine."

Vane straightened from his slouched position and leaned forward. "I thought we had established that you are a dreadful liar, Isabel."

The lady did not disappoint him. Primed with renewed outrage, she leaned forward until they were almost nose-to-nose. "I did not give you leave to use my Christian name, Lord Vanewright."

He could almost hear her molars grind together when he replied with a cocky grin, "My coach, my rules." Taking advantage of her speechlessness, Vane reached down and gently gasped her just above her injured ankle.

"What are you doing?" she demanded, attempting to wiggle free.

"Quit squirming," he said sternly. "You will only hurt yourself."

Completely undone by his high-handedness, Isabel fell back against the leather cushion. "Good heavens, is there no end to your torment?" she wailed as dramatically as an actress.

Vane chuckled.

Unfortunately for Miss Thorne, he was just getting started.

Chapter Six

"Merciful heavens, what happened to you?"

Isabel smiled wanly at their housekeeper as Lord Vanewright carried her over the threshold and into the small front hall. "Good afternoon, Mrs. Allen. It appears you were correct when you warned us that shopping on Bond Street was fraught with peril and unsavory characters."

Delia focused on what mattered most to her. "Oh, Mrs. Allen, you should have seen the lovely evening dress we found! I vow I shall perish if it is sold before we have the opportunity to return to the shop." She gave her sister a side glance, disgusted that Isabel had ruined the afternoon by tangling with a pickpocket.

Isabel sighed. There was no point in reminding Delia that they could not really afford the expensive dress. Such details mattered little to her sister. Isabel started when the earl murmured in her ear, "Shall I carry you to your bedchamber?"

A wordless exclamation was uttered by the

housekeeper. Surprised by the brazen suggestion, Isabel turned her face toward Lord Vanewright's, resulting in her nose brushing against his chin. "No you shall not! The drawing room will suffice, my lord."

Trailing after the trio, the housekeeper said, "Miss Thorne, forgive my impudence, but who is this gentleman? And why is he carrying you about town as if he has the right to put his hands on you."

"Not a word from you," she warned him sternly. With her arms wrapped about his shoulders, she could feel his body quaking with laughter. "Mrs. Allen, allow me to present Lord Vanewright. My lord, this is our housekeeper, Mrs. Allen. She is looking after us during our brief stay in London."

"Mrs. Allen, would you mind opening the door to the drawing room? Miss Thorne had a terrible fright with a pickpocket and I want to see her settled comfortably before the surgeon arrives."

"The surgeon?" Isabel echoed, struggling in the earl's arms to be released.

Mrs. Allen stepped around the couple and opened the door. "A pickpocket? In a dressmaker's shop you say? Is no place safe, I ask you?"

"Isabel stumbled into the thief and rescued Lord Vanewright's snuffbox," Delia explained as she retrieved a pillow from a chair and placed it on the sofa.

Isabel marveled that the earl was not winded by his efforts. He carried her to the sofa with an ease that suggested he appreciated the outdoors and had a casual familiarity with manual labor. She was almost disappointed when he lowered her onto the sofa.

"When did you have time to summon a surgeon?" she demanded, annoyed by the unexpected expense.

"I ordered my coachman to fetch him." His look was inscrutable as it rested on her grim features. "Are you in pain?"

"As I have told you over and over again, I am fine," she said through clenched teeth. "Ow! Stop that." She slapped his hand away when he deliberately probed her wrapped ankle to prove that she was lying to him—again.

"Uh-huh," he said, his tone suspiciously flat. He glanced at the housekeeper. "Mrs. Allen, would you be so kind as to fetch a shallow basin of warm water for Miss Thorne's ankle and a pot of tea to settle her nerves."

Eyes blazing, Isabel glared at the presumptuous man. "See here, Lord Vanewright. You have no right to bully me or my staff!" Before she said something that she would come to regret, Isabel cleared her throat. "Yes, Mrs. Allen, I believe a cup of strong tea would benefit us all."

Rudeness was clearly not the way to get rid of the man. From the sparkling glint in his eyes, the earl was having too much fun baiting her.

"Nothing else to say, Miss Thorne?" he asked, sitting down in the chair to her left even though no one had invited the arrogant man to remain.

"Not at this time," Isabel said haughtily. "I am saving my strength for the surgeon."

Isabel Thorne crossed her arms over her breasts and huffed. "Lord Vanewright is wasting good coin on a frivolous matter."

"Then it is mine to waste," Vane smoothly replied.

Miss Thorne was not very appreciative of his attempts to help her. As he glanced down at the worn sofa, which was likely older than the lady sitting upon it, he wondered if it was pride that pricked her temper—or him.

He rather hoped it was him.

"Mr. Stern, when you are finished torturing me, you may deliver your bill to me," Miss Thorne said tightly, grimacing at the pain of the surgeon's examination.

Vane's fingers curled around the back of the sofa. "Mr. Stern will do no such thing. After all, I owe you a debt, Miss Thorne, and I address all of my obligations."

His calm declaration was met with stony silence.

Excellent. He had won this minor skirmish with the lady.

He peered over the stubborn woman's shoulder as the surgeon examined her bare ankle. Even to his untrained eye, her ankle appeared to be slightly discolored, the flesh puffy. Miss Thorne, however, did have lovely toes. Slender and straight. He could imagine himself nibbling on those sweet tender digits. He doubted the straitlaced lady had ever permitted a gent to suckle her toes or measure the arch of her dainty foot with the tip of his tongue.

Miss Thorne inhaled sharply at the surgeon's prodding, pulling Vane from his pleasant musings.

"That is quite enough, Mr. Stern," she ordered. "A little rest will take care of my bruised ankle rather nicely. You may keep your saws in your case."

"So disagreeable," the middle-aged surgeon chided lightly. In his experience, most patients were surly, so he took little offense at her crisp tone. "A pretty lass like yourself should be flirting with your man."

Miss Thorne glanced upward at Vane. Once again, Vane was startled by the impact of her frank perusal, even when those beautiful light brown eyes were clouded with pain and frustration. "Lord Vanewright is not my *man,* good sir. I barely know him."

"Well, my dear, if you want my advice—"

She wrinkled her nose. "I do not."

The surgeon ignored her soft protest. "Might I suggest a little less vinegar, Miss Thorne." Kneeling at her feet, he winked at her shocked expression. "It will give your man reason to return after I'm gone."

"Of all the—" Miss Thorne scowled at Vane. "What if I do not want him to return?"

Chuckling, Mr. Stern's intelligent gaze shifted from the outraged Miss Thorne's blushing cheeks to the quiet determination he noted on Vane's face. "Something tells me that the decision is out of your hands, Miss Thorne."

Before his patient could form a proper response to his outrageous remark, Mr. Stern deftly changed the subject back to her bruised ankle.

Hours later, Vane arrived at Lord and Lady Heppenstall's ball. Although he was running late, he was in high spirits. After paying his respects to his host and hostess, he avoided the ballroom and headed down the hall to the card room. There he found his friends. Sin, Frost, Hunter, and Reign were seated at one of the tables, while Dare watched. Vane glanced about the room, but there was no sign of Saint.

"Good evening, gents!" Vane said as he approached the table. "Who's winning?"

Not glancing up from his cards, Frost replied, "Clearly not you since you are late again. Did you happen to encounter Saint on your way into this crush?"

There was no room for him to join the game, so he accepted the glass of brandy Dare offered him and positioned himself between Sin's and Hunter's chairs. "I haven't seen Saint in three days. I thought he was called away from town for a few days."

"That's odd," Hunter mused. "When I called on his residence yesterday, his butler turned me away and claimed Saint was too ill to receive visitors."

Reign snorted. "I have never known Saint to take to his bed unless he had a willing female under him."

Sin pounded his fist on the table. "Hear, hear."

"I must concur," Frost said, collapsing his cards into a neat stack and giving them all a sweeping glance. "He was patronizing the Golden Pearl last evening, and from what I saw of him, I can assure you all that the gent was neither infirm nor out of town."

Vane took a sip of his brandy. "Then why lie to us?"

Sin stirred in his chair. "Perhaps he has a new mistress and isn't in a mood to share."

"Or be teased," Reign added.

"No sharing." Frost wiggled his eyebrows suggestively. "Truly, our friend has grown positively missish on us."

"I don't think it is a new mistress," Vane said, his own problems with women flickering in his mind. "Saint's liaisons tend to be brief. He's told me many times that a kept female is more trouble than she's worth."

Not that Vane was in any position to judge.

Setting aside his cards, Hunter said, "Well, there was that one time—"

Dare abruptly kicked the leg of Hunter's chair with such violence, the man jumped.

Shooting Dare a murderous glance, Hunter shrugged at everyone's unspoken question. "Then again, I might have misspoken."

"Do you have something to share with us, Hunter? Dare?" Vane asked.

It was strange enough that Hunter was allowing Dare's actions to go unchallenged. Then again, Dare had married Frost's younger sister, Regan. If Hunter attacked Dare, Frost would feel honor-bound to defend his brother-in-law.

Hunter's handsome features tightened into a mocking smile. "Nothing worth getting my nose bloodied for. Are we playing cards, gents, or turning into a sorry bunch of gossiping spinsters?"

"Count me out," Sin said, tossing his cards toward the center of the table. "I'm a happily married man. I would rather fondle my pretty wife in Lord Heppenstall's back gardens than speculate on Saint's latest conquest."

Dare was still boring holes into the back of Hunter's skull with his hostile stare, but he nodded at Sin's words. "I'll take Sin's chair."

"Between the two, I would rather take Sin's wife," Frost teased, and was rewarded with laughter from his friends. Even Sin joined in, because he knew his lady would likely geld Frost if he were foolish enough to touch her. "Besides, she clearly is the softer choice compared with setting my arse on Heppenstall's uncomfortable chairs!"

Sin shook his head and laughed. "Juliana speaks fondly of you as well, Frost." He gestured at the Earl of Rainecourt, who also had a wife awaiting his return to the ballroom. "Reign?"

The earl waved him off. "Tell Sophia that I will join her after I win my money back from Frost."

Vane uncoiled from his position against the wall. "I'll walk with you, Sin. I have yet to pay my respects to my mother this evening."

As the two men said their farewells to their friends, Frost said, "Vane, you may want to pay your respects to Reign's poor wife. His losses will likely keep him from the ballroom the entire night!"

Sin and Vane threaded their way down the crowded passageway toward the ballroom. The orchestra was in fine form and was playing an energetic country dance. The cheers and clapping from the onlookers could be heard even at a distance.

"Saint isn't the only one who has been absent from Nox," Sin observed aloud.

Vane feigned innocence. "Me? Well, in my defense, I was enjoying a mistress."

Walking with his hands clasped behind his back, Sin quirked his brow in a questioning manner. "Was?"

"It seemed best to part ways." Vane hedged. He had not seen the dressmaker's bill yet, but he was confident that Bridget would try to beggar him with her demands.

"Best?" Sin seemed to taste the word. "The last time

you thought it best to part ways with a mistress, she tried to crack your thick skull with a chamber pot."

Vane grinned at the forgotten memory. He had been seventeen, greener than spring oats, and the fair lady in question had caught him seducing her cousin. He could not even recall the murderous wench's name, but he still had a dent above his right ear from the crockery she had broken over his head.

"Oh, Bridget liked me well enough."

"Bridget Corsar?" A glimpse of the former rogue surfaced in Sin's expression as he recognized her name. "A fine woman. Very enthusiastic in temperament, if I recollect."

"Very," Vane confirmed, sounding a little wistful. "However, it seemed prudent to give her up before my mother decided to carry out her threat."

Sin frowned. "Your mother? What did Lady Netherley have to do with Miss Corsar?"

"Nothing. And I intend to keep it that way." Vane walked in silence until he was satisfied no one could overhear them. "Can you believe my mother wanted an introduction?"

"You jest!"

If only he was. "When my mother learned of my budding friendship with Miss Corsar, she naturally concluded it was an affair of the heart."

"Naturally."

His frustration increased as he recalled the discussion with his mother. "How was I supposed to tell my dear mother that the only thing I wanted from Miss Corsar was a vigorous and thorough—"

"Debate," the marquess interjected smoothly as they passed two elderly matrons. "Good evening, ladies."

Vane also inclined his head to the two women. "I vow, Sin, I will be a raving madman if my mother persists with her ridiculous attempts at matchmaking. For two years I have tolerated her mischief with humor, but no more." He halted, and placed his hand on Sin's shoulder. "I cannot engage a lady in polite conversation without worrying that the lady in question is conspiring with my mother."

"You are being ridiculous."

It annoyed Vane that his friend was not taking him seriously. "Am I? Last month, my mother told Lady Sankey that she would happily pay any willing miss a king's ransom if she was clever enough to trick me into marriage."

"And who told you this?"

"Lady Sankey, when I discovered her disrobing in my bedchamber." His hand tightened on Sin's shoulder when the marquess surrendered all sense of decorum and started laughing. "God's teeth, Sin! Lady Sankey cannot be a day under sixty! Can you not fathom what my mother has done? Although she denies it, my mother has placed a veritable bounty on my head. If this gets out, every female from the lowest scullery maid to your grandmother will be dreaming of ways to compromise me into marriage."

Sin sobered, and urged Vane to continue walking since they were drawing attention. "Fortunately for you, my grandmother has long departed this world. However, you might want to avoid my sister this season."

"Oh, go stuff your advice in your arse!" Vane snarled as he shook off the marquess's staying hand. He abruptly stopped, and pivoted so he was face-to-face with Sin. "I thought you, above all whom I consider my closest friends, would understand and not make a mockery of my misery."

He walked away before he did something foolish like punch the arrogant bastard.

"Vane . . . wait!"

A curse was on his lips when his friend seized his arm. "I've had enough of your advice for one evening, Sin."

All mirth had vanished from the marquess's features as he steadily met Vane's angry gaze. "Forgive me, I didn't know this was troubling you so much. You have always spoken of it as an annoyance . . . a battle of wills between you and your mother. What does your father have to say about this matter?"

"It has never been addressed." He and his father were quite adept at avoiding all things of importance. "Even so, he has never been secretive about his disappointment in me. That I do not deserve the Netherley title."

No, that honor belonged to his brother. Unfortunately for his mother and father, his brother was dead, and Vane was their only living son.

The reluctant heir.

"Nonsense. You are more than worthy," Sin said loyally. "If your father ever spoke those words, he said them with grief in his heart. Everyone knows he took your brother's death hard."

Vane solemnly nodded. "As did my mother, though

she hides it well. It is probably why she is so determined to see me settled with a wife. I'm all they have left to continue the family line."

"And it is a lousy reason to marry."

They had reached the ballroom. From the corner of his eye, Sin caught sight of his beloved Juliana. Sensing her husband's attention, she turned and smiled at them. Vane inclined his head in her direction.

"If you want my advice, let your mother play her matchmaking games. You have foiled her efforts for two seasons, and this spring will be no different. What's the worst that can happen?"

"Besides marriage?" Vane's thoughts drifted to Isabel and Delia Thorne. How could he pursue a harmless flirtation with his mother looking on? Even if his friends could only see the humor of his awkward predicament, Vane was no longer laughing. His mouth curled with revulsion. "Celibacy."

Chapter Seven

"Milady, Miss Isabel Thorne."

Isabel curtsied. "Lady Netherley," she said as she carefully glanced sideways at the butler. In her note, the marchioness had begged Isabel to be discreet, and servants were a great source for information if one bothered to make inquiries.

"Thank you, Squires," the marchioness said, rising from one of the drawing room chairs. "That will be all."

"Very good, madam." The servant closed the doors, the sound making Isabel's heart leap in her chest.

The marchioness extended her hand toward Isabel. "Pray join me."

Her nerves rather than pain made Isabel's limp more pronounced as she approached Lady Netherley. At first glance, there was little physical resemblance between the seventy-two-year-old woman and her son Lord Vanewright. She was short in stature; age and childbirth had rounded her face and girth. Her once strawberry-blond hair had darkened into brown hues, and silver threaded her bound tresses, especially near her temples.

It was Lady Netherley's eyes that reminded Isabel of the earl's. Like her son's, her eyes were a warm shade of blue-green. While Lord Vanewright's gaze tended to have a cynical cast, though, the marchioness seemed to convey kindness and humor even if it wasn't warranted.

"Oh, my, why did you not tell me that you were hurt," Lady Netherley said, her face clouding with concern. "Should I summon Squires?"

Isabel smiled reassuringly at the older woman. "Your butler's assistance is not required. The surgeon assures me that it is simply bruised, and it is mending nicely." She did not even have to use the walking stick the man had suggested.

Although she had met Isabel only twice, the marchioness did not hesitate. She wrapped her arm around Isabel's waist and helped to ease her onto the nearest sofa. "Perhaps a pillow," she muttered, frowning at Isabel's foot. "Or I could have Squires bring a basin of warm water?"

"Do not bother. My ankle is fine," she said firmly. Obstinacy was another attribute mother and son had in common. "Besides, once you hear my tale, you will agree a few bruises were worth the outcome."

Lady Netherley's gaze lifted from Isabel's foot to her face. A sly grin brightened her features. "You have good news for me?"

Isabel nodded. "You were correct. Lord Vanewright was indeed at the dressmaker's shop at the designated hour. It was not very difficult to make him believe our meeting was by accident."

She did not add that the earl had been dallying with another lady in one of the private rooms.

Lady Netherley beamed at her. "Excellent!" She sat down next to Isabel on the sofa and affectionately patted her hand. "I knew when I was introduced to you while I was visiting Cotersage that I could count on you, Miss Thorne."

"Vane, what on earth are you doing here?"

Vane turned his head when he heard his name, and mentally winced. Dare's wife had just entered the dressmaker's shop with two of her friends. Any hope that his friends would remain ignorant of his small errand had vanished. He thanked the clerk and strode toward the three women.

"Good afternoon, Regan. Miss Bramwell. Miss Tyne," he said, cordially bowing. He pivoted the toe of his right boot in the direction of the door, his thoughts on escape. "Do not allow me to distract you from your errands."

Regan grabbed his hand and tugged him closer. "Oh, no, you do not escape me that easily!" She rolled up on her toes and placed a chaste kiss on his cheek.

Although they were not related by blood, Regan was a sister of his heart. As Frost's younger sibling, she had literally been raised by the Lords of Vice. Each of them had contributed to her unconventional education. Vane had shared with her his passion for chemistry—and, inadvertently, his penchant for playing with fire. Fortunately, Nox's kitchens suffered most of the damage, and Regan had been sent away to a boarding school. Though Vane suspected her five-year banishment from London had more to do with Dare than with the fire.

Not that the separation had quelled the attraction between Regan and Dare. His friend had married Regan within weeks of her return to London.

Vane could hardly blame Dare. Beautiful, intelligent, and adventurous as any Lord of Vice, Regan was a treasure, one he had also contemplated claiming for himself. However, he did not envy having Frost as a brother-in-law.

Dare was a brave man, indeed!

"I cannot believe Dare has allowed you out of the house without a footman or two to look after you and your friends."

Regan rolled her eyes. "You are a fine one to lecture me. I heard that you tried to chase down a pickpocket in this very shop!"

"Not alone. I had a little help," he said drily, thinking of the courageous Miss Thorne.

Her two companions, Miss Tyne and Miss Bramwell, smiled at her light scolding.

Regan continued as if Vane had not spoken. "Besides, we have two men just beyond the door. I would never hear the end of it from Dare or Frost if I wandered London alone."

His friends had good reason for their concern. Last spring, Regan had become separated from the footman watching over her, and a madwoman had pushed her into the busy street. It was a miracle Regan had not been trampled to death by a horse or wagon.

Vane shifted slightly to include Regan's friends in their conversation. "Miss Tyne and Miss Bramwell, you both look lovely as always. And Miss Tyne, forgive me for not congratulating you on your recent betrothal. My mother tells me the wedding will take place in the autumn."

Miss Tyne blushed at his attention. "Thank you, Lord Vanewright. Yes, the wedding will take place in September."

Regan's blue eyes narrowed on him. She poked his chest with her finger. "You think you are clever, do you not?"

"Often enough," Vane quipped. "And you disagree?"

"All the compliments and flummery will not distract me from my original question," Regan said, nodding to her friends for support. "You have not told us why you are here."

Even though he doubted Regan would blush if he told her that he was waiting for his mistress to appear from one of the private rooms, Vane was reluctant to confess the true reason why he had returned to the dressmaker's shop.

He had purchased the poppy evening dress for Miss Thorne.

Vane had observed her face when she and Delia were arguing over the dress. Once he had seen the Thorne sisters' modest dwelling, he understood Isabel's casual dismissal of an evening dress that she clearly desired.

It was the least he could do for her. After all, she had rescued his snuffbox from the young pickpocket.

Still, he doubted Miss Thorne would wear his gift if

she was aware that several ladies of the *ton* knew its origin. He could trust Regan to remain silent. However, Miss Tyne and Miss Bramwell did not owe him their loyalty. If word got out, the gossips could shred Miss Thorne's reputation within an evening.

"Didn't I?" He leaned forward and kissed Regan on the cheek. "It's a pity I do not have more time for explanations."

"Now, see here!"

Vane ignored Regan's frustrated outburst. "Ladies, I am certain we will meet again. Regan, tell your husband that I will be stopping by Nox this evening."

His errand completed, he walked away as quickly as decorum permitted.

"Dashing in front of a pickpocket!" Lady Netherley exclaimed as she poured tea into Isabel's empty cup. "I cannot decide if that was the bravest or most foolhardy thing I have ever heard."

"My only thought was to slow his escape," Isabel explained, feeling calmer after spending the past two hours with the marchioness. "It was Lord Vanewright who was supposed to catch him."

Her nervousness was to be expected, since her experiences with the *bon ton* were rather limited. Isabel had spent all her life in the quiet village of Cotersage. Even though her mother was the daughter of a viscount, her marriage to a commoner severed all ties between her family and London society. If Lady Netherley had not been visiting a sick friend in the country, Isabel would have never met this unpretentious, sweet-natured woman.

"I hope my son thanked you for your bravery."

A faint smile played upon her lips as she thought about their encounter. "Only after he lectured me for taking a foolish risk."

"Although I applaud the originality of your introduction, I must agree with Christopher."

"Christopher?"

"My son," Lady Netherley replied. "It is a lovely name, is it not?"

"Indeed."

"Oh, everyone refers to him by his title, or simply Vane, as he prefers, but he shall always be my Christopher."

"You are his mother. Of course, such intimacy is appropriate."

Lady Netherley picked up a spoon and stirred her tea. "As it is between a man and wife."

Isabel tried not to choke as she swallowed her tea. "And you believe my sister is the perfect lady for Lord Vanewright?"

"I do. A mother knows a thing or two about her son, and the moment Mrs. Whitechurch introduced me to you and your sister, I sensed that Delia was the key to my quandary."

"You mentioned that Lord Vanewright has resisted your matchmaking efforts over the years."

"Christopher can be rather stubborn about certain matters, but I am certain you and I will bring him around."

"Me?" Isabel said, startled that she was being included.

"Obviously, my dear. From what I recall of your sister, Delia is no more interested in marriage than my son. Together, we must conspire and think of ways to bring them together. Delia is quite beautiful, and Christopher appreciates true beauty. Nature will take its course, and soon I will be preparing for a wedding. What do you think of a summer wedding?"

"A summer wedding would be wonderful," Isabel said, feeling more than a little guilty that she and the marchioness had brought Delia to London under false pretenses.

Lady Netherley was correct. Delia had no desire to marry. Like a caged exotic bird, her sister longed for her freedom. Marrying the first gentleman she encountered in London was not part of her sister's plans. Nevertheless, Isabel had seen curiosity in Delia's gaze whenever it settled on the handsome earl. Some marriages began with even less.

No, whether Delia liked it or not, she held her family's welfare in her delicate hands. Becoming the Countess of Vanewright, and eventually the Marchioness of Netherley, would save her family from financial ruin. It would also give Delia all the things that she craved out of life. Wealth. A place in the *ton*. Respect. The freedom to fulfill every whim and secret desire.

"Miss Thorne. Isabel?"

"I beg your pardon, Lady Netherley," Isabel said, embarrassed that she had been caught woolgathering. "You were saying?"

The marchioness glanced at the closed door. Fearing that they might be overheard, she lowered her voice.

"My son is clever. He will be suspicious of anything that I say or do, so I will be depending on you to be my eyes and ears."

Isabel carefully set down her teacup. "I will admit that I have some concerns about this plan. I am not certain I can meet your expectations, Lady Netherley, since it will require me forming a friendship with Lord Vanewright. To be frank, I do not believe your son has any desire to speak with me again."

The marchioness smiled at her. Beneath all that sweetness, there was a kind of shrewdness that prickled the tiny hairs at the nape of her neck.

"Never fear, my dear. You will encounter my son again."

Chapter Eight

"Brace yourself, dear brother. I am moving in with you and I am in no mood for arguments."

Vane opened one eyelid to see his younger sister, Ellen, standing in the open doorway of his library. Like him, she was blessed with the dark hair of their sire and their mother's clear blue-green eyes. She was a pretty little thing with a flawless complexion, a lean, almost boyish build, and too much intelligence for her own good. At seven-and-twenty, she was still unmarried, which was another thing they had in common. As a small child, she had been his best friend, playmate, and fellow slayer of dragons.

"And you thought disturbing my nap would sweeten my disposition?"

"Susan is arguing again with her husband," his sister announced as she strode into the room without waiting for an invitation. "She has brought the children with her. Not all of them, mind you, but I saw at least six of the twelve. When I left, our sister was telling Mama that she will not sleep under the same roof with Pypart until he has apologized properly to her."

"For what?" Vane asked, repositioning himself so that he was resting on his elbows. He had resigned himself to the thought that the nap he'd been anticipating had come abruptly to an end. "According to Pypart, he has made his apologies. Numerous times."

Ellen gave him an exasperated look. "Of course he has. Our brother-in-law's sins are many." She walked over to the sofa and slapped at his boots. Obliging her, he shifted his legs until they were planted on the floor. She sat down at the end of the long sofa.

"Pypart isn't a villainous brute, Ellen. He is simply flawed like most of God's creations. His problem lies not in the fact that he cannot seem to resist sticking his co—" Vane caught himself and tried to amend his words of civil company. "Himself in ladies other than his wife. It is his damnable regret afterward and his need for absolution. He should do like any other self-respecting gent and *lie* to his wife."

Ellen laughed. "Especially to our sister. Mama tells me that Susan chased her husband around the bedchamber with a brass bed warmer."

"That does not sound horrible."

Unholy glee lit up his sister's eyes. "It was filled with hot coals."

Vane winced in sympathy. "Fortunately for Pypart, he is quite light on his feet." All of his indiscretions had kept his brother-in-law fit.

"She beat him soundly when she caught him." Enjoying herself, Ellen twisted so they were face-to-face.

She clasped both of his hands, silently encouraging him to sit up. "According to Mama, Pypart's clothing ignited as he was showered in a hail of burning coals and his wife's hellish temper."

"Hellish temper is right. When I was a small lad, Susan used to take a broom handle to me if she caught me misbehaving." Or whatever else was within reach. "I pity her children. All of them are probably sporting half a dozen dents in their skulls for their transgressions."

Vane and Ellen laughed, though it was not out of cruelty. Their elder sister had behaved like a second mother rather than a sibling because of their differences in ages. Susan had already married when their mother had given birth to Vane, and eighteen months later to Ellen. With an unfaithful, albeit apologetic husband, and twelve children who needed a firm hand and guidance, their sister had little patience to spare for her younger brother and sister.

"Well to be fair, Mama was always reluctant to punish us," Ellen said, releasing his hands so she could toy with a lock of his dark hair. "Susan thought if Papa had beaten you once a week, you would not have fallen in with those womanizing scoundrels that you call your friends."

It sounded like something Susan would have said. "The Lords of Vice? The rumors that you've heard are exaggerations and lies, dear sister," Vane said with feigned outrage.

"Mmm," Ellen said, tugging on his hair. "And what of that gambling hell you call Nox?"

Vane put his arm affectionately around his sister. "A club of charitable deeds." He ignored her burst of laughter. "No, seriously, our club provides certain amusements for the lost souls wandering about London." He failed to mention the fallen doves Madame Venna sent to Nox each evening or the depravity that often took place in the private rooms upstairs.

"I'll wager these lost souls fill the Lords of Vice's coffers rather handsomely."

"Nox provides its own rewards to all who pass through our doors," he said with as much dignity as he could muster.

In truth, Nox was one of the more notorious clubs in London. Founded by Vane and his six friends, and situated near the more fashionable clubs of St. James and Covent Garden at 44 King Street, Nox was a veritable den of corruption if the papers were to be believed. The Lords of Vice as the seven of them were often called had desired an elegant place to meet and play away from the disapproving scrutiny of the *ton*.

It was Hunter who solved the dilemma of a site when he donated the now eighty-eight-year-old house that had been a gift from his grandmother. In a joint venture, all seven of them contributed resources and labor to renovate the old building.

Vane could not recall who had originally suggested opening the lower half of the house to guests and potential club members, but such a mercenary scheme was likely Frost's idea. With Mr. Charles Berus as steward, the gaming hell paid for its costly upkeep as well as the staff's wages.

Everyone who entered Nox passed under a stained-glass rectangular panel with the words *Virtus Deseritur.* The Latin phrase translated into "virtue is forsaken," and was a generous gift from one of the gentlemen's former mistresses. Over time, it became the Lords of Vice's apt motto.

Not that Vane intended to share Nox's true origins with his younger sister. The rumors about the club and its wickedly depraved founders were often understated for polite society's ears.

The delicate arch of Ellen's left eyebrow lifted when Vane said nothing more about the club. "And what does Mama have to say about Nox?"

Vane slid his finger down the length of his sister's nose. "Our mother has the good sense not to ask questions about matters that would only upset her. Perhaps you should do the same."

Ellen wrinkled her nose in distaste. "Not much fun. Besides, if I behaved myself I would still be listening to Susan's tirade. Can you believe that I caught one of our nephews imbibing the contents of my scent bottles?"

"Which one?" Vane asked, highly amused. At last count, their sister had five sons.

She rolled her eyes. "Does it matter?"

"Perhaps to Susan" was his dry reply. "While she may often rail at their sire, she is rather protective of her brood. I hope you alerted her so she could dose our nephew with an emetic."

Ellen smoothed the wrinkles from her skirt. "How do you think I made my escape? I slipped out while

Susan was screaming for Mama." She leaned forward and rested her cheek against his shoulder. "So may I reside with you this season? I am tidy and relatively quiet. You won't even notice that I am here."

"And if I refuse?"

She sighed and straightened. "Then I will dedicate myself to the task of helping Mama find you a suitable wife."

Vane gave her a look of disbelief. "You devious little blackmailer. I am very disappointed in you."

"A tragedy to be certain." Ellen enraged him further by stifling a yawn. "Do we have a bargain? You offer me shelter and I will not meddle in your affairs."

"Done," he said curtly.

"Excellent!" She leaned over and kissed him on the cheek before rising. "If you do not mind, I will occupy the bedchamber that I used last time."

"Ellen, when did you become such a brat?"

"And when did you become such a pouter," she countered. "Trust me, dear brother, you could use an ally in our family. Once Susan calms down, I am certain she and Mama will scour the balls and routs in search of the perfect bride for you."

Although it came as no surprise, Vane rubbed his brow and cursed.

"Exactly." Ellen nodded, pleased that he understood his precarious situation. She casually crossed the room, pausing when she had reached the door. "Do not fret. I'll keep an eye on Mama and Susan. It is the least I can do to repay your generosity."

After his sister departed, Vane stared at the empty

doorway wondering if Ellen was a willing pawn in his mother's plans. He loved her dearly, but he could not afford to trust her.

"Where did you get that dress?"

Delia and Mrs. Allen glanced up as Isabel entered the small parlor. Her afternoon with Lady Netherley had gone better than she had expected, but she had left the marchioness's town house feeling irritable and tired. Anticipating a quiet moment to herself, she was surprised to find her sister clutching the poppy evening dress they had both coveted in the dressmaker's shop.

Holding the dress against her front, Delia gave her a sly grin. "Can you believe it is a gift?"

Isabel reached out and touched one of the sleeves. The dress they had admired had been unfinished. Someone had instructed the seamstress to complete it. "No," she said flatly. "This is a mistake."

Lady Netherley had offered to pay their expenses while she and Delia resided in London, but Isabel had refused out of pride. Accepting more of the marchioness's charity would have eased their financial woes, yet doing so seemed dishonorable. She had told the older woman several times that she could only encourage her sister to receive Lord Vanewright favorably, but she could not promise that the couple would marry.

"Not at all." Delia handed her a card. "A boy from the shop delivered the small trunk minutes before your arrival."

This was one of Lord Vanewright's calling cards. "The earl was here," Isabel said, astounded by his mother's intuition. She had predicted that they would see him again.

"The card was delivered with the trunk." Delia preened for the housekeeper. "What say you, Mrs. Allen? Do you think I will be mistaken for a countess?"

Isabel managed to choke on her own spit at her sister's casual query. She coughed into her hand, fighting to catch her breath and composure.

"Oh, Miss Delia . . . more like a grand duchess," Mrs. Allen said, her worried gaze switching to Isabel. "A cup of tea with a spoonful of honey will soothe that irritated throat. Delia, you can show me the rest of it later."

"Rest?" Isabel croaked after the housekeeper left the room.

Delia gestured to the trunk at her feet. "Lord Vanewright thought of everything. Dress, gloves, shoes . . . a matching reticule and fan. There is even a petticoat and—"

Isabel held up a hand. "Say no more," she entreated, staring at the trunk with an expression of appalled astonishment. "We cannot accept these gifts from Lord Vanewright."

Her sister protectively hugged the evening dress to her chest. "Why not? The earl clearly wanted me to have them."

She glanced up at Delia at her claim. "Are you certain? The trunk was delivered to you by name?"

"Well, no," her sister conceded. "Mrs. Allen thought the boy had made a mistake, too. Then the boy said the trunk was to be delivered to the Thorne residence. Nevertheless, Lord Vanewright knew I desired the dress. He overheard us arguing. I am certain of it."

Whether he was aware of it or not, Lord Vanewright was playing right into his mother's hands. "It was very kind of the earl. Even so, we cannot accept this trunk. We must return it immediately."

"You cannot do that!" Delia protested. "Turn over his card and read his note. He would be insulted if we spurned his generosity."

Scowling, Isabel turned the calling card over.

Lord Vanewright's handwriting was as lavishly bold as the man himself.

It reminded me of you. With gratitude.
—V

"It takes true skill to be considerate and thoughtless with a single deed." Isabel allowed her hand to drop to her side. The earl had sent the dress to Delia. As much as she coveted owning such elegance, no gentleman would have looked at the brilliant poppy color and thought of her.

Her knowing gaze rested on her sister's face. "You do understand that we cannot keep the dress," she said gently.

"Of course we can," Delia argued, sounding devastated, while she crushed the upper portion of the bodice with her fingers.

"Delia," Isabel said, striving for a reasonable tone. "We are strangers to town. One misspoken word of the origins of the dress and your reputation will be in tatters."

"I do not care."

Isabel recognized that mutinous jut of Delia's chin. "You will if no respectable hostess will receive you. Then there is Lord Botly. When he learns of our presence in town, he will not be pleased."

"You might be wrong."

"Perhaps." Even so, Isabel was highly doubtful. "If you recall, after Father's death, our mother journeyed to London to see the viscount. When she returned, she locked herself in her bedchamber for days." No amount of pleading from her daughters had opened the door. It had been Mrs. Willow who had coaxed the fragile Sybil from her room. "You and I both know that her father has not forgiven her for marrying beneath her. We are nothing to Lord Botly and his family. It would be foolish to give him just cause to guarantee that everyone in London agrees with him."

Delia's hazel eyes filled with tears. "But I want it! The dress will be perfect for Lady Benyon's ball this evening."

Isabel turned away, her throat constricting with emotion. "No one gets everything that they want." *Especially not us Thorne women.*

Mrs. Allen shuffled in with a tray laden with tea for both women and a plate of biscuits. "Goodness, you two have not been arguing again, have you?"

Isabel cleared her throat. "Mrs. Allen, I have another task for you," she said briskly. "I need you to find me a responsible lad to carry out an errand for me."

* * *

A few hours later, Vane's sleep was interrupted for a second time when his butler carried a trunk into library. "Forgive the intrusion, milord. This arrived moments ago, and the young man delivering it insisted that I was to bring this to you immediately."

Swinging his long legs off the sofa, he scrubbed his face wearily. "Place it on the desk, Jemison. Did the lad mention who sent it?"

The servant grunted as he relieved his arms of their burden. "No, milord. I was told, however, that his mistress included a note."

"Mistress?" Vane's forehead furrowed, wondering if Miss Corsar was returning miscellaneous articles of clothing that he might have abandoned at her residence. He would have never been so careless as to leave anything valuable behind, but considering their abrupt parting she might have decided to remove all traces of his presence in her life. "Open the trunk."

Vane stretched his arms over his head before he sauntered over to the desk. He started swearing the second he saw the poppy evening dress. "Ungrateful chit. Does she have to get her way on everything?"

Jemison handed him the folded piece of paper.

Vane parted the edges of the paper and read.

Dear Lord Vanewright,
In polite circles, when a lady accepts intimate gifts from a stranger, she might be mistaken for the liberal sort who is willing to dally in the private room of a dressmaker's shop with any gentleman.

If my sister and I have given you such an erroneous impression about our character, then please accept our sincere apologies. I pray you will not take offense because I am returning your generous gift. Such a beautiful dress should be worn and appreciated. If you cannot return it to the shop, I have no doubt that London is filled with worldly ladies who will accept your gifts without hesitation.

Most Humbly,
Miss Thorne

"Humbly?" Vane sneered as he shook Isabel Thorne's letter at the butler. "The woman is not even acquainted with the word. She is annoyingly stubborn and opinionated. Between her candor and her age, it is no surprise that she is unmarried!"

Yes, it was hypocritical of him to judge her when he was older and more experienced. She had also deduced that he had been the one in the private dressing room with Miss Corsar. If he had been a younger man, he might have blushed. Miss Thorne must have come to the conclusion that he was the vilest of scoundrels. His attempt to make amends and show his gratitude had only confirmed her suspicions.

"If you say so, milord," Jemison said, closing the trunk and securing the straps. "Any further instructions?"

"Yes," Vane said, coming to an impulsive decision. "Have my phaeton readied. I will be taking the trunk with me. I need to run an errand before I prepare for my evening."

Chapter Nine

Isabel had never attended a town ball. She assumed there was little difference between Lady Benyon's ball and the ones she had attended at Cotersage. The moment she had disembarked from the post chaise with her sister at her side, however, she realized that anything she'd experienced before this night paled in comparison. As they entered the glittering front hall, Isabel felt she had walked into a different world where extravagance was merely a tool of measurement in a world of the *ton*.

Lady Netherley's good word had secured their invitations, but it was yet to be seen if she and Delia belonged. With a sliver of envy in her heart, Isabel observed the elegantly dressed ladies around them. The amount of jewels and gold adorning these ladies' throats, arms, and ears clearly established their position in polite society. Her own bare limbs were a reminder that she did not truly belong in this world.

Isabel turned to reassure Delia and gasped. Her sister had already removed her black cloak and was handing the garment to a servant. Instead of the green evening dress Isabel expected to see, Delia was attired in the beautiful poppy-colored evening dress.

The one that had been returned to Lord Vanewright that very afternoon!

Isabel untied the ribbons at her throat, allowing a servant to remove the cloak from her shoulders. Murmuring her thanks, she took her sister by the arm and marched her away from the receiving line.

"What are you doing?"

"Where did that dress come from?"

"Oh, you know very well the answer. Otherwise you would not be on the verge of an apoplectic fit."

"The trunk was returned to Lord Vanewright."

"Fortunately, he thought it best that I keep it."

"What?" Her high pitch caused several guests to stare at the two women. Isabel offered their spectators an apologetic smile. When they moved on, she glared at her sister. "When did you speak with Lord Vanewright?"

Delia appeared vaguely annoyed by the question. "I do not know. He appeared on the doorstep when you went upstairs to lie down. Mrs. Allen allowed him to stand in the front hall. She did not think you would approve of me inviting the earl into the parlor."

"Why was I not told of this?"

"I told Mrs. Allen not to mention it. I knew it would only upset you. Besides, I wanted to surprise you. Did I not predict that the dress would be flattering?"

Isabel closed her eyes, trying to keep from yelling at her sister. Delia knew exactly how Isabel was going to react once she learned that Lord Vanewright had returned to the house with the dress. The clever girl had charmed Mrs. Allen to secrecy, and she had come downstairs already wearing her cloak. Her sister was counting on Isabel not to make a scene at Lady Benyon's ball.

"Without a doubt, everyone will be envious of your dress this evening," Isabel said, meaning every word. "What did Lord Vanewright say when he returned with the dress?"

Delia was already looking past her, openly admiring a group of gentlemen who had recently arrived. "The earl asked to see you, but Mrs. Allen told him that you were not receiving visitors. In truth, he seemed relieved by the news."

"Oh . . . oh, really," Isabel said, stung.

"Do not worry. Lord Vanewright did not stay long. He said that he was returning the dress to its owner."

"Did he even bother reading my note?" she seethed aloud. "What else did he say?"

"Very little, actually. Lord Vanewright just told me to tell you that he had already found the lady who appreciated the dress. He was simply returning it to her. Naturally I thanked him. After all, the earl has been generous to both of us. Do you not agree?"

"Yes."

"And do not fret. Lord Vanewright assured me that no one will learn who purchased the dress for me. So fear not, dear sister, my reputation is safe."

Isabel finally noticed that one of the nearby gentlemen was leering at Delia. She stepped in front of her sister and glared at the man until he glanced away. They had just averted a disaster with Lord Vanewright only to face another one.

"Come along. We need to greet our hostess, and find Lady Netherley."

In this crush of guests, Isabel was going to require assistance protecting Delia's virtue.

"Vane, what an unexpected surprise," said Sophia Housely, Countess of Rainecourt, as she greeted him. At her side stood her friends Lady Frances Lloyd and Juliana Braverton, Marchioness of Sinclair.

Vane bowed, acknowledging each lady according to her rank. "Good evening, ladies. How so?" he asked Sophia.

Wearing a blue dress that happened to be her husband's favorite hue, the beautiful blonde was clutching her white walking stick with gold top. Partially blind since childhood, the countess depended on her friends and walking stick to navigate the crowded ballroom.

It was Juliana, Sin's wife, who replied to his question. "Upon our arrival, Reign predicted we would see less of you this season than Frost—and you know how he detests these private balls."

Frost detested private balls because they were often hosted by doting mothers who hoped to secure a titled husband for their young daughters by parading them up and down the ballroom like fine mares wearing golden bridles. While the earl had no intention of marrying one of these muslin-clad fillies, it amused him to arrive unannounced just to disconcert his hostess and the hovering mothers since his title and wealth opened all doors to him. No one dared to refuse him, even if he was the devil himself.

The *ton*'s hypocrisy never ceased to amaze Vane and his friends.

Vane gave Juliana and Sophia a knowing glance. "So your husbands have been gossiping about me, eh? And branding me as some kind of coward, too."

"No one was accusing you of being a coward," Lady Frances said hastily, her mahogany tresses adorned with tiny white flowers. "I believe the general consensus was that you were not tempting fate this season."

"Diplomatic as always, Lady Frances," Vane said with a slight smile on his lips. "If you are willing, I would be honored to dance with you later."

Lady Frances inclined her head. "No, it is I who is honored, my lord. After all, any attention you bestow upon a lady this season will certainly stir speculation among the gossips."

"It will, indeed," Vane agreed, though he was not concerned that the young woman would misinterpret the polite gesture. It was common enough knowledge within their circle of friends that Lady Frances was pining for Mr. Derrick Griffin, though the gentleman seemed to view her as nothing more than a good friend. "I will consider it a favor. It will spare me hard looks from our hostess, and no one will be able to accuse me of shirking my duties in the ballroom."

"Such flattery will go to Fanny's head," Sophia scolded lightly. "No wonder your mother is convinced you need her help in this endeavor."

"Lord Vanewright does not mean to be rude," Lady Frances said, coming to his defense. "He is simply being practical. Would you not agree, my lord?"

It was a pity that his heart only held admiration for the lady. Lady Frances was an extraordinary woman. From the corner of his eye, Vane noticed that Griffin was watching them. Ignoring the varying expressions of surprise on the three ladies' faces, he gallantly took Lady Frances's hand and kissed it. "Both of us may benefit from the flirtation. Do not glance in his direction, however; Griffin apparently has taken offense to my presence."

Juliana had been acquainted with the Lords of Vice long enough to know that an unspoken provocation from any of the gentlemen could escalate into fisticuffs. "No fighting."

"It never even occurred to me," Vane lied. A riotous brawl always livened up a ball. He released Lady Frances's hand. "Griffin seems content to leave you on the shelf. Perhaps he needs a reminder that you will not wait for him forever."

Although she was slightly taken aback by his knowledge of her unspoken love for her childhood friend, she swiftly recovered. "I look forward to that dance, Lord Vanewright," she said as she glanced coyly in Griffin's direction.

Juliana slapped the collapsed blades of her fan on his wrist to gain his attention. "You have done enough mischief for one evening. You might want to seek out your disreputable friends in the card room before your mother decides to introduce you to that young lady in the poppy-colored evening dress."

"What lady?" Vane turned his head, searching for the lady who had caught the marchioness's eye.

"I do not know her," Lady Frances murmured. "However, I covet her dress. A beautiful color."

Sophia tilted her head, attempting to glimpse the lady her friends were discussing. "Perhaps Lady Benyon will provide an introduction for us."

Isabel Thorne and her sister had been invited to Lady Benyon's ball. Who had invited them? The old house the Thorne sisters were renting, with its worn furniture, suggested that the ladies were lacking funds and connections. Vane mentally chastised himself for not procuring the invitations himself. His family's name could open many of polite society's doors to the ladies.

Anticipation hummed in his blood as he caught sight of his mother and the lady wearing the poppy evening dress. As his gaze traveled from the skirt upward, Vane cursed under his breath. It was Delia, not Isabel, who was wearing the dress. Delia laughed at something his mother was saying, and he caught a brief glimpse of Isabel's face. She did not look happy, which only seemed fair, considering his current mood.

Did the stubborn woman have to fight him on every trivial thing?

"What is it?" Sophia asked, the first to pick up on his annoyance. "Do you know the ladies?"

"No," he said curtly. Though he was certain his mother was planning to remedy it. Fortunately, he was willing

to accommodate her. "If you will excuse me, ladies."
He bowed and headed toward his mother with a dangerous gleam in his eyes that had people stepping out
of his path.

"But the card room is in the opposite direction," Juliana said to his back, sounding exasperated and a little
annoyed.

Vane sympathized with the sentiment.

Isabel stood stiffly beside her sister while Lady Netherley and her daughter Lady Susan were debating which
parks and gardens the Thorne sisters should visit.

"A carriage ride through Hyde Park should be done
first," Lady Susan recommended, and then added,
"though superior equipage is as essential as your carriage
dress. After all, the point of drive is to be seen by the
ton."

Isabel's already flagging spirits plummeted. She and
Delia were getting about town with the assistance of
hackney coaches. She could not afford to add the purchase of an elegant carriage and horses to their growing bills.

Lady Netherley gave her a friendly pat on the arm.
"Do not look so worried, my dear. You and Delia have
us to watch over you." She turned to her daughter. "We
could all do with a nice drive through the park. Such
outings are much more fun in large groups, do you not
agree, Miss Thorne?"

"I-I suppose," Isabel replied, her hesitancy earning
her a sharp look from Delia, which she ignored. She was

barely speaking to Delia because of her trickery with the evening dress.

The elderly marchioness considered the matter settled. "Oh, and you two must see the Chinese Pagoda at St. James Park. It was only last year that they installed gas lighting."

"My sister and I are looking forward to seeing more of London," Delia said with unfeigned enthusiasm. "It is a pity that our mother was unable to join us this trip."

Isabel's stomach fluttered at the mention of their mother. She wanted to pinch Delia for even mentioning it. Lady Netherley frowned at her sister.

Oblivious to the emotional undercurrents, Lady Susan asked, "Is your mother ill?"

In unison, the sister gave opposing responses.

Isabel tried to appear apologetic. "Forgive us." She leaned closer and whispered. "My mother's condition is something that is rarely discussed outside the family."

Lady Susan's mouth formed a soundless *O*. "I understand completely," she said, leaving Isabel baffled since she had not really offered an explanation at all. "Then you have family in town?"

"Well, we have—ooph!" Delia stepped away and glared at Isabel.

"Forgive me, I did not intend to step on your toes. I hope I did not *ruin* anything," she said, giving her sister a meaningful look.

"The evening is still young," Delia replied with a light laugh.

Lady Netherley also laughed. "In a crowded ballroom, bruised toes are to be expected."

Isabel could tell by Lady Susan's expression that she was not satisfied with their answers, so she added, "Our father passed away, and we have little family left. Fortuitously, your mother has offered her friendship and her indispensable guidance during our stay in town."

Lady Susan's shrewd gaze switched from Isabel's carefully blanked expression to her mother's not-so-innocent one. "How old are you?"

"Susan, really," an amused masculine voice drawled, startling Isabel. "And I'm usually considered the rude one in the family."

Isabel spun around to see Lord Vanewright standing behind her.

Chapter Ten

Vane allowed his fingers to dance lightly over his heart as he acknowledged his mother with a bow. "Good evening, Mother. As usual, you look so lovely, our father should worry that someone will steal your heart."

He did not bother asking if his father had joined her. After losing not one but two virile sons, the man had slowly distanced himself from his wife and remaining children.

He critically studied his sister. "You look well, Susan. Ellen tells me that you and the children are living under our father's roof again. So tell me, what are your plans when you are not scaring young ladies or bashing your husband's head in with a bed warmer?"

"Christopher!" he mother exclaimed, walking over to him and placing her fingers on his lips. "Ladies, pray ignore my disrespectful son."

Vane casually slipped his arm around his mother's waist and gave her a brief hug before he released her. "I suspect you have warned your new disciples about me already."

"Disciples?" She shook her head. "Sometimes I think your nurse dropped you on your head."

Vane grinned, completely besotted with his mother. It was one of the reasons why she had gotten away with her matchmaking mischief. "No, my dear mother, I believe it was Susan and she was wielding a broomstick at the time."

Susan huffed. "I chased him with a broomstick once. *Once.* And he behaves as if I beat him every morning," she said to Isabel, who was edging away from their merry group.

"You have the wrong man. Perhaps you are confusing me with your husband," he said cheerfully, earning a baleful glare from his older sibling. "So tell me, sister, are the rumors true? Have you swapped out your broomstick for a bed warmer?"

Before Isabel could think of a clever excuse to leave, Vane touched his mother on the arm and changed the subject. "Mother, it is unlike you to be forgetful when it comes to introducing me to beautiful young ladies. Who are your companions? I do not believe we have been introduced."

His mother's eyes boggled with amazement. "You are asking to be introduced?"

Now it was his mother who was being rude. "I can be civilized."

He noted that Isabel visibly sagged with relief. The poor girl must have been holding her breath, wondering if he was planning to mention that he'd already had the pleasure of holding her in his arms.

Delia appeared to be the adept liar in the Thorne

family. She offered him a guileless smile. "Lady Netherley, this is your son?"

Clever girl, Vane mentally applauded. If he had not been present in the dressmaker's shop, he might have believed her demure guise.

"Oh, I am forgetting myself this evening. Yes . . . yes, he is. Miss Thorne and Miss Delia, may I present to both of you my son, Christopher Courtland, Earl of Vanewright. Christopher, I would like you to meet Miss Isabel Thorne and her sister, Miss Delia Thorne."

Isabel and Delia curtsied. "Lord Vanewright," both sisters politely murmured.

Vane formally bowed, which caused his sister's right eyebrow to rise a solid inch. He shot her a quelling glance. Both Susan and their mother seemed surprised that he could behave himself.

"Miss Thorne . . . Miss Delia, I am honored to meet you both." And his remark was sincere. With Isabel and Delia in attendance, this evening would prove entertaining. "How long have you two been acquainted with my mother?"

"Not long at all," his mother said, crossing in front of him to stand next to Isabel, as if she needed protecting. "However, with Lady Benyon occupied with her duties as hostess, I could not resist taking it upon myself to look after these young ladies. Can you believe this is their first visit to London?"

A noncommittal sound rumbled in his throat as his eyes narrowed. He suspected there was more to the tale than his mother was telling, but he did not challenge her. Besides, it would be much more amusing to charm the information out of Delia or intimidate Isabel into confessing. As he silently pondered which course would be the most entertaining, his mother accidentally gave him the opening he needed.

"Christopher, I was originally planning to appeal to one of your unmarried friends. However, now that you are here, perhaps you could invite Miss Thorne to partner you in a dance."

He showed plenty of teeth as his gaze clashed with Isabel's startled brown eyes. "My pleasure," he purred.

"Oh, that is not necessary," Isabel said to the marchioness, giving him an apologetic look. "Delia is a much better dancer than I."

"I would be honored, my lord," Delia said, moving close enough that her poppy-colored skirt brushed against the leg of his trousers.

Vane took an intimidating step toward Isabel. "You are too generous, but I will risk my toes." He extended his bent arm, encouraging her to accept his invitation.

Isabel moistened her lips. "Lord Vanewright, I must—"

"Accept," he finished. When she stared at him blankly, he explained, "You are the elder, Miss Thorne. It would be a breach of etiquette if I danced with your sister first."

"And when have you ever cared about etiquette?" Susan asked, sounding amused.

Vane bit back a nasty retort. Isabel was already skittish and would probably refuse to leave his mother's side. Instead, he tried a more diplomatic approach. "Never. I was only thinking of Miss Thorne and her sister. Why cause unnecessary speculation? Do you not agree, Lady Netherley?" he asked, using her title so she understood that he was annoyed.

"Christopher is correct, Miss Thorne," his mother said, all but taking the poor girl by the hand and slapping it on his arm. "Do not fret, I will watch over your sister during your absence to make certain no scoundrel absconds with her."

As Vane led his reluctant companion away, he could have sworn he heard her mumble.

"But who will protect me?"

To the casual onlooker, Lord Vanewright appeared courteous and almost protective of the lady he escorted. Only Isabel was aware that the hand he had placed over her own was to prevent her from fleeing.

When she was satisfied that they could no longer be observed by Lady Netherley, Isabel said, "Do not be offended, but I do not wish to dance."

She might have omitted *with you,* but the young earl grimaced as if she had been so rude to speak the words aloud. His hand tightened over hers.

"Strangely, Miss Thorne, neither do I," Lord Vanewright said grimly. "Let us find someplace quiet for this intimate conversation."

He seemed to know everyone, Isabel silently marveled as he greeted ladies and gentlemen while guiding her away from the guests who had congregated to admire the dancing. He did not take the time to introduce her, and she knew it was deliberate on his part. The only reason he had asked her to dance was that etiquette demanded it. Once he returned her to Delia and his family, the earl would be free to dance with her sister.

"A little farther," Lord Vanewright said in a clipped tone, nudging her down a narrow passageway. With no one about, she wondered if he was using one of the servants' corridors. He opened a door and stuck his head through the narrow gap. "This will do." The earl pushed the door open and waited for her to enter.

It was a narrow anteroom decorated with olive-flocked paper. Across the room four white doors provided a pleasant contrast with the dour color. The number of doors suggested that this room connected to a larger drawing room. Lord Vanewright took her by the arm and led her to one of the benches lining the room. Spectacular gilt pier glass mirrors had been mounted between the doors, and the panels of glass and crystal glittered like diamonds.

Isabel sat down, and could not resist stroking the thick tapestry covering. Lord Vanewright made no move to join her on the bench. He simply watched her as she admired her surroundings.

Feeling foolish, she slowly raised her gaze to meet his. His eyes were not as kind as his mother's, but Isabel grudgingly conceded that his stare was compelling. His thoughts were unfathomable, but she felt the strength of his gaze. This was a gentleman who was used to getting his way.

"Forgive me, Lord Vanewright," she said, hoping her humility would assuage his wounded pride. "I have a bad habit of uttering opinions without fully explaining myself. I pray you did not take my refusal to dance as an insult." Her hand made a sweeping gesture at her legs. "Although I have not admitted it, my ankle still pains me and I fear my clumsiness will embarrass both of us."

His hard expression relaxed into mild concern as his gaze dropped to her feet. "Why did you not mention this sooner?" He drew her gaze to the firm line of his jaw as he rubbed it. "Confound it, you did not even protest when I practically dragged you out of the ballroom."

Lord Vanewright was torn between annoyance and embarrassment, which surprised Isabel. She doubted the earl felt a need to apologize for his actions very often.

"I thought it would be obvious. You and I have unfinished business to discuss." Ignoring the slight twinge of pain in her ankle, Isabel stood. She was taller than most ladies. Generally, she viewed her height as a physical flaw; she seemed to tower over many of her male acquaintances. She could not say the same for Lord Vanewright. Four inches taller, with a lean muscular build, he made her feel almost delicate.

The earl seemed to study her from head to toe as he took an intimidating step toward her. "Indeed we do, Miss Thorne."

"The dress," they both said in unison.

Instead of finding it amusing, they glared at each other. Then they started speaking at once.

"The dress was a gift. Never have I encountered—"

"Did you even *read* my note? I told you that my sister and I could not accept such a gift! Imagine my shock when I saw—"

"Are you always so stubborn? You make it impossible

for someone to show his gratitude! And you insult me further by giving the damn dress to your sister," Lord Vanewright all but snarled.

It was this declaration rather than the earl's ire that silenced Isabel's angry tirade.

"What do you mean, *give*?" she demanded, resisting the urge to poke the obnoxious gentleman in the chest. Ladies could not go about poking thickheaded earls, even when they deserved it. "Delia told me that you insisted that she keep the dress, even after I explained why—"

"The evening dress was meant to be yours."

That brought her up short. "I beg your pardon?" she said faintly.

Lord Vanewright sighed. Perhaps he was troubled by the notion that she was standing on her bruised ankle. It would explain why he took her by the elbow and encouraged her to sit on the bench she had abandoned earlier. He sat down next to her, taking up the remaining space on the bench.

"Despite your protestations that afternoon at the dressmaker's shop, I knew you desired the dress. I was in the position to grant you a boon for rescuing my snuffbox, so I purchased it. For you."

Not for Delia. "My sister told me—" Isabel bit her lower lip, realizing she was on the verge of sharing confidences with a gentleman she did not truly know. "Never mind. Delia looks magnificent in the dress. I could not have done it justice."

Lord Vanewright had pivoted so that his knees were

a hairbreadth from touching her skirt. "Do you truly believe that rubbish or is that what your sister told you so you would not demand she hand over the dress?"

"I did not even know that you had delivered it until we arrived—" Isabel glanced away, annoyed that her tongue seemed to have a will of its own this evening.

"An admirable stratagem," the earl said as understanding warmed his eyes. "She was wagering that you would not cause a fuss once you arrived at Lady Benyon's town house."

"Delia was aware of my concerns," she said simply.

"Your concerns. Ah, yes, you must be referring to my dastardly deed of purchasing the dress that has caused you nothing but strife."

Isabel tilted her head and stared at him. "Are you teasing me, Lord Vanewright?"

"Yes, I believe I am," he said, sounding completely unrepentant. "However, I may relent if you will favor me by calling me by my nickname. Everyone calls me Vane."

Isabel laughed. "I am not surprised." Her hand fluttered to her mouth as his eyes narrowed. "Not surprised, my lord, because you are so handsome," she blurted out, and then winced. She was babbling.

"We should return to the ballroom." Isabel stood, but he snatched up her hand before she could flee.

"So you think I'm handsome?" he murmured, clearly pleased with her declaration.

"No—Yes! Of course any lady would consider you handsome." Inspiration struck. "My sister was the first to comment on your masculine beauty. Oh, and your strength. She marveled about how effortlessly you carried me into our house," she said, relieved that she could speak of Delia in a favorable light to the earl.

After all, Lady Netherley was expecting Isabel to do her part to nudge Delia and Lord Vanewright toward matrimony.

"How very kind of her," he said, rising since Isabel was not being subtle about her desire to leave the anteroom. "And what of you, Miss Thorne? Did you praise me as well?"

Isabel was entering dangerous territory. To deny that she found him appealing would be nothing short of a lie. It would also be insulting. If she had any hope of convincing him that Delia should be his countess, then they needed to be friends.

"I admired your eyes and your hands," she confessed. Though she had never had such a conversation with her sister, her admission was the truth. "Delia was right when she praised your strength, and yet you were so gentle when you tended to my ankle. I did thank you for that, did I not?"

"Thank me again, Miss Thorne."

Before she could guess his intentions, he lowered his head and kissed her. The kiss was light, almost chaste. Nonetheless, the brief caress made her head swim and her knees quake.

That wonderful mouth, a mere inch from her lips, curved into a triumphant smile. "Perhaps we have discovered something else you like?" He moved closer to kiss her again.

"No."

He stilled but did not move away. "No? Are you certain?"

No.

Isabel did not dare reveal how conflicted she felt. She almost wanted him to kiss her again to prove that she was moved more by curiosity than desire. "I am not in the habit of kissing strangers."

"Kiss me again, and I promise to allay that particular worry."

He licked his lips in anticipation, and the sliver of space between them closed.

"I am betrothed." When he paused, the truth triumphed over her blatant lie. "Well, almost betrothed. I believe. There is a man visiting the village we live in. He is a natural philosopher like my father and he has been helping me go through my father's papers and journals. We have been spending a lot of time together, and, well, I am optimistic."

This was more half-truth than truth, but she refused to quibble. And Lord Vanewright appeared to be only partially convinced.

Isabel allowed herself to exhale when the earl straightened.

"Almost betrothed, you say? I did not realize. Forgive me."

Whether or not he was mocking her, Isabel was too relieved to care. "It was my fault. I should have spoken up sooner."

Lord Vanewright slapped his palm to his forehead and grimaced. "Small wonder you were so upset about the dress, eh? Your gent would not have taken kindly if he learned another man was buying his almost be-trothed gifts."

"I suspected as much. You *are* mocking me!" Isabel shook her head at her own stupidity, and headed for the door to the anteroom.

"Miss Thorne. Isabel. Wait!" He circled around her before she had reached the door and blocked her way.

"Permit me to pass."

Lord Vanewright held up his hands to surrender. "I confess, I was teasing you. I've just never encountered a lady in your precarious quandary before."

Even though she had no intention of ever marrying Mr. Ruddel, let alone seeing the man again, the earl's remarks stung just the same. "If that was an apology, I would consider it mediocre at best."

"Point taken." He leaned against the door and crossed his arms. "And very judgmental of you, I might add. Nevertheless, I am offering you my sincerest apologies and friendship if you will accept."

"Why?"

For a few seconds, he appeared perplexed by the question. "Why? Because you are probably the only un-married lady in town who isn't obsessed with the notion of marriage. Worse still, marriage specifically to me. That makes you unique and rarer than a large pink dia-mond. No, Miss Thorne, I insist that we become friends. You alone will make this season bearable."

Chapter Eleven

Three nights after Lady Benyon's ball, Vane was enjoying a casual evening with his friends and their wives. Everyone had gathered at the Sinclair town house because Sin turned out to be an excellent host. Three years had passed since Sin had married Juliana, and last September his wife had delivered the Sinclair heir, Henry Alexius Braverton, the new Earl of Crossington. Now seven months old, young Henry had his mother's green eyes and Sin's dark hair. Judging from the manner in which Juliana, Regan, and Sophia were fussing over the lad, he also possessed his father's uncanny charm. Perhaps he was the first of the next generation of the Lords of Vice.

"Henry has your looks, Sin," Vane said, watching the baby giggle as Regan teased him with a small piece of ribbon.

"Aye, he is a handsome devil," Sin said, his voice laced with pride and affection. "And he has his father's lusty appetite. Is that not so, *lybbestre*?"

The golden-haired marchioness blushed at her husband's teasing, her eyes promising retribution. "Let us pray he does not inherit his father's penchant for mischief."

Sly, knowing glances were exchanged among Vane, Sin, Hunter, Saint, Dare, and Reign. While Juliana, Sophia, and Regan were well aware that the Lords of Vice had earned their notorious reputations, some tales were not to be retold; otherwise, these husbands would never be welcomed in their wives' beds.

Keeping himself apart from the domestic scene, Frost was seated in one of the japanned beechwood armchairs. With his fingers casually curled around the bold ornament scrolls of the armrests, and reclining against the chair's regal high back, the earl looked like a king awaiting the evening's amusements. Vane's estimation was probably not far from the truth—Sin was not the only one who excelled at mischief.

"Regan, you seem to have bewitched young Henry," Frost said to his sister.

Regan beamed at the baby before she spared her brother a glance. "Babies love everyone. Including you, dear brother." To Henry, she cooed, "Is that not right, little man?"

"Are you breeding, dear sister?"

Used to her brother's frank speech, Regan ignored the other women's soft gasps and replied with equal candor. "I do not believe so. What about you? Any bastards in the family, well, besides you, of course?" she asked sweetly.

Frost barked with laughter, his unusual turquoise-blue eyes gleaming with admiration. "I do not believe so," he said, echoing her words.

Dare looked as if he could happily murder his brother-in-law in front of everyone. Vane half expected the man to leap from the settee and stalk across the room.

Saint, who was sitting beside Dare, seemed to also pick up on their friend's growing ire. "Quit while you're ahead, Frost. I doubt being related to you by marriage will prevent Dare from pounding out his displeasure on your pretty face."

"I concur," Dare said, his eyes narrowing on Frost. "Quit pestering my wife."

Uncomfortable with the sudden tension in the drawing room, Sophia reached for Reign's hand. Her husband squeezed to let her know that all was well. Vane felt a pang of sympathy for the young countess. When she was a girl, her parents had been murdered during a violent altercation.

"I believe I will check on our daughter," she said to Reign.

"Give her a kiss from me," Reign said, pressing his lips to his lady's hand. The scathing look he gave Frost could have melted stone. The earl was very protective of Sophia, though she had proved that she was stronger than she appeared.

Regan cuddled Henry in her arms as she stood. "Juliana, I think your son needs tending."

The marchioness exchanged a quiet look with Sin before she rose from her chair and held out her arms. "Here, give him to me." To the Lords of Vice, she said, "Try not to break the furniture in our absence."

Hunter saluted Frost with his glass of brandy. "She said nothing about lumping on your pate."

"An entertaining evening, I must say," Saint said as he, Vane, and Hunter settled in for the drive back to Nox. The night was still young, and the men had planned to pass the rest of the evening at the club. "Never expected to witness a pugilist demonstration in Sin's drawing room."

Hunter chuckled. "Marriage has clearly not softened Dare's fist."

"Frost was fortunate that Dare did nothing more than bloody the man's lip," Vane said, admiring their friend's restraint. "He should be spitting out teeth for his careless remarks."

Saint closed his eyes. "Frost isn't cruel. It's obvious Dare and Regan never told him."

"Told him what?" Hunter asked, his gaze sliding from Vane to Saint.

So Frost was not the only one who didn't know. Vane hesitated, reluctant to gossip about one of his closest friends.

"What?"

Saint's eyes snapped open. "Hunter, Regan was with child. She lost the babe," he said solemnly.

Hunter cursed under his breath. "When?"

"A few weeks after Henry was born," Vane replied. "She wasn't far along, but—" Dare and Regan had been excited about having a child, especially after holding Sin and Juliana's son in their arms.

"Why did no one tell me?" Hunter demanded, annoyed that no one had bothered to share the sad news with him.

Vane shrugged. "You were north when it happened. Besides, I thought Dare told you. No one really talks about it."

"Dare should have told Frost," Saint muttered after a few minutes of silence.

Vane frowned, feeling the need to defend their friend. "Dare already blames himself for not taking better care of Regan. He doesn't need Frost blaming him, too."

Hunter sighed. "Dare isn't to blame. And Regan . . . she's young. There will be other babes."

Vane agreed. Regan was strong and healthy, and too stubborn to allow anything to stand in her way. The next child she held in her arms would most likely be her own.

"Just don't tell Frost."

Hunter's upper lip curled at Saint's warning. He might have been ignorant of the loss of Dare and Regan's child, but the man wasn't stupid. "I'd like to keep my teeth, too!"

Isabel untied her sister's stays. She did not mind playing lady's maid; she had often performed the task at home. Mrs. Allen sent one of her daughters upstairs to assist her and Delia as they prepared for an evening, but Isabel saw no point in making the poor girl wait up for them.

"I liked Lord and Lady Wodgen," her sister said, exhaling noisily and making a low sound of relief after she was freed from her stays.

Isabel laid the undergarment over one of the chairs

to allow it to air out. "As do I. It was a pleasant way to spend an evening."

Thanks to their benevolent benefactor, Lady Netherley, the two women had been invited to a card party. No more than twenty-five people had been present, and Isabel had felt honored to have been included. They had played whist and speculation, and later there had been a hot supper. Isabel had expected to see Lord Vanewright again, but he and his friends had not been invited. When she'd asked about the oversight, Lady Netherley muttered something about a regrettable incident and quickly changed the subject.

It was her whist partner, Lady Kempe, who brought up the Lords of Vice. "I mean no disrespect to their families, but it would be best to refrain from engaging in conversation with those wicked gentlemen." The countess gazed pointedly at Isabel, much to her chagrin.

Intrigued by these mysterious men, Delia asked in hushed tones, "Who are these Lords of Vice?"

"Frost, Sin, Reign, Hunter, Dare, Vane, and Saint. Handsome devils," Lady Howland murmured, ignoring Lady Kempe's wordless admonishment for praising such villainous creatures. "And difficult to avoid during the social season. Much is forgiven when a man has a respectable title and wealth, and a family has a daughter or two to marry off."

Lady Kempe nodded as she played a card. "Well, except for Lord Wodgen. He has not quite forgiven Frost and Vane for their mischief."

Vane. The countess could not possibly be referring to Lord Vanewright. Stunned, Isabel stared across the table at Lady Kempe. "Vane. You speak of Lord Vane-wright?"

The older woman seemed to relish Isabel's surprise. "Didn't Lady Netherley tell you that her son was one of the notorious founders of that troublesome club, Nox? I suppose not, considering how she dotes on him."

Isabel sat back in her chair, no longer interested in the cards on the table.

"Now, Myra, one could hardly fault Lady Netherley," Lady Howland chided her friend. "After all, she and her husband lost their eldest boy, William, during the Battle of Villers-en-Cauchies in 1794."

"Netherley's true heir was a lieutenant colonel in the Fifteenth Light Dragoons," Lady Kempe added. "Such a decent young man. His death was a tragedy for the family and the *ton*."

Lady Howland's eyes misted. "And then they lost Arthur. He was a beautiful boy. When did he drown?" she asked Lady Kempe.

"I believe it was 1804. Vane was ten years old when his seventeen-year-old brother drowned attempting to save the passengers in an overturned coach that had plummeted off a crowded dock into the river."

"Simply terrible," Delia murmured, casting a side glance at Lady Netherley, who was seated two tables away from them and thankfully ignorant of their grim discussion.

Isabel felt nothing but pity for the marchioness and her family. "I had no idea."

"Vane is all the Netherleys have left," Lady Kempe said, her expression revealing what she thought of the surviving son. In her opinion, Lord Vanewright did not measure up to his heroic brothers. "Well, there are the two girls, of course. Needless to say, no one is surprised that Lady Netherley has taken it upon herself to see that her son settles down with a respectable young lady."

"Sin and Reign have settled into good marriages," Lady Howland reminded her friend. "And just last season, Dare married Frost's younger sister, Lady Regan." Her expression grew speculative when it alighted on Delia and Isabel. "How long have you two been acquainted with Lady Netherley?"

Isabel had called trump, and that put an end to their conversation about Vane and the Lords of Vice.

"Your turn." Dressed in her shift, Delia took Isabel by the shoulders and spun her about. "So what offense do you think Lord Vanewright and his friend Frost committed against Lord and Lady Wodgen?"

If the *ton* had dubbed the gentlemen the Lords of Vice, the possibilities were endless. "It is nothing that concerns us," Isabel said primly, though her certainty sounded hollow even to her ears.

Chapter Twelve

"Why this sudden desire to ride in Hyde Park? No wait, let me guess. Your celibacy has come to an end," Saint said, giving his horse's neck an affectionate pat. "How long did your vow last? Five days?"

"Longer than that."

Vane endured his friend's ribbing because his vow had been halfhearted anyway. Giving up Miss Corsar had not been a trial. Once he had settled her accounts with her creditors, he had not given her another thought.

"So who is she?"

Vane did not pretend to misunderstand the marquess. "Actually there are two ladies."

"*Two.* God's blood, you and Frost never do anything in half measures!" Saint exclaimed, amused and a tad envious of Vane's good fortune.

"Since my mother and sister will be joining them, your wicked thoughts will earn you a place in hell, gent," Vane replied with a soft chuckle. "No, by my oath, I believe I have found the perfect female companion this season."

Saint made a vague gesture with his hand. "And here I thought they were all special to you."

Vane frowned. For the marquess, one lady would do as well as any other. "No, Isabel Thorne is different. She claims to be almost betrothed and has assured me that she has no interest in courting any gent's favor while she is in town."

His friend grimaced. "Almost betrothed? A bit shilly-shally for a man on the verge of committing himself, do you not think?"

Vane had also thought Isabel's almost betrothed predicament was rather odd, but he kept his opinion to himself. "The man was foolish to allow his lady to wander London without him. He does not exist as far as I am concerned. What matters is that Isabel is the one lady my mother cannot sway."

The two gentlemen rode in companionable silence for several minutes.

"You mentioned there were two ladies," Saint reminded him.

Immediately the vision of Delia wearing the poppy-colored evening dress he had purchased for Isabel flashed in his mind. "Ah, the younger sister, Delia. A delightful young woman"—if one liked greedy ambitious creatures. "If I were a betting man—"

"You are."

"That I am," Vane readily admitted without shame. "I'd wager Delia is the one my mother is hoping will entice me to give up my sinful ways. She is a charming creature and quite beautiful. And like most of the simpering ladies my mother finds, is amenable to marrying me for my title."

Saint grinned, but swiftly sobered as a thought occurred to him. "Do you think the sister is conspiring with her?"

"Isabel?" Vane pondered the possibility, and then he shook his head. "No, the lady is unacquainted with guile. Once she starts hearing rumors about the Lords of Vice, she will be terrified to leave me alone with her younger sister."

Protective mothers and chaperones were nothing new. "It sounds like you have it all worked out," Saint said, cocking his head in Vane's direction. "So why have you brought me along?"

Vane shrugged. "To provide a distraction. Keep me from throttling my mother, and who knows, mayhap Delia is the lady who might be capable of claiming your heart."

"Utter trumpery!" Saint scoffed, his noble features hardening as he stared off into the horizons. "Everyone knows I have no heart."

"Lady Netherley, is that not your son riding toward us on a dapple gray horse," Delia asked as she craned her neck to get a better look.

The seventy-two-year-old marchioness tipped her parasol back and squinted at the two approaching gentlemen. "Yes, it is. Though I must confess I am amazed. Usually he has other business to attend to when I ask for such favors." Lady Netherley shared a conspiring smile with Isabel, silently letting her know that it was her and Delia's presence that had prompted her son's cooperation.

"Who is the handsome gentleman with him?" Delia asked.

Neither Lady Netherley nor her daughter Lady Susan had the opportunity to reply. Lord Vanewright guided his horse alongside the marchioness's carriage while his companion circled to the side closest to Delia.

"Good afternoon, Mother. Susan." Beneath his hat, his blue-green eyes seem to lighten with humor as he met her gaze. "Miss Thorne and Miss Delia, if I had known you would be joining my mother and sister, I would not have tarried."

Isabel felt the full impact of the earl's charm. Wearing buff riding breeches and a dark blue coat, he looked rather dashing on his beautiful dapple gray gelding. If she had not been already seated, she would have asked for a chair.

Recalling his friend, Lord Vanewright formally introduced her and Delia to Simon Jefferes, Marquess of Sainthill.

Good heavens, *this* was Saint. Another one of the Lords of Vice. The knowledge must have shown on Isabel's face, because she could have sworn both gentlemen's lips twitched as if they were trying not to laugh.

"Vane, you are correct," Lord Sainthill said, his blue eyes scrutinizing Isabel's face. "Almost to a fault. I envy you, my friend."

Twenty minutes later, Lord Vanewright had suggested

that the ladies should disembark from the carriage and enjoy the park as pedestrians. Lady Netherley eagerly agreed, claiming that her bones had rattled long enough to produce a variety of aches and pains.

While the coachman shook out a large wool blanket for the marchioness and Lady Susan to sit upon while they admired their surroundings, Isabel, Delia, Lord Vanewright, and Lord Sainthill ambled ahead discussing London, the weather, and Lord Fiddick's masquerade ball, which would take place weeks from now.

Isabel wasn't certain if it was planned or by accident, but somehow the two couples slowly separated as their conversations also went in different directions. Delia was ahead with Lord Sainthill listening intently to her words. It was an intriguing pairing, one that Lady Netherley would not be pleased about.

"You do not have to fret about Saint," Lord Vanewright said, startling her from her musings. "On occasion, he can be respectful."

Isabel could not confide to the earl her true concerns. "I was not questioning your friend's—"

"Of course you were, Miss Thorne," he countered, even though he did not appear to be insulted that she might be questioning Lord Sainthill's intentions. "Let me guess. Someone mentioned that Saint and I are sometimes referred to as the Lords of Vice."

She paused and stared off at the water. The sunlight caused its surface to glitter like diamonds in the distance. "Saint was mentioned, but yours was the only one of the seven names that I recognized. You told me that your friends called you Vane. When Lady Kempe—"

"Lady Kempe." His jaw tightened in anger. "Meddlesome woman. She apparently thought she needed to scare you off."

Good grief, their conversation was becoming decidedly awkward. Isabel looked away and delicately cleared her throat. "Not precisely. The countess and Lady Howland are aware that your mother has high hopes of you finding a bride this season."

The earl bowed his head as if the weight of it was too much to bear. "Lady Howland, too. How the devil did you get cornered by those two harp—er, ladies," he demanded, indignant that his private business had been openly discussed with her.

"No one waylaid me with gossip," she assured him. "We were playing whist at Lord and Lady Wodgen's house, and Lady Kempe happened to mention you and your friends."

"Christ! Whist at the Wodgens's." Lord Vanewright closed his eyes as he struggled with his temper. His right hand folded into a fist. "Of all the nonsensical rubbish . . . and the Wodgens—just wait until Saint hears about this!"

Isabel touched the earl on the arm, stilling his attempt to march toward Lord Sainthill and Delia. "Please do not tell him. No harm was done—no one else overheard the quiet discussion. Perhaps it was imprudent of Lady Kempe and Lady Howland to speak about you and your friends thusly."

"Perhaps?"

Isabel winced at his sarcastic tone. "Well, it isn't as if they revealed what you and your friend Frost did to earn Lord and Lady Wodgen's contempt. Delia asked Lady Kempe several times . . ."

Lord Vanewright threw his head back and began laughing.

Her nose wrinkled in bemusement. Perhaps the Lords of Vice had played some kind of prank on the Wodgens. "The countess refused to say. I even asked Lady Nether-ley about it, and she called it a regrettable incident."

The earl sobered at the mention of his mother. "You discussed this with my mother?"

"I had no idea that everyone would be so secretive about the discord between the Lords of Vice and Lord and Lady Wodgen," she said, becoming exasperated that the earl was annoyed at her. "Do you want to tell me what you and Frost did that offended the Wodgens?"

A slow, devilish grin creased his face. Isabel found herself smiling back at him.

"Oh, no, Isabel Thorne, you will have to spend more time with me before I tell that particular tale!"

Chapter Thirteen

No one was more surprised than Vane that the mistrustful Isabel Thorne had a bad habit of intruding on his thoughts at odd moments. Her temperament and stature were far removed from his usual requirements for a female companion. He preferred curvaceous temptresses who were as generous with their smiles as they were their bodies. Most were simple, cheerful wenches who enjoyed his attentions, but understood that a man's nature was fickle.

Isabel was precisely the type of female he painstakingly avoided. Oh, her looks were pleasing to a gentleman's eye. Her light brown eyes bespoke intelligence and compassion and her mouth was generous, even if her breasts and hips were less so. Instead of discouraging him, her willowy stature haunted him. More than once he had contemplated the soft, scented flesh that was hidden underneath muslin and whalebone. Had she shared her body with another man? Instinct and her nervous reaction to him told him that she was untouched. Vane avoided virgins at all costs. The thought of breaching Isabel Thorne's maidenhead should have cooled his ardor.

Regrettably, his cock refused to listen to him. It twitched at the mere thought of undressing Isabel and relieving her of her virginity.

Then there was his mother's interest in the Thorne sisters. It was an ominous sign. His mother longed for him to marry, and she had ceased to be subtle about it.

Not that Vane could fault the poor woman. After all, her surviving son was a notorious rake. Her ambitions would remain fruitless as his mistresses' wombs. *Ah, there she is!* Vane smiled to himself as he finally caught sight of the lady he had been searching for over the past hour while wandering about the museum.

Unfortunately for Isabel Thorne, he had inherited a few of his mother's shortcomings. Lack of subtlety and patience being forefront in his mind as he strode toward her and her sister. He knew the moment she had sensed him. He noted a stiffness in her shoulders as her sister whispered of his unavoidable approach. Adorned in a pale pink gros de Tours wool-and-silk spencer and an embroidered white skirt, she did not turn to acknowledge him until he was before them.

"Good afternoon, Miss Thorne . . . Miss Delia," he said genially, tipping his hat and bowing to the sisters. They curtsied. "What an unexpected pleasure to encounter you both. If the past hour has been any indication, you have spared me from an exceedingly dull afternoon."

The delicate arch of Isabel's brows lifted in feigned

astonishment. "Intellectual pursuits bore you, Lord Vanewright?"

"On the contrary, Miss Thorne," he said, earning him a puzzled frown. "I enjoy all challenges, be they of an intellectual or a sporting nature. Nonetheless, what is the point of knowledge if it cannot be shared?"

Delia, looking like spring in a rose-pattern print dress and a straw hat and veil, tittered nervously as she glanced at her sister. "Then you have something in common with my sister, my lord. Isabel believes our minds will atrophy without constant stimulation of history and the arts."

"This is only our second tour of the museum, Delia. Our lives cannot revolve around rides in the park and shopping," Isabel said in a lecturing tone. "Papa would expect more from his daughters."

At the mention of their father, Delia's cheeks turned a rosy pink hue. Vane was curious, but he held his tongue. While teasing Isabel was highly amusing, he did not wish for his encounter with the sister to end too soon.

Vane nodded at the gallery ahead of them. "I assume you were about to tour the Greek antiquities before my approach."

"Yes," said Delia.

"No," replied Isabel. She gave him an apologetic smile. "Forgive me, yes, we were about to tour the gallery, but our friend is indisposed."

More than mildly curious about their absent friend, Vane tilted his head. "Friend?"

Isabel's face was clouded with her concern. "Yes, Lady Howland."

"Lady Howland," he parroted as he glanced about, half expecting to see his mother or, God help him, Lady Kempe jumping out in front of him. "Is she alone?"

Isabel and Delia had identical looks of bewilderment on their faces.

"Of course not! Perhaps I should explain. All the walking left Lady Howland feeling breathless," Isabel explained. "We escorted her to one of the small retiring rooms, but there were few places to sit so my sister and I decided to explore the gallery until Her Ladyship can rejoin us."

"Then you leave me no choice," he said, relishing Isabel's guarded expression. "I shall be your escort until your chaperone returns."

"Lady Howland is not our chaperone!" Delia protested, chafing at the restrictions placed on her freedom. "Isabel is six-and twenty, and a more-than-adequate companion. I told Her Ladyship several times, but she seems to be partially deaf when it suits her."

Isabel winced at Delia's unintentional cruelty, and a pang of sympathy rose in Vane's chest for the lady who seemed to be both mother and sister for her sibling. To Vane, she said, "I had expressed a desire to see the collection Mr. Townley had assembled, and Her Ladyship offered to share her opinion on the artifacts. It is regrettable that her health was not up to the task. Perhaps we should visit the museum another day."

"Nonsense!" he said, startling both women. "Lady Howland is resting"—he did not bother adding that the lady would have gathered the two young ladies to her ample bosom and fled were she aware the Thornes were in his company—"and you have a charming escort who is willing to discuss sculpture, ancient coins, and weaponry . . . anything you and your sister desire."

Delia moved closer to him, confirming that she was on his side. "Say yes, Isabel!"

The lady knew she had been outmaneuvered, but she was too polite to comment on it. Instead, she said, "Wheedling is unbecoming in a lady."

"So is pouting," Vane observed, grinning when Isabel hastily bit down on her lower lip. "Though you might be the exception, Miss Thorne."

The outrageous gentleman had the audacity to wink at her. *Wink.* As Lord Vanewright anticipated, Isabel surrendered gracefully. There was no point in arguing with Delia and the earl. Two peas in a pod, they were. Lady Netherley had chosen her son's bride wisely.

Isabel scowled at the thought.

"This vase not to your liking?" Lord Vanewright murmured in her ear. She started, unaware that he stood so close to her.

"I . . . uh." She blushed, appalled at how unsophisticated she must have appeared to the earl. It was humiliating to admit it, even to herself, but she had not been paying attention to the marbles she had expressed a desire to see. She cleared her throat discreetly and tried to speak once more. "I was worrying about Lady Howland."

It seemed plausible, even if it was a lie. This unexpected meeting with Lord Vanewright seemed like a boon, and she did not want to squander it. Although she was certain Lady Howland would disapprove of them being escorted in public by one of the notorious Lords of Vice, this was a chance for the earl to spend time with Delia.

"Ah, I see," he said, trying not to laugh. For reasons unbeknownst to Isabel, she managed to provide him with an endless source of amusement. "And this particular high relief on the vase made you think of Her Ladyship?"

"Well, yes," she said, sounding uncertain even to her ears. She peered at the marble vase and gasped. Good grief, she had been absently gaping at unclothed Bacchus as he merrily celebrated with his equally naked companions. "No! Definitely not!"

Lord Vanewright's laughter filled the room, drawing everyone's attention. "Lying is not your forte, Miss Thorne."

With her head held high, she walked past him, determined not to dignify his erroneous comment with a rebuttal. Excelling at lying was nothing she wanted to gloat about.

Delia glanced away from a bas-relief of two griffins fighting two female warriors and asked the retreating Isabel, "What did I miss?"

"Nothing important," she muttered as she walked up to a statue of a female holding a cluster of grapes in one hand and a thyrsus above her right shoulder. A panther rising up on its hind legs was at her feet.

"That is Libera," Lord Vanewright said, coming up from behind until he stood next to her. "She is called the female Bacchus."

"At least she has the good sense to keep her clothes

on," Isabel said, coolly looking over her shoulder at Delia. "My sister loves stories. Perhaps you could explain why those female warriors are battling griffins."

"Attempting to get rid of me, Miss Thorne?" the earl said, circling her as she strolled to another statue.

"No."

A gentleman would have respectfully yielded to her not-so-subtle hint and excused himself. Isabel had to remind herself that Lord Vanewright was no gentleman.

She concentrated on the statue. It was safer than staring at the handsome earl who might one day be her brother-in-law. The statue was almost five feet in height. It was another female, and blessedly, she was clothed.

"This is Ceres, is it not?" she asked, frowning as she stared at the conical basket in the figure's left hand. It held leaves and flowers. When her question was met with silence, she added, "My sister is easily bored, and you said that knowledge should be shared."

"No, you are definitely attempting to rid yourself of my presence." He did not appear to be surprised by that revelation. "What do you fear, Miss Thorne?" He took a step toward her.

"N-nothing," she stammered as she watched his eyes narrow. "I just thought you might enjoy my sister's company."

His eyes flashed with the heat of unexpected anger. "You do not know me well enough to tell me what I should or should not enjoy."

He inclined his head, his gaze never leaving hers. "But you will, Isabel Thorne."

With a final nod, he joined her sister.

Isabel watched as Delia brazenly flirted. She should have been relieved that she had won this skirmish with the earl, but she was troubled.

Why did the gentleman's parting words sound like a threat?

Chapter Fourteen

"Well, well . . ."

Isabel turned her head at the low masculine drawl and discovered that the man was as captivating as his voice. Striding toward her like a marauder in evening clothes, the dark-haired gentleman with unusual turquoise-blue eyes looked like he was capable of practically anything. Rules, she suspected, did not apply to this man.

"You must be one of the seven Lords of Vice people keep warning me about," she said, risking a side glance to the young lady she had been speaking to before the gentleman's interruption. She discovered that her companion had fled.

This did not bode well.

Taller than Vane by three inches, he had black hair that fell loosely around his narrow face. She would rarely apply this word to a man, but he was beautiful. Whether he was an angel or the devil had yet to be determined.

"Saint was not exaggerating. A man might give up

many things with the proper enticement. Are you Vane's?" he asked, those enthralling blue eyes studying every aspect of her.

Isabel could feel her pulse beating at her throat at his close scrutiny. "Vane's what?" she replied, fighting the urge to open her fan and hide behind it.

"Temptation, Miss Thorne," he said silkily. "A foolish man's downfall."

She did not like what this gentleman was implying. "Lord Vanewright isn't a fool."

The dark-haired stranger inclined his head. "It is best that you remember your own words."

"Which Lord of Vice are you?"

"Frost." His white teeth flashed as he smiled. "Ah, I see my depraved reputation precedes me. I hope you aren't too disappointed with the man."

"Begging for compliments, Frost?" Vane said coldly, stepping in front of Isabel.

"Or attempting to frighten off the *Thorne* digging into Vane's ars—side," quipped another dark-haired stranger as he joined the two men.

Belatedly, Isabel realized she was wrinkling Vane's coat. She mumbled an apology and stepped away from the three gentlemen.

"I thought only to introduce myself to the lady," Frost protested. "Saint's high praise of the Thorne sisters had me curious."

The gentleman who had followed Vane snorted indelicately at their friend's explanation.

Isabel let out a soft squeak as a tall blond gentleman

brushed by her. Another Lord of Vice, she presumed, wondering if one had to be a veritable giant to be considered for membership at their club.

"Regan sent me over because she feared there was a fight brewing," the newcomer growled. "Please do not disappoint me. Especially you, Frost."

"Now that we aren't hindered by Juliana's fondness for her furniture, I'm willing if you are, Dare," Frost said. The deadly menace in his voice had Isabel inching away.

"If you will—" Her voice faltered when all four gentlemen recalled that she was witnessing their quarrel. "Pray excuse me."

"She is terrified," one of the men murmured.

"And this surprises you?" was Vane's thunderous reply as he glared at Frost.

"Do not blame me," Frost grumbled. "Miss Thorne and I were getting along famously until we were rudely interrupted."

Vane pushed by his friends until he was standing in front of her. "We will save the introductions for another time. Let's get you some air. You are looking a little pale."

Vane and Isabel did not speak until they had reached the stone terrace. "What did Frost say to upset you?" When he'd noticed that his friend had managed to corner Isabel, a fierce need to protect her had risen within him. He had been prepared to challenge Frost, and the realization shook him to the core.

"I was not upset," she hastily replied, moving away from him. "I was just startled that he knew who I was. Honestly, he seemed concerned about you."

Vane smirked. "Frost? Worried about someone other than himself? You are mistaken."

When another couple emerged from the open doors, he took Isabel by the arm and escorted her away from the house. With torches lighting their way, they followed the garden wall.

"The others . . . they are members of your club?"

He nodded, admiring the lavender dress she had donned this evening. He longed to trace the graceful curve of her neck, allowing his lips to taste the dip at her collarbone.

"And good friends. We've all known one another since we were lads, and like most brothers we have misunderstandings, jealousy, and arguments. Even so, I would trust them all with my life. There was no reason to fear them, including Frost."

Isabel circled the nearest torch so she could study his face. "I was not afraid of your friends. I am, however, curious. What did Lord Sainthill tell Frost about me and my sister?"

"I was not privy to their private conversation," he admitted, even though it was simple enough to deduce that Saint must have told Frost how Vane had initially encountered the Thorne sisters and of their encounter in the park. It must have amused Frost immensely considering Vane's ridiculous vow of celibacy. "I imagine Saint praised your intelligence and beauty."

Uncomfortable with flattery, she backed away from

the torchlight. Her heel caught on an unseen stone, and she stumbled. Before he could catch her, she managed to keep her balance by reaching for the stone wall.

"And graceful," she said mockingly.

"Lovely, too," he added. Seizing the opportunity, he backed her against the wall.

"Pretty lies, Lord Vanewright," she said, almost desperately, as she became aware of his proximity. "I suspect all ladies are lovely to you."

He frowned slightly and shook his head. "Not particularly. Then again, I pursue only the ones who I want to kiss."

"You do not want to kiss me," she blurted, her gaze searching for the open terrace doors that were no longer in view. "And we should not even be here. We should—"

"End this ridiculous argument," he said, silencing her by bringing his finger to her lips. "Especially when there are more pleasing exercises we can do with our lips."

To avoid his finger, Isabel turned her face away and moistened her lips. "Lord Vanewright . . . Vane," she said, remembering that he had asked her to call him by his nickname. "I believe we should return to the ballroom before we are missed."

Ignoring her request, Vane tilted his head and studied her profile. She was breathless, and he'd wager her heart was pounding. Was it fear or anticipation that was making her tremble? Several seconds later, a low chuckle rumbled in his throat. "Sweet Isabel, has no man ever stolen a kiss from your lips?"

Her eyes blazed at his amusement. So did her pride. "Of course! Dozens of times," she brazenly lied.

Vane braced his palms against the wall, effectively caging her with his body. "Then one more gent will hardly make a difference," he teased, before his mouth slanted over hers and swallowed her gasp.

Isabel froze as his lips moved tenderly over hers. This might not have been her first kiss, Vane silently mused, but it would be the one she would remember. Although he teased her lower lip with a tantalizing flick of his tongue, he made no attempt to deepen the kiss. He did not wish to frighten her. His friends had seen to that. He just wanted to demonstrate to Isabel, and maybe himself, that the attraction he felt when he looked at her was not one-sided. And when all was said and done, his mother's machinations and Isabel's absent suitor from Cotersage proved little hindrance when he finally put his hands on her.

Vane ended the kiss before someone caught them and reported back to his mother that her son was ravishing Isabel Thorne in the gardens. Her dazed expression and slightly swollen lips mollified his masculine pride. Yes, whether she would admit it or not, the lady was not immune to his kisses.

"Are you planning to gloat?" she asked once she found her voice.

Since it was exactly the sort of behavior that she expected from a Lord of Vice, Vane decided he liked her best when she was unbalanced. With great deliberation, he removed a leaf from her bound tresses and tossed it away. "Let's return to the ballroom. After we dance, I will introduce you to my friends and their wives. I am certain that tempers have cooled during our absence."

Unfortunately, Vane could not make the same claim for his unruly body.

Chapter Fifteen

Vane waited impatiently for the housekeeper to open the front door. He had become a regular visitor at the Thorne residence, but it was beginning to annoy him that he was not their only caller. He scowled as Mrs. Allen opened the door and another gentleman departed the house. Vane did not recognize him; nor did he care to discourage the gent from leaving.

The gentleman caller met Vane's stern gaze, nodded warily, and then scurried off. Vane was rather pleased with himself until he noticed that the housekeeper had witnessed the silent exchange.

"Do not bother telling me that Miss Thorne and Miss Delia are not at home." He motioned with his head at the hastily retreating figure of the sisters' last caller.

"Miss Delia is not at home," Mrs. Allen said tartly. "However, Miss Thorne is in the study. If you will wait here, I will see if she is receiving visitors."

"That will not be necessary, Mrs. Allen," Isabel said from the doorway. "Lord Vanewright, will you join me?"

Vane did not need a second invitation. He followed Isabel into the study and shut the door. A minute later, the housekeeper opened the door. She did not openly threaten him, but the look she gave him told him that she would make him suffer if he laid a hand on Isabel.

Isabel seemed to be oblivious to his silent exchange with her housekeeper. She had picked up an open book on the satinwood secretaire, and whatever she had glimpsed on the pages made her sad.

"Did you receive some troubling news?" he asked, discarding his hat and gloves on the nearest side table.

Her forehead wrinkled. "Troubling?" she asked, the pain and confusion clearing from her expression. "No. Why do you ask?"

It was a calculated risk, but instead of keeping his distance, Vane crossed the room until he had reached her side. "First, the stranger that departed your house upon my arrival."

The shy smile that brightened her face was as potent as brandy. "Mr. Fawson was hardly a stranger. I have been corresponding with him for more than a year," she said, shutting the book and hugging it to her chest.

Jealousy was a ridiculous, petty emotion. It crawled up his spine, its venomous claws digging into his throat. Vane wanted to know why this Fawson fellow was writing Isabel, but he held his tongue. He had no right to ask. She was simply his friend, nothing more. He tugged at his cravat and cleared his throat. "And second." He tapped the leather-bound book with his finger. "You looked sad when I entered the room, and I believe this book is responsible."

Isabel turned back to the secretaire. "Should I ring Mrs. Allen for some tea?"

"Equivocating will not work with me," Vane said, gently shifting her until he was almost embracing her. "You can confide in me. Was Fawson a creditor?"

He immediately dismissed the notion at her surprise.

"What made you think—oh," she said softly, gazing morosely at a worn rug beneath her feet. "No, Mr. Fawson called on me for an entirely different reason."

Vane gritted his teeth in frustration. If he thought Isabel would permit him to use his resources to settle with her London creditors, he would have made the offer weeks ago.

"Pray tell, Mr. Fawson is not the mysterious suitor that you are almost betrothed to, my lady?"

She blushed at his teasing remark. "Oh, no, Mr. Fawson isn't . . . he was here to make an offer on this journal."

"Why would Fawson be interested in an old journal?"

Isabel handed him the book. "It belonged to my father. He was a natural philosopher and inventor. He was always scribbling his thoughts and experiments in one of his journals, or on any piece of paper he could find. It's all I have left of him."

Vane thumbed through the journal, his own intellectual curiosity heightening as he admired detailed sketches and paragraphs of speculation and the results of experiments.

"My mother mentioned that your father was killed in an accident," he murmured, not taking his gaze from the page, though he sensed that she nodded.

"I was thirteen years old when my father died. There was an explosion in his private laboratory. Fortunately, he worked in one of the outbuildings a short distance from our cottage. Otherwise we might have all perished in the fire."

Vane's gaze sought hers. Although she was standing next to him, he needed assurance that she was unharmed. "Who is Fawson?"

"He represents a gentleman who is an inventor and natural philosopher like my father." Her brown eyes were eloquent with emotion as she gazed at the journal in his hands. "Much of Father's work was destroyed in the fire. However, seven of his journals and numerous papers were spared because he had stored them in his study."

"A fine legacy for his daughters." Vane shut the journal with a decisive *snap* as it suddenly occurred to him how valuable it would be in certain scientific circles. "Good God, Isabel, you could be sitting on a small fortune." He handed the book back to her.

Her look was unreadable as she accepted the volume, then slid it back onto the bookshelf. She closed glass doors made up of complex wooden cross-bandings and locked each one with a small key.

"I am not a fool, Vane," she said tersely. "When my father died, numerous gentlemen called on my mother to inquire about my father's work. Initially my mother was so distraught, she turned them all away. A few months later, one of them returned and offered to pay her handsomely for any writings that existed on the carriage steering mechanism my father had dabbled with when they had corresponded. When I was older, I came across a brief article in a newspaper about an innovative steering mechanism for carriages. The inventor was the same man who had visited my mother years earlier and bought my father's papers. No credit was given to my father."

Vane did not have to ask Isabel her feelings on the matter.

"It wasn't thievery," she said, examining the small key in her hand. "After all, the gentleman had paid for those papers, and my mother gave them freely. It's just—" She heaved a weary sigh. "My father, Morgan Thorne, was a remarkable man. I always thought I might be able to get his papers published so he could be honored for his work. However, this has proven to be a difficult task. Mr. Fawson and the gentlemen he represents would rather purchase my father's notes and sketches and put their name on his work than assist me in honoring a dead man who has already been forgotten."

Not by you, Vane thought. "I could make some inquiries on your behalf," he said measuring his words. Isabel could be awfully prickly when it came to accepting anyone's help.

Her expression grew wistful. "You are too kind. However, it is more complicated than it appears." She walked around him to the center of the study and opened her arms. She slowly pivoted on her heel as her gesture encompassed the dingy interior of the study. "It breaks my heart to part with any of my father's work."

Vane moved to her. "Then don't."

Isabel impulsively reached out and lightly touched his face. Her next words stopped him from leaning in and kissing her. "Only a man who has never wanted for anything could stand by his convictions. Regrettably, I have not been as noble. I have to balance a daughter's love for her father with practicality. Each paper I sell provides a roof over my family's head and food on our table. His work has given Delia the season in London that she deserves. My father would have wanted to see her happy."

What about you, Isabel?

He already knew the answer. Much like his mother, Isabel worried about her family. She rarely spoke of her mother, but Vane had already deduced that Mrs. Thorne had depended on Isabel to manage their household after her husband's death.

"Forgive me, I am being selfish, boring you with my troubles." She gestured for him to sit on the settee. "I did not expect to see you this afternoon. I hope you are not too disappointed that Delia is not at home."

Vane studied Isabel's elegant profile as she explained why her sister had left the house without her. If the lady could read his thoughts, she would be dismayed.

No, he was not disappointed at all that Delia was out for the afternoon.

Chapter Sixteen

"Father, you should have called one of the servants to help you," Vane scolded as he caught sight of his eighty-year-old father, his arms full of pots overflowing with lush greenery.

"Christopher," the marquess said. His low, raspy voice held a hint of surprise and breathlessness from his exertion. "Was your mother expecting you?"

"No." Without asking permission, Vane gathered up the four small pots and nodded toward the open door. "Were you heading outdoors?"

Lord Netherley brushed the soil from his gloved hands. "Yes. Yes, of course, but there is no need for you to do that. I was perfectly capable—"

"Where do you want them?" Vane asked, cutting him off. As long as he could remember, the conservatory and the gardens had been his father's favorite mistresses. He often wondered if his sire bedded down on one of the benches at night; it was rare to see both of his parents in the same room.

"I was taking the pots to the east wall," his father

explained, the slight hitch in his breath, causing Vane to slow his pace as they stepped outside into the sunshine. "You can place them on the bench. I'll go get the others."

The muscle along Vane's jaw tightened. *Damn stubborn man,* he thought. "Leave them. I'll collect them for you." As he leaned over to place the pots on the bench, he belatedly noticed that his coat was smeared with dirt. He had been so distracted by his father, Vane had forgotten to remove the garment. "Do you need anything else? Should I call Squires?"

The marquess squinted at him from under the straw hat he had slapped on his head. His blue eyes were clouded with cataracts, but his gaze was still sharp. "Squires is not as young as he used to be. He's probably napping in the butler's pantry."

"Squires is twenty years younger than you," Vane said drily, and the marquess chuckled, his sun-weathered face creasing with humor. His father had been teasing the family butler over his need for an afternoon nap for years. "I'll get the rest of the pots."

However, his father had already turned away and was inspecting the pots on the bench. He was probably worried that his son had bruised the fragile vines. Shaking his head, Vane shrugged out of his ruined frock coat as he headed for the conservatory.

He had not planned on visiting his parents' town house. With Susan and her destructive little monkeys wreaking havoc, Vane was content to keep his distance. Nevertheless, his time with Isabel had put him in a contemplative mood. He had called on the Thorne residence in the hope of breaking down those invisible walls the distrustful young woman had erected. His goals had hardly been noble. Even if Delia had been at home, Vane had intended to find a way to corner Isabel and perhaps steal a few kisses. Instead, he had spent part of the afternoon with a lady who was heartbroken because she had to part with her father's work to pay her creditors.

Vane had discovered something about himself this afternoon. He was not the thoroughly selfish bastard he knew he was capable of being. Frost, and possibly Saint, would certainly have manipulated Isabel to gain what they wanted. He was not proud of his actions, but he had done the same. For some reason, though, that had changed: He could no longer treat Isabel in a callous manner.

When he returned to his father, he had discarded his coat and waistcoat. There was nothing that could be done about his shirt. If he had been alone, he might have untied his cravat and removed his shirt. When he was more lad than man, however, his mother had forbidden him from stripping down and overwhelming the female staff with his physique. Ah, those were the days. He recalled with fondness that there was a time or two when he had managed to get the maids to remove their clothing as well.

"Sun already getting to you, Christopher?" the marquess asked, leaning on the shovel he was gripping. "You have an odd expression on your face."

"I'm fine, Father." Vane walked by his father and put down the pots. "What are you planting?"

"I intend to entwine the honeysuckles and virgin's

bower so it grows into a lovely tangle and provides shade for the alcove." He placed a trembling hand on one of the pots and chuckled hoarsely. "Though I shouldn't have to explain a virgin's bower to a Lord of Vice, eh?"

Vane's gave him a sheepish shrug and glanced away. It was fortunate he did not share Isabel's propensity for blushing, but he felt his face burn under his father's knowing perusal.

"I do not have your enthusiasm for gardening, Father," Vane said. "I don't have the patience for it."

"True enough," the marquess said genially, straightening as he prepared to use the shovel.

Vane stepped forward and reached for it. "You should let someone help you. If not someone from the staff, then hire some jobbers for the manual labor."

His father surrendered the shovel easily. "I ask for help when I need it." He slowly lowered himself onto the bench and began removing his gloves. "If I don't, I have to deal with your mother. The woman likes to make a fuss."

"On that, we can agree." Vane gestured at the ground. Someone had already cleared the section of withered vines and rocks. "How much space do you want between each hole?"

"This will suffice," the marquess said, measuring the distance with his hands.

Silence settled between father and son as Vane stabbed the earth with the blade of the shovel. Neither one of them ever had much to say to the other. There were many reasons. No common interests, different temperaments, even his father's advanced age. Lord Netherley had been fifty-one years old when Vane had been born. All reasonable excuses, Vane silently mused, but they only scratched the surface of their complicated relationship.

The real problem was . . . he was never supposed to be Lord Vanewright. The title had belonged to William, his father's true heir. A brother he had never met, but one he had come to secretly despise. William, the perfect son. At twenty-five, he had been a lieutenant colonel in the Fifteenth Light Dragoons and by all accounts was loved and respected by all. On April 24, 1794, his heroic older brother was slain in the Battle of Villers-en-Cauchies. His lady mother was already pregnant with Vane when she learned of the death of her firstborn. When he was a boy, one of the servants had told him that his mother had been so grief-stricken by her loss that there were concerns she might miscarry the child in her womb.

On September 1, his mother delivered a healthy son to replace the one she lost. Even then, he was a superfluous addition to the family. It was Arthur who had been burdened with taking William's place—an unenviable position, to be certain. Vane paused for a second and wiped the moisture collecting on his brow. How old had Arthur been? Seven, perhaps, or thereabouts. He had grown up watching his father mold Arthur into a young man worthy to replace the heroic William. Unlike Vane, Arthur never seemed bothered by the expectations placed on him.

Then again, he never lived long enough to enjoy his eighteenth birthday. He died a hero. Just like William.

His father had taken one look at his remaining son and found him lacking. The marquess retreated to the conservatory, and Vane was sent away to school. It was an arrangement that both of them were content with.

"Was there a particular reason why you decided to honor us with a visit?"

Vane's thoughts flickered to Isabel. Her sadness had filled the gloomy study when she spoke of her father. He had wanted to offer her more than a sympathetic ear, but Isabel had too much pride to accept anything more. He grimaced. "Not particularly."

"Well, I am pleased we have a private moment to speak," the marquess said gruffly. "You and I have a few things to discuss."

Vane stilled. "Business?"

The marquess gestured broadly with his hand. "After a fashion." He placed his palm on the seat of the bench to help him stand. When Vane moved to assist him, his father waved him away. "I'm fine. Just a bit of stiffness that will fade once I get moving. No, I wish to discuss your upcoming marriage."

It was a jest. Then again, Vane never credited his father with much of a sense of humor. He slammed the blade of the shovel into the earth and rested his hands atop the handle. "What marriage?"

"The one your mother assures me will be taking place soon." The marquess turned away to pick up one of the pots, missing his son's expression of unadulterated fury at his mother. He carefully schooled his features into something more acceptable.

"And did my mother give you the name of my soon-to-be bride?"

His father was not fooled by Vane's calm demeanor. He knelt down and gently tapped the side of the pot to free the plant from its confines. Vane did not offer to help.

"It's time, Christopher."

A chill settled in his spine. "Perhaps you will be kind enough to explain to your wife that I prefer to select my own bride," he said coldly.

His father did not look up from his task, and the slight only infuriated Vane further. "Is that what you are doing? Selecting a bride? Yes, Christopher, your legendary reputation has reached even my old ears. I am well aware that you've been happily sampling every willing miss within reach. I also am aware that you have no intention of marrying any of them."

"And what business is it of yours?"

The marquess might have been on his knees, but he was not cowering. He gave Vane a withering glance. "By God, you are my heir! Every decision you make is my business. Now, about this search for a bride—"

"Are you even listening? I am not searching for a bride. Mother is—although she has had little success since I refuse to cooperate."

"Then you will start cooperating."

"No."

"Perhaps you have forgotten that I am your father."

"No, my lord, that particular fact is one I can never overlook."

"Good. Then heed me, my boy, when I tell you that your wild ways have reached their zenith. You have duties to me and this family, and by damn you will fulfill them even if I have to take that shovel from you and beat some sense into that thick skull of yours."

"You are welcome to try."

"Do not challenge me on this, Christopher," his father warned as he dropped the plant into its awaiting hole with uncharacteristic roughness. "Your mother is expecting you to select your bride this season, and you will not disappoint her."

"You are asking too much."

"No, my fault is in not asking more of you. It has made you arrogant and disrespectful. Well, this afternoon it ends."

Vane opened his mouth, prepared to tell his elderly father that he could go to the devil with his demands.

"I am dying, Christopher."

The quiet confession forced Vane to swallow his bitter oath. "Dying is inevitable for us all."

"I am an eighty-year-old man and not remotely senile. I do not need a condescending lecture from my son."

"Is this merely speculation or have you been examined by a physician?"

"I haven't told your mother, but I suspect she has guessed by the frequency of Dr. Ramsey's visits."

"You're lying," Vane said flatly.

"Am I?" The marquess's raspy chuckle filled the air.

It soon disintegrated into a mild coughing fit. "Well, time will prove one of us right. In the meantime, perhaps you will appreciate a more direct threat. Your mother has gone to great efforts to find you a bride. You will accept the lady she has handpicked for you."

Never. Vane swallowed, attempting to free the muscles in his throat from their sudden paralysis. "And if I refuse?"

His father staggered onto his feet. "I will beggar you. Not one penny until I'm dead and the Netherley title is within your grasp. And don't expect your mother to take pity on you. She will respect my wishes, and my man of affairs will make certain of it."

"According to you, my impoverished state will be blessedly short."

"Do you provoke me, Christopher?"

Vane had no doubt that his father was telling the truth. The real question he needed to ask himself was— *What do I intend to do about it?*

"Am I to have no opinion when it comes to picking a bride?"

The marquess snorted. "Until now, you have had nothing useful to offer on the subject. However, I will leave the final decision to your mother."

"You are condemning me to marry a lady I will never love." In his current mood, he despised the very notion of this mysterious lady.

"You do not have to love her. Just do your duty and bed your lady. When she gives you an heir, you will learn to look upon her with a kind eye."

Choking on his suppressed rage, Vane tossed aside

the shovel and walked away from his father with Isabel's fateful words echoing in his mind.

Only a man who has never wanted for anything could stand by his convictions.

Chapter Seventeen

"It seems unsporting to throttle an eighty-year-old man even when he deserves it."

Seated in a parcel-gilt mahogany chair covered in the crimson caffoy that could be found in many old drawing rooms, Vane watched as Saint's valet prepared His Lordship for their evening. After his enlightening discussion with Lord Netherley, he had driven to Nox in the hope of running into one of his friends. The club's steward, Berus, had told him upon his arrival that the private rooms were empty and were currently being cleaned by the staff. Distracted by an unexpected delivery at the back, Vane was too restless to wait idly for one of his friends to arrive.

"My father is stronger than he looks. The years he had dedicated to his gardens have made him as tough as most jobbers." A wily bastard, too, Vane silently added. His father and mother had more in common than he had thought. "I cannot allow him to get away with this."

Saint turned, lifting his arms so the valet could slip a light blue silk taffeta waistcoat embroidered with silver silk thread into place. Over the past eight months, he had allowed his usually short dark chestnut hair to grow out until it covered his ears. The soft waves reminded Vane of the Greek statues they had admired together in the museum. If a man could be called beautiful, Saint was worthy of the description, even if he did possess a devilish temper when provoked.

"Between you and Dare," Saint said, his white teeth flashing as he smiled and turned again to appease his valet, "I count myself fortunate that my sire had the decency to expire in his mistress's bed when I was too young to be any use to him or my mother."

For his friend, it was an old wound that had never quite healed so Vane remained silent.

Saint did not have much faith in families. Often he viewed them as a damn inconvenience. In general, the Marquess of Sainthill was not Vane's first choice when it came to sharing his private woes about his family. At times like this, he usually sought out Dare's opinion. His friend was acquainted firsthand with the frustrations of dealing with a father who never quite appreciated his son's worth. He also sympathized with Vane's unspoken resentment toward William.

Dare's older brother, Charles, the former Lord Pashley, was no one's idea of a hero. Abusive and unfaithful to his wife and family, and possessing a temperament that bordered on madness, Charles had been Dare's boyhood tormentor and rival. No one had been particularly shocked by the man's violent end.

"Have you spoken to your mother about the argument you had with your father?"

"I did not trust my temper." Vane brushed back the strands of hair that were making his forehead itch as a soft growl of frustration escaped his lips. "I doubt she knew of my father's plans to confront me. Nevertheless, she will not defy him. If I fail to live up to my obligations, my father will cut me off until I bow to his demands."

Saint tilted his chin up. The valet appeared to be oblivious to their conversation as he concentrated on tying his friend's cravat. "It seems you have two choices: either marry a silly chit who meets your parents' approval, provided you can stomach bedding her. Or—"

Vane could sense Saint's smile. "Or what?"

Saint murmured something to the servant, and the man quietly withdrew. His friend took a minute to admire himself in the mirror before he replied. "Well, you could always buy an army commission and pray for a merciful bullet to put an end to your misery."

Despite his dark mood, Vane discovered that he could still laugh, which probably was his friend's intention all along. "You are a rotten friend, Sainthill. Leave me to my suffering!"

Saint braced his arms on Vane's chair and grinned. "Then you will need brandy. Bottles and bottles. And women. Greedy strumpets and fashionable Impures of the *ton*."

"No." Vane shoved the marquess aside as he came out of his chair. "No females. They're at the heart of my troubles."

Yours as well, my friend, he thought, but he did not bother pointing out the obvious. He had enough problems. He did not need to ruin the evening by provoking a fight he had no desire to win.

Saint clapped his hand on Vane's shoulder. "With the help of your fellow Lords of Vice, you will drown in a potent river of debauchery."

It sounded like a damn fine evening for two unmarried gents!

"Do you see that gentleman in the gray waistcoat?"

Isabel discreetly searched the crowded room for the latest male who had captured her sister's attention. Thus far, Delia had spent the evening flirting with several admirers rather than listening to the talented soprano Lady Kerfoot had invited to perform for her guests.

"Do you see him?" her sister whispered, using her fan to hide her rude behavior.

Isabel craned her neck. Ah, yes. Gray waistcoat. The gentleman was seated seven chairs to their right. He had straight blond hair and a friendly countenance. The man noticed her curiosity and winked at her. Isabel hastily glanced away. In her opinion, the gentleman was too friendly.

"I see him," Isabel murmured.

"Do you think you can secure an introduction from Lady Kerfoot?" Delia offered a coy smile to the blond stranger. "He has lovely eyes."

You cannot see his eyes from this distance! Isabel wanted to yell, but she held her tongue. Her gaze returned to the gentleman. The poor sot was mouthing *I love you* to Delia, and she was preening under his lovesick regard. What the young gentleman didn't realize was that he had competition. Having men reduced to fisticuffs on her behalf would be the highlight of the evening for her sibling.

"I will appeal to Lady Netherley for an introduction," Isabel whispered to Delia. The elderly marchioness had arrived late to the recital and was seated behind them. However, she was certain the lady would seek her out to inquire about the progress Isabel had made in securing Delia's interest in Lord Vanewright.

How could she report that she was failing?

Delia only seemed mildly curious about the earl, and Vane . . . Isabel's gaze dropped to her clasped hands on her lap. Lady Netherley would not be pleased if she learned that her son preferred Isabel's company to Delia's.

Oh, the entire plan was hopeless!

As Isabel had predicted, Lady Netherley approached her and Delia minutes after their hostess announced that there were refreshments in the adjoining chamber. Since the marchioness could not discuss her plans openly, she acquiesced to Delia's shy request to become better acquainted with Lady Kerfoot, not realizing her sister's true intentions.

Annoyed with the entire evening, Isabel did not attempt to interfere. Perhaps it was unkind of her, but she hoped the blond gentleman was a greedy fortune hunter. It was exactly the sort of gentleman her manipulative younger sister deserved.

Isabel started when Lady Netherley clasped her hand. "How are you this evening, Isabel. You seem distracted. Is something amiss?"

"No, not at all," she lied, softening her deceit with a smile. "I do not wish for you to think me unsophisticated, but three hours of music was tiring."

The marchioness's eyes lit up with amusement. "My backside is aching as well. Look about, I doubt you will find a single guest sitting the rest of the evening."

Isabel searched the room, realizing the older woman was correct. She laughed, and some of the tension of the evening faded. "Good. I feared I was the only one."

With her gaze occasionally straying to Delia, Isabel followed Lady Netherley to one of the open windows.

The marchioness did not mince words. "We have little time to discuss this, so tell me quickly. How fares our plan? Have you seen Christopher?"

In this, Isabel could answer her truthfully. "Yes, my lady. Lord Vanewright has become a frequent visitor to our humble drawing room."

"Good . . . good," Lady Netherley nodded, her blue-green eyes gleaming with approval. "And what of Delia? Has she fallen in love with my son?"

"Uh—I . . ." Isabel gave a vague helpless shrug. How could she tell such a blatant lie when her sister was across the room flirting with the blond gentleman who had caught her eye? "It is too soon to tell, my lady. However, Delia has never uttered an unkind word about Lord Vanewright."

"And what about you?"

Startled by the question, she stammered, "I—I beg your pardon?"

"Has Christopher been treating you kindly?" Lady Netherley asked, her eyes sharpening on Isabel's face.

"Naturally. Lord Vanewright has been the perfect gentleman."

The marchioness almost seemed disappointed by her companion's response. Before Isabel could press, the odd expression had vanished and the older woman was beaming at her.

"You are a generous soul, Isabel." The marchioness took her by the arm and patted her hand. "We need to find you a respectable man who will appreciate your sweet, compassionate nature. Someone who can relieve you of the burden you carry on your young shoulders."

Isabel hoped she did not look as appalled as she felt. "You are too kind, madam."

"Do not fret, Isabel," she said with genuine affection threading her soft voice. "You must think with your limited prospects that such a man does not exist. You must learn to trust me. I have an instinct for these delicate matters of the heart."

Unable to think of anything polite to say, Isabel simply nodded.

Vane sidestepped the two fighting men who had thrown themselves into his path and staggered toward the table where Saint, Frost, and Hunter were awaiting his return from the much-needed task of relieving himself.

Dare, Sin, and Reign had joined them at Nox where their evening had begun. They had remained downstairs in the common rooms, where they had spent hours playing cards, drinking, and debating politics and the latest news in the papers until Frost and Saint had almost come to blows over their differences of opinion.

Later, Dare and the others had departed with some reluctance. His friends had made promises to their wives. One of the ladies of the *ton*—Vane could not recall which one—was holding a music recital, and while Dare, Sin, and Reign had cleverly avoided the boring affair, the gents were obligated to join their wives for a late supper elsewhere.

He idly wondered if Isabel and Delia had attended the gathering.

The brandy Vane had been happily pouring down his gullet for hours had done its job. Instead of a tavern, Saint had brought them to the residence of Lord Ravens, a gentleman who had gained a certain reputation for his intimate gatherings.

Vane did not particularly care for the man. If there was truth to the rumors, the earl had a predilection for hurting his lovers, something Vane abhorred even if the consent was mutual. Some years ago, there had been an idle discussion of offering Ravens membership at Nox, but nothing had come of it.

To his surprise, Lord Ravens had greeted Saint as a close friend, which was something else he needed to ponder further with a clearer head. At the moment, his brain was pleasantly numbed and the desire to throttle his sire had waned into disgust. Vane had not cursed his father's name in hours, which he assumed was a good sign that he was drunk.

"Our merry group has grown in my absence," he said in lieu of a greeting. "G'evening, ladies." He managed to bow without falling.

"Vane, did you get lost in this maze of a house?"

Hunter asked. During Vane's absence, he had collected a pretty redhead who was petting His Grace's straight dark hair as if he were her favorite stallion.

"Thought you walked all the way home to piss," Frost said, his tongue thick from drink. A brunette with green eyes was seated on the rug, positioned between his friend's long, outstretched legs. He felt the curious stroke of her heavy-lidded gaze, but it was apparent that she had picked Frost for the evening.

"Where's Saint?" Vane asked, slurring his words as he finally noticed that the marquess was missing.

Frost shrugged. "He mentioned that he had a small task to perform. I hope she isn't too disappointed."

Hunter and the two women burst into laughter at Frost's jest. Clearly his friends believed Saint had slipped away to fuck one of the many females their host had provided for his guests. They were probably right. Not that Vane cared one way or the other.

"Come join us," Hunter invited. "Do you have a preference in hair color or shape or will any female suffice?"

Vane swayed on his feet as his mind conjured the sort of female he desired, a brown-eyed beauty with a tall, slender build and long hair that ranged from golden to light brown. "I won't find her here," he said, surprise lacing his voice.

After his argument with his father, he had no business sniffing after any lady, and that included Miss Isabel Thorne.

"Vane, you underestimate Lord Ravens," Frost said, raising two fingers to signal a servant. "I am certain he can provide you with—"

"He has nothing I want." Vane shook his head as if he hoped the action would clear his muddled brain. "Enjoyed our evening as always. I will see you tomorrow. Tell Saint that I have gone home."

Chapter Eighteen

It was long past midnight, and yet Isabel had been too restless to retire for the night. On the drive home from Lady Kerfoot's, Delia had proclaimed herself half in love with two of her new admirers. All four gentlemen had vowed to call on the Thorne sisters, much to her sister's elation. In high spirits, she invited Isabel to claim any of her castoffs.

Isabel shut the book she had been reading and rubbed her weary eyes. She should have never brought Delia to London. Everything about their stay was fraught with risk: Delia's flirtations, Lady Netherley's demands, her common sense whenever Vane was near, and the unforeseen disasters lurking just beyond her careful planning. This evening, Isabel had overheard Lord Botly and his wife as they discussed their recent visit to the theater with their hostess.

Isabel doubted the man who denied their very existence would welcome his granddaughters with open arms.

Without any time to explain, Isabel had grabbed her

sister by the hand; they lingered in the garden until the Botlys had departed. They had averted one disaster, but how long would their luck hold? Sitting alone in the study, Isabel had read her book and sipped the medicinal cordial Mrs. Allen kept hidden in the kitchen. She'd prayed it would calm her frayed nerves.

Vane was correct. She was not cut out for subterfuge.

A muffled shriek escaped her lips as something struck the window with a *crack*. Isabel tossed the book aside and dashed for the door. Fear had spurred her to action, but she had no specific plan except to run upstairs. Her bare feet skidded to an abrupt halt when she heard the noise a second time. A third. Frowning, she realized someone was throwing something at the window.

Isabel had the good sense to retrieve the iron poker from the hearth before she approached the window. She flinched and jumped back a step as another small object, most likely a pebble, struck the glass pane. Warily, she drew back the curtain.

Vane stood below the window.

Relief flooded her limbs. Still clutching the iron poker, she unlatched the window and opened it. "Are you drunk? You gave me such a fright! I have a good mind to bash your skull in with this poker."

His handsome face crinkled into an irresistible grin. "You will have to let me into the house if you want to dent my skull."

"I am doing no such thing, Lord Vanewright," Isabel said primly. "Go home before the watch sees you and mistakes you for a housebreaker."

"Take pity on me, Isabel," Vane entreated, his arms extended. "A few minutes so I may bid you a proper good night, and then I will take my leave."

Her eyes narrowed as she glanced at the empty street. "Where is your coach?"

"I told my coachman to drive onward and then circle back." Hatless, he staggered back a step to keep his balance. "I did not want to cast suspicions on this house. I wouldn't do that to you and your sister."

Isabel hesitated. "The hour is late."

"And yet, here we are, Isabel. You and I," he pointed out unnecessarily. "Let me in. A few minutes. What harm can I do?"

Her forehead wrinkled as she frowned at him with undisguised suspicion in her gaze. "Have you been drinking?"

"Yes," he conceded, "and you would be, too, after the day I've had."

Isabel bit her lower lip and cast a guilty glance in the direction of the study where she had abandoned a glass of cordial on the table. She was in no position to judge.

"Delia is asleep, and I am not properly dressed for visitors."

Vane chuckled. It was low, sensual, and full of unspoken promise. Her stomach fluttered as warmth pooled in her limbs.

"Since I have no intention of being proper, your state of dress hardly matters, does it?"

Madness had brought him to the Thornes' residence. Madness and a considerable amount of brandy. When he had ordered his coachman to drive down Isabel's street, he had told himself that he had no intention of stopping. Then he had noticed the oil lamp burning invitingly through the window of the study. Isabel had not retired for the evening.

A sudden need to see her seized him by the throat. It prompted him to pound on the small trap door and to order his coachman to halt. He hastily disembarked from the coach before he could think of a single reason why he should not summon her to the window.

As he had approached the town house, the small sliver of conscience he possessed almost hoped Isabel would have the good sense to turn him away. If she let him into her home, he was afraid he would not be able to keep his promise and leave.

"I *will* use this poker if you misbehave," she said fiercely.

"I consider myself warned, Miss Thorne."

Isabel nodded. "Very well. Come to the door and I will let you into the front hall—but no farther. You may bid me good night and then take your leave."

"Upon my word," he said humbly, praying he was telling the truth.

A minute later, the front door opened. Isabel must have brought the oil lamp from the study and placed it on the small round table in the front hall to illuminate the interior.

"It is fortunate you did not wake the entire household," Isabel said in lieu of a greeting as she stepped aside so he could enter the hall. She promptly shut the door.

"I will count my blessings later." Vane reached up to

remove his hat, and then remembered that he had left it in the coach. "Forgive the late hour. I was on my way home and saw the light in the study."

"The drive home took you down our street?" she said, sounding unconvinced.

"This evening it did."

Perhaps it was impolite to scrutinize a lady in her current state of undress, yet Vane could not resist. She was captivating. Despite her protestations, Isabel's attire covered her from her neck to her feet. She wore a simple white muslin dress—or perhaps it was her chemise. It was difficult to tell without untying the white pelisse robe decorated with plumetis embroidery. Even her arms were covered. Several layers of muslin, embroidery, and lace were denying him from even the slightest glimpse of the tempting flesh underneath. Fortunately, his experience with the female form was quite extensive, and no amount of muslin was likely to quell his curiosity or imagination.

"So you've come to bid me good night," she said crisply as she touched her hair in a nervous gesture.

Isabel had forgotten to don her lace cap. She had braided her hair into a single plait. The heavy length fell over her right shoulder and over the soft curve of her breast. She had not braided her hair to entice, but the casual styling would have only been seen by her family, or a lover.

Without thinking, Vane reached out and caught the plaited length of hair with his bare hand. Isabel gasped at his brazenness, but she did not pull away.

"I have often wondered and I was correct. It does

feel like silk," he murmured, entranced by the texture and weight.

She gently tugged her braid from his loose grasp. "Did you have a pleasant evening?"

The courteous question was meant to put distance between them. It was on the tip of his tongue to warn her that it was too late. After all, she was the one who had decided to open the door and invite him in.

"Well enough, I suppose." He shrugged. "And you?"

"Pleasant." Isabel crinkled her nose in a delightful manner and laughed. "Though it sorely tested my appreciation for the musical arts."

So she had attended the recital. If Vane had not been so furious after his encounter with his father, he might have sat beside her and discovered what she had found so amusing about the evening.

"I had a nasty argument with my father this afternoon," he admitted, surprised that he wanted to tell her about it.

Isabel appeared to be equally taken aback. Her wary expression faded as concern weakened her resolve to keep her distance from him. "It is difficult to remain cross with the ones we love."

"You have a generous heart, Isabel," he said, dragging his hand through his uncombed hair. "Unfortunately, I am not so forgiving."

She sighed, accepting that she could not dissuade him from his rigid stance. "A generous heart. Your mother paid me a similar compliment."

Suspicion roiled in his gut, mixing with the brandy. "When did you speak to my mother?"

"At Lady Kerfoot's house. I encountered her at the recital."

"Did she mention me or my father?"

"Are you are referring to the argument that you had with your father?" She shook her head. "No, Vane, there would be no reason to discuss something so personal. Your mother loves you."

"My mother loves getting her way," he said bitterly. As did his father.

"Now you are being petulant and unjust." Isabel walked over to the door. "Perhaps we should say good night before you decide to provoke a fight with me."

Vane backed her against the door before she could guess his intentions. "Too late," he said, pinning her wrists over her head. "I have been fighting you since I saw you sitting on your pretty backside on the dirty floor of the dressmaker's shop."

She glared up at him. "Fighting? I retrieved your precious snuffbox, you disagreeable and ungrateful man!"

He leaned against her, holding her in place with his body. At once, he noticed that Isabel Thorne was not wearing stays. Instead of stiff whalebone, her soft breasts and belly molded against his body.

"I have also been fighting myself," he admitted. "I am so weary, Isabel."

There was a slight tremor in her voice when she spoke. "You just need to sleep off the brandy."

Vane only wished it were so simple. "We both know it is more complicated than that, Isabel."

Her face blanched as a desperate look crept into her gaze. "You promised to go home straightaway."

With his fingers still gripping her wrists, Vane lowered her muslin-clad arms to her sides. He took a deep breath and savored the feel of her body against his. Isabel would not escape him until he was ready to let her go. "And so I shall, my lovely Isabel. All I require is a kiss, and then I shall take my leave."

Isabel's heart was pounding. She silently wondered if Vane could feel it. Despite their clothing, she felt every unyielding contour of his body as he pressed her against the door.

Even so, she was not afraid. She would never have opened the door if she had truly feared for her safety. "Do I need to remind you, Lord Vanewright, that I belong to another?"

"Ah, yes, you are referring to the mysterious gentleman who has *almost* committed himself to you, are you not?" His brandy-laced breath filled her nostrils.

"He exists," Isabel said tersely. *After a fashion.* "And I do not believe he would be pleased if I were kissing other gentlemen during his absence."

Vane grinned down at her. With his left forearm braced above her head, he used his other hand to caress her plaited hair. "Has your beloved gent seen you with your hair down, Isabel? Felt your body against his without your whalebone cage? Has he seen incredibly expressive brown eyes glow with desire in the middle of the night?"

"Of course not! It would be unseemly to allow him such intimacies—" Her eyes rounded in dismay: She had unwittingly allowed him to trap her with her own words.

"And yet, I have the pleasure of experiencing them all," he said, his eyebrows coming together as he studied the soft uneven tail of her long braid. "Personally, I would not give a gentleman who can resist your wiles too much of my esteem. No offense, but the man sounds like an arse."

Isabel silently agreed. Mr. Ruddel was an arse. Fortunately, he was not *her* arse. Nonetheless, there was no reason to point out the fact that she had no intention of marrying the man. She had already revealed too much of her feelings to Vane.

"Your opinion is duly noted, my lord."

He tickled her cheek with the end of her braid. She made a soft choking sound in her throat. If she were not so vexed with him, it might have been misconstrued as laughter. "Quit that at once!" she snapped, turning her face upward to avoid the itchy hairs.

Vane's mouth slanted over hers.

Belatedly Isabel realized he had once again used trickery to get what he wanted from her.

The kiss he had demanded. The kiss she had unintentionally promised.

A gentle farewell as he made his way home in the darkness.

Although it was difficult since her movements were hindered, Isabel closed her eyes and willed her body to relax. Reacting to the subtle changes, Vane shifted his stance and allowed her a little freedom before his hips pressed enticingly against hers. In tandem, his lips brushed hers, silently encouraging her to give him access.

Of late, she seemed to be taking all sorts of risks. Reckless undertakings usually were met with disastrous results. Even knowing this, her lips parted and she took a small part of him inside of her. Isabel moaned as Vane stroked her tongue with his, a clever, tantalizing dance meant to imitate the mating of male and female flesh.

Isabel was aware of the rigid rod pressing against her lower belly, of her own body's response. There was an almost painful tightening between her legs and an answering wetness that might have shamed her if Vane knew of it.

His right hand covered her left breast as Isabel opened her mouth, craving more than the teasing sweeps and flutters from his clever tongue. She suckled the nimble flesh and his fingers dug into the fabric of her pelisse robe.

Neither one of them uttered a word. He had demanded a kiss, and those were the unspoken rules. If they ended the kiss, he would have to stop touching her. She would have to let him go.

Isabel started when his callused hand found her bare breast. When had he slipped his fingers through the slit of her robe and under her chemise? Her nipple contracted as his fingers found her areola. Her breath caught in her lungs as his fingers glided over the tiny bumps that circled the aching flesh.

Vane muttered an unintelligible oath against her lips as he reached between them and adjusted his swollen manhood. She bit his lower lip for slight separation and he returned the mild reprimand. Isabel moaned with pleasure when he pushed her against the door again. This time she felt the broad head of his manhood press into her. Even through the layers of fabric, she trembled as the blunted flesh found her womanly core.

His hips ground against her in a rhythm that had her blindly reaching inside his evening coat and under his waistcoat. Isabel grabbed fistfuls of his shirt and pulled him closer. Vane's hand cupped her breast as his thumb caressed her nipple until she thought she could not bear it.

Their tongues tangled and all Isabel could think was that it wasn't enough. She wanted more of him. Suddenly her clothes were too confining and she despised the limitations of her body. She wanted him inside her, so deep he would always be a part of her. Isabel wanted to drink him as if he were a potent wine until she was drunk with pleasure. Allow him to cover her like a sheet until his scent clung to her skin, marking her as his.

Vane sensed her frustration. The frantic rocking of his hips told her that he hungered for the easing only her body could provide. Unlike her, he intended to do something about it. Without warning, he tore his mouth away from hers and ripped her pelisse robe and chemise with one violent tug, exposing her left breast.

No, she thought wildly, *the rules.*

She had forgotten that rules meant nothing at all to a Lord of Vice.

Every cell in her body was vibrating with need when his mouth latched onto her exposed nipple. He suckled as if he was starving for succor only her body could provide. Isabel tried to push him away in a feeble attempt to make him stop, but felt helpless as a ripple of pleasure rolled down her body. Her legs parted automatically, allowing his manhood and the damp muslin to rub the sensitive flesh between her legs.

Suddenly, instead of pushing him away, Isabel was struggling to pull him closer. She bit her lower lip to prevent herself from screaming. The frantic pumps his manhood was striking against her womanly core were her undoing. Her breasts and womb pulsed with a startling pleasure she had been unaware her body was capable of.

Vane did not lift his head until she was breathless and too weak to fight him. He kissed her tenderly on the lips and allowed her to stand without his assistance.

"You . . ." Isabel gave up speaking. She sagged against the door and tugged the torn pelisse robe over her exposed breast. She pretended not to notice the several bite marks on her pale flesh.

A part of her was pleased to note that Vane was not unaffected by that madness that had claimed them. His shirt was ripped, and the prominent bulge in his trousers looked painful to her untrained gaze. She tensed, waiting for him to demand more from her.

"I will take my leave. Good night, Isabel."

Vane was leaving.

"*That* was a farewell kiss," Isabel said, bewildered by the hurt and anger she heard in her voice. Her lower lip quivered. She stepped away from the door so he could leave. If he stayed, she might be tempted to dent his skull with the iron poker.

It was either that or cry.

Vane opened the front door and hesitated at the threshold. "That wasn't a farewell kiss."

Isabel stared at him, mutely willing him to leave before he confessed something that would make her despise him for the rest of her life.

"I never expect to take—No." He gave her a sheepish look. "It is too late for this discussion. And I promised. One kiss and I would leave."

"A farewell kiss," Isabel prompted, finding her voice as her eyes filled with tears.

The scoundrel had the audacity to grin at her. "What you might want to ponder as you climb into your chaste bed is what would have happened if I had stayed. I doubt either one of us would have been happy with the consequences."

Isabel winced and closed her eyes. *Lady Netherley. Delia.*

When she opened her eyes, she discovered that he had already shut the door. She took a deep breath.

She gasped when the door abruptly swung open. Vane leaned against the door frame. "Have you received an invitation to Lord Fiddick's masquerade?"

She seemed to live her life in half measures. She was almost betrothed to Mr. Ruddel, and this evening she had almost been ravished by a madman.

"No, I do not believe so."

Vane winked at her. "You will. And do not disappoint me by not attending. I will not be pleased if I have to search London for you. Nor will you."

Isabel waited until the door closed before she sat down on the bottom step of the staircase.

Chapter Nineteen

Two days before Lord Fiddick's masquerade ball, a box arrived for Isabel. She recognized Vane's bold handwriting on the note his servant hand-delivered.

"His Lordship wanted me to convey his high hopes that you will accept his gift, Miss Thorne. He was most specific that the costume is for you, and not for your sister."

Alone in her bedchamber, she removed the lid and peered inside. Bemused, she broke the wax seal and read the words scrawled within.

Behold the witch who bespells men into beasts.

—V

Isabel picked up the white mask encrusted with gold spangles and glass beads and brought it up to her face. Catching a glimpse of herself in the mirror, she began to laugh. She was still laughing when Delia walked into the bedchamber.

"Mrs. Allen said there was a delivery for you," her

sister said, mildly offended that Isabel had not told her about the mysterious box. Delia paused as she noticed the mask.

"It appears I no longer need a costume for Lord Fiddick's masquerade," Isabel announced, withdrawing the mask from her face. "Even so, I can think of an embellishment or two that will improve the impression I hope to make."

Vane and Saint stood near the balustrade of the gallery overlooking the front hall. Impatient, he had been waiting for Isabel and Delia to arrive.

"Is there a significant meaning to the masks you have chosen this evening?" Saint inquired, his mouth twisting into a knowing smirk.

At Vane's suggestion, the Lords of Vice were wearing formal evening attire and half masks representing various beasts. Saint was a hawk, Dare an owl, Hunter a lion, Sin an alligator, Reign a fox, Frost a snake—his choice amusing everyone. Vane had claimed the wolf mask for himself.

"It seemed appropriate since most of the *ton* believes we are beasts walking about on two legs," Vane explained to the marquess.

"Very true," he said, his forearms resting on the top of the railing as he surveyed the crowd below waiting to greet Lord and Lady Fiddick. "Have you seen Regan, Juliana, and Sophia's costumes? The ladies collaborated and are attending as the Moirae. I believe Sophia is portraying Clotho, Juliana is dressed as Atropos, and Regan is Lachesis."

Vane's attention kept shifting back to the Fiddicks' front door. "The Moirae . . . are they not depicted as old crones in Greek mythology?"

All three women were exceptionally beautiful. Even masked, no one would mistake them for ugly hags.

Saint chuckled. "I never said that they were striving for an accurate representation."

A small commotion below had both gentlemen leaning over. Vane grinned at Saint as he realized that Isabel and Delia had arrived. Even masked, he would have recognized them: Very few women matched their willowy statures. Delia strode through the threshold first wearing a light blue round dress with silver netting. Isabel had told him that her sister would be attired as a sea nymph. Her costume evoked approving murmurs from nearby guests.

Saint apparently approved of Delia's costume as well.

"Hmm, this hawk might make an exception and plunder the sea for prey this evening."

Before Vane could reply, Isabel entered the front hall. Her half mask in place, she had donned the white stola he had selected for her. To cover her bare arms, a gold silk palla was pinned at her right shoulder and draped across her body.

The guests around her started to laugh and applaud when they glimpsed her small companion.

"By God, is that a *pig*?" Saint clapped, enjoying the spectacle as Isabel used a plaited leather tether to lead her pig toward her host and hostess. "Who is Isabel supposed to be?"

Neither Vane nor Saint had noticed that Frost had joined them. Lifting his black reptilian mask from his face, he peered down at Isabel, his eyes glittering with undisguised appreciation.

"Is it not obvious? The lady is Circe."

Her grand entrance had been shared with a pig.

Isabel would never forget Lord Fiddick's expression when she handed him the pig with her compliments. It seemed the most practical solution, since she did not relish strolling about the ballroom with an animal nibbling on the hem of her dress all evening.

Masked guests circled her, slowing her progress to the ballroom. Had Vane witnessed her entrance? She had searched for him, but of course everyone was masked and he had not revealed the nature of his costume.

She had lost Delia before she had greeted Lord and Lady Fiddick. There was no sign of her pale-blue-and-silver costume. By the time she had reached the ballroom, an hour had passed. During her search, she had stumbled about Lord Sinclair and his wife, Juliana; received numerous invitations to dance, one of them from the Duke of Huntsley; and spent half an hour standing beside Lady Netherley in the hope that Vane would find her.

Eventually, the tight mask and the overly warm ballroom took their toll on her high spirits. Excusing herself from the small group of people surrounding the marchioness, Isabel left the ballroom and ascended the large staircase. She removed her mask. Someone had mentioned that several rooms had been prepared for guests seeking solace from the music and confusion, and it was exactly what she needed before she renewed her hunt for Vane and her sister.

What Isabel had not expected was to find them together.

Her hand still poised to open the door, she silently stepped to the side so the couple could not see her. The large mirror mounted on the wall provided her a glimpse of their reflections without risk of discovery.

Both of them had removed their masks.

"You are not being very discreet, Delia," Vane said, and Isabel could hear the humor in his voice.

"Nor are you," her sister countered. "I suspect neither one of us is burdened with such principles as Isabel."

Isabel recoiled as Delia spoke her name. They were speaking too softly for her to hear everything that was being said. She tilted her head and closed her eyes to concentrate. Her desire to eavesdrop on their private conversation had nothing to do with her own confusing feelings for Vane. Lady Netherley would want to be apprised of these latest developments.

"I do not feel reasonable," Vane muttered. "What do you want, Delia?"

Her sister laughed smoothly. "Perhaps you are asking the wrong question, my lord. Here, allow me to demonstrate."

Isabel's eyes opened at the deafening silence. With dread, her gaze sought out the mirror and her heart stopped. Entwined in a passionate embrace, Vane was kissing Delia.

A soft gasp escaped Isabel's lips.

Her body tensed as Vane tore his mouth away from her sister's ravaged lips, his hand still protectively clasping Delia's shoulder. "Who's there?"

Isabel backed away from the partially opened door. A confrontation was the last thing she desired. Whirling away, she hurried down the corridor.

"Isabel!"

She ignored Vane's order to halt, and made her way down the staircase. When she reached the landing below, she brought her half mask to her face and moved through the crowd. With her face covered, no one knew who she was, and Isabel was grateful for her anonymity. Stepping behind an alabaster column, she watched from afar as an unmasked Vane searched the sea of guests. A look of pure frustration darkened his features, but he had yet to give up his search for her.

Isabel strolled away from the column, and used the steady stream of merry revelers to conceal her movements, though the ruse was unnecessary. Vane had decided to search other parts of the house for her. She did not realize she was holding her breath until pain in her chest forced her to exhale.

"Pardon me," a gruff, unfamiliar gentleman muttered as he tried to pass by her. Noting her attire, he stiffened, and Isabel braced herself for a stern lecture on the choice of her brazen costume this evening.

"Are you Miss Thorne? Miss Isabel Thorne?"

Isabel's mouth parted in surprise. Although she had only glimpsed him from a distance, she was positive this masked harlequin was her grandfather Lord Botly.

Unprepared for this inevitable encounter, she meekly

replied, "No, my lord. I am Circe." She curtsied and moved away from him.

Isabel would rather risk running into Vane than confront her indomitable, unforgiving grandfather who had preferred to ignore her and Delia's existence. He probably had come to warn her off. After all, this was his world, not hers.

But it could be her sister's world if Delia and Vane married.

"No, damn you, I did not mean your costume. I—"

Isabel did not hear the rest; Lord Botly's explanation was muffled by the surrounding noise. She made her way toward the main staircase. With no sign of Vane, she descended the stairs, all thoughts centered on fleeing the house before she was caught again by the two gentlemen she intended to avoid.

Collecting her cloak from a helpful servant, Isabel continued out the front door with her half mask in place. Once the wind caught her hair, an ominous sign of the storm that was approaching, Isabel belatedly noticed that the congested coaches and carriages all looked more or less alike in the gloom. Undeterred, she strove onward, ignoring the curious stares from coachmen and footmen, hoping that when she reached the end of the long, snaking line of equipage she would find a hackney coach willing to drive her home.

A brutal gust of wind caught her skirt and cloak like a sail and pushed her sideways. Casting aside her half mask, Isabel struggled with her unruly cloak. A drop of cold rain hit her on the forehead, and she glanced up at the dark sky.

Lightning flashed overhead.

"Isabel!"

An unflattering yelp escaped her lips as firm, rough hands seized her by the shoulders and spun her around. Hatless, Vane was scowling at her.

"Only a madwoman would wander out into the night in the middle of a thunderstorm!" he yelled to be heard over the wind.

"What concern is it of yours, Lord Vanewright?" she sneered, attempting to push him away. "Go back indoors!"

Back to Delia.

"Tell me what is wrong. I will fix it if I can."

Even under the dim lamplight of the nearby coaches, Isabel could see the sincerity in Vane's face.

She swiped at the wetness on her cheek, praying he would mistake it for rain. "There is nothing for you to fix. Everything is as it should be," Isabel said, striving for the calm that always eluded her whenever she was around him. For better or worse, Vane had a bad habit of tilting the axis of the life she had built for herself. "Just go."

The wind caught the some of her hair and whipped the strands about, nearly blinding her. Vane closed the space between them and smoothed the offending wisps away from her eyes.

"It was the kiss," he said bluntly. "What were you doing? Spying on us?" He cursed under his breath. The coarse vulgarity directed at her made her cheeks burn in shame.

"Of course not!" she replied, outraged by the mere

suggestion that such a reprehensible purpose had brought her to that door. "I had spotted Lord Botly in the crowd, and I wanted to warn Delia," she lied. "When I went searching for her, I did not expect"—the lump in her throat seemed to double in size—"I did not mean to eavesdrop. Not precisely. I felt awkward, and did not know what to do, particularly when I saw you and my sister . . ." She trailed off, unable to finish.

Vane tucked a strand of loose hair behind her ear. The gesture was absent, almost tender. "You saw Botly. Did he approach you?"

"Later, when I—he asked me if I was Miss Thorne. I told him that I was Circe and slipped away before he could question me further."

The rain was becoming a nuisance. Isabel reached back and tugged the hood of her cloak over her head. Her elegant coiffure was ruined. All she wanted to do was crawl into her bed and never leave it. In the coming years, Delia and Vane could bring their children to visit their bedridden spinster aunt.

"You ran from me."

The steady intensity of his eyes flustered her. "N-no."

"It upset you to see me and Delia kissing."

Was he deliberately being cruel? Her heart was ripped from her chest when she saw them kissing. Sheer tenacity and pride kept her from dissolving into tears. "Not at all. In fact, I am very happy for you both."

The blackguard had the audacity to grin at her. "How many times do I have to tell you that you are an atrocious liar, Isabel? Admit it. You wanted to slap my face for kissing Delia."

Isabel gritted her teeth. "Calling me a liar gives me reason enough, Lord Vanewright."

She squeaked as he backed her up against the side of the waiting coach, his body sheltering her from the elements and preventing her from escaping. "If you do not have the sense to return to the ball, then I shall. Move aside!"

"Poor little Isabel. How much did you glimpse through the narrow gap of the door? What did your sharp dainty ears overhear? Did you see me put my wicked hands on Delia? See me pull her against my aroused body, caress her tempting lips with my mouth? Did you feel a flutter of excitement in your own belly because you knew exactly what it felt like to have my—"

"Yes! I saw it all and I am sorrier than you will ever know. There . . . are you happy?" She pushed against his chest, but somehow her frantic efforts to escape only brought him closer. The warmth of his body seeped into her, taking away the chilly dampness of the stormy night. "P-please, I beg of you. Just let me go."

Vane startled her by giving her a vigorous shake. "Either you weren't paying attention or you might want to consider a good pair of spectacles, Isabel. You did not see me kissing Delia."

Her lips trembled with fury. "Now who is the liar? I saw *you*—"

"No! You saw Delia kissing *me*!" he shouted at her. "Your clever brain took snippets of a conversation and glimpses of supposed misdeeds, and wove it all into a tragic tale of love lost worthy of Shakespeare."

"I know what I saw," she said, though there was little conviction in her voice.

"Heed me, Isabel Thorne, for I will only say this once. Delia followed me into the informal parlor with the purpose of discussing my attentions to you. When I refused to speak of our friendship, she decided to twist the meaning of my words and concluded that my interest in the Thorne sisters was because of *her*. Before I had a chance to deny it, your sister had wrapped herself around me like a choking vine and you were running down the passageway, convinced I was the worst kind of scoundrel."

Was it possible that Vane was telling the truth?

The pain in her heart eased at the glimmer of hope his confession had given her. "I thought—" Isabel shook her head, ashamed by her behavior. "You were right to call me a madwoman. I should have stayed and demanded an explanation."

And slapped his face for good measure!

Deducing her thoughts, Vane's lips twitched. He placed his finger against her lower lip. "Hush."

Oblivious to the discomfort of the rain or their surroundings, he stroked her lip, the gesture igniting every nerve in her body as if she had been struck by lightning.

"Now pay attention. I do not want any misunderstanding between us," he said, his eyes dark and wild as the sea in a summer storm. "A lady filled my thoughts all evening, but it wasn't Delia whom I longed to drag into my arms and kiss until she was warm and adoringly befuddled. It was you, Isabel."

His admission staggered her. "No, it cannot be true."

"Stubborn woman," he admonished softly. The teasing, almost husky quality of his voice should have warned her that her denials were mild hindrances to a man such as Vane. "How can I prove myself to you?"

"There is no need—"

Vane lowered his head and kissed her.

Chapter Twenty

She tasted of tears and rain.

Vane had been longing to put his hands on Isabel ever since he'd observed her grand entrance as Circe, complete with a tethered pig waddling along at her heels. Although Isabel would deny it, she was charming the *ton* with her beauty, quiet nature, and subtle wit. Lord Fiddick was probably still regaling everyone about Miss Thorne's offer to change any of his disagreeable guests into pigs. When she presented the small pig as a gift to the earl and his wife, Lord Fiddick laughed so hard his face turned an alarming crimson hue.

Fiddick and the *ton* were not the only ones under Isabel's spell.

With each meeting, Vane craved more from the lady. Dances and stolen kisses had whetted his appetite and imagination. There were nights when all he could think about before exhaustion claimed him was Isabel. He hungered for her caress, the softness of her lips, the shy awareness that crept in her expression when she sensed the desire he often tried to conceal from her.

Satisfied that the storm had chased away even the most daring, Vane pressed Isabel against the wall of the coach and deepened their kiss. The kiss Delia had given him might have appeared pleasurable, but he had felt nothing—that was, until he realized that Isabel had stumbled across them. Then he was bloody furious. Delia was an obvious little minx. He should have guessed her intentions the moment she entered the room.

Kissing Isabel was different.

She was sunshine and innocence, and coaxing shy endearing kisses from her filled him with a tenderness that he thought he was incapable of giving to anyone.

Isabel also maddened him with a wild, hot-blooded animal lust.

Vane had lost count of how many times that he wanted to forget that she belonged to someone else and toss her over his shoulder. If she would have him, he would carry her off and keep her in his bed until the fever in his loins cooled.

Isabel made a soft breathy sound against Vane's cheek as his lips nibbled their way down to her bare neck. It was such a lovely neck, he silently mused, wondering if she would allow him to buy her a diamond necklace. Paste would not do for Isabel Thorne.

His hand slid possessively around her waist. "Damn your *almost* betrothed circumstances. The gent doesn't exist here in London. Come away with me," he said, nipping her neck.

Thunder rumbled overhead.

"What?" she asked, sounding bemused. "Delia—"

Vane pulled back, and cupped her face with his

gloved hands. "You were already planning to abandon Delia," he said, kissing her again because he preferred to keep her off balance. If Isabel had little thought for the man who desired her hand in marriage, the man was less than nothing to Vane. "Let us leave. Now."

He wanted to take his time when he peeled her out of her damp garments. She deserved a proper bed, not a careless shag against the coach.

Her brown eyes were large and luminous. "How can we? No, it is too reckless!"

"We have the rest of our lives to embrace our responsibilities." Vane could tell by her frown that she was considering his wicked proposition.

"But—"

Vane sealed off her words with a lingering kiss. With a gentle touch of his fingers, her lips parted and his tongue slid over her lower teeth. Proud of the lovemaking skills he had honed at a young age, he teased and tempted her without words.

If that did not work, he was desperate enough to beg. "Say yes."

His heart was caught in his throat when Isabel remained quiet. Then she began to nod. It took him a moment to grasp that she was agreeing to come with him.

"Yes."

Isabel offered him the shy, brilliant smile that always managed to bring his cock to life.

Vane pounded on the side of the coach. "Maston, are you awake?"

"Not likely sleeping with all this rain trickling down my back" was the coachman's gruff reply.

Wide-eyed, Isabel glanced warily up at the man who had been sitting silently on his perch. Clearly she hadn't even noticed that they weren't alone—something for which Vane would gladly reward Maston with a cask of porter.

"This is *your* coach."

"Indeed." With his hand firmly around her waist, Vane guided her forward until he could open the door. "No need for you to climb down, Maston. I have the door."

"'Bout time, I say," the older man grumbled. "I couldn't decide if you were kissing or drowning the lass."

Before Isabel could reconsider, Vane nudged her into the interior. Exchanging rakish grins with Maston, he slapped the side of the coach and said, "Take us home."

Whisked away into the night by a handsome rogue, while overhead the heavens roiled with lightning and thunder. Isabel could not imagine anything more daring or romantic.

Vane did not give her much time to dwell on her decision. Within the dark confines of the coach, he seduced her with his mouth and hands. He whispered dark carnal promises in her ears, and she stroked the proof of his desire. The short journey ended before she had caught her breath. Her legs were so weak with the need he had built within her, Isabel had to lean on him as they made their way to his house.

There was no opportunity to explore his residence. The servants had already retired for the night, and Vane explained in hushed tones that his younger sister had moved into his house while his older sister and her family invaded the Netherley town house.

The thought of encountering one of his sisters doused some of her ardor. Sensing her dismay, Vane quickly explained that his sister was still out enjoying her evening and would be gone for hours. Then he led her up to his bedchamber.

Isabel was too nervous about being discovered to resist.

Before they reached the bedchamber, he surprised her by backing her up into a small alcove. Vane brought his finger to his lips to silence any questions. He brushed her lips with a brief kiss and disappeared down the passageway.

Isabel closed her eyes and listened to Vane's footfalls. A door opened, and Vane greeted another man, though she could not hear what was being said. Most likely, it was his valet, who had been waiting up for his master. After the servant was dismissed, Vane returned to her side.

"Poor little love," he crooned, pulling her into his arms. "Too much adventure, eh? I did not mean to leave you so long, but I forgot about my valet. I normally do not have late-night visitors, so Cheswick is rather distressed that I will not be requiring his services this evening." He took her by the hand, and they walked down the passageway.

His revelation was so unexpected she had the oddest urge to laugh. If half the rumors about the Lords of Vice were to be believed, one would expect Vane to keep a veritable harem in his house. Isabel had not been wrong about the earl's character. Joy took wing in her heart as she realized that she was the first lady he had allowed to invade his private world.

Vane opened the door to his private bedchamber, and beckoned her to enter. Once she stepped into the room, he closed the door and locked it, ensuring that they would not be disturbed.

"Are you cold?" he asked as he briskly moved about his bedchamber to light a few candles and then crouched down in front of the hearth to tend to the coals.

Isabel glanced at the windows as thunder ominously rattled the glass panes.

"Not really." Even though her hair was still damp, her cloak and Vane had kept most of the rain from soaking into her evening dress. He had removed her sodden garment the minute she had stepped into the front hall.

"A little brandy will warm you," Vane said, glancing back over his shoulder with a knowing smile. "And naturally you have me."

"Naturally," she echoed, uncertain of his meaning.

"There," he said, brushing his hands together.

She could hear the satisfaction in his voice. Vane bit the tips of his gloved fingers and pulled, swiftly peeling them from his hands. He had discarded his evening coat and waistcoat once he had entered the room. The distinctive click of glasses colliding and a splash of liquid filled the silence of the bedchamber.

Isabel wrapped her arms across her chest and waited for him to return to her.

He took a sip of brandy. "I could go down to the cellar if you prefer wine," Vane said, offering her the glass.

Isabel did not want him to leave her alone. "The brandy will suffice." She accepted it, trying not to dwell on the intimacy of drinking from the same glass. "Thank you," she murmured and took a tentative sip. The liquid warmed her almost as fast as one of Vane's kisses. She silently recalled that her father used to enjoy brandy now and then. When she was finished, she handed the glass back to him.

"You look . . ." He paused as he sought for the proper word. ". . . terrified."

Isabel could not help but grin. "A little," she admitted, turning away from him. Her gaze settled on his bed, while she recalled all the fascinating things he had whispered in her ear.

Vane came up from behind and nuzzled her shoulder. "What are you thinking? I get nervous when you frown like that. It's usually a sign that I will not like your thoughts."

She sighed. "I cannot help but believe that my sister should be here in my stead." Isabel allowed the back of her head to rest on his shoulder. "Delia suits you better than I. She's the adventurous one." *More beautiful, too.* Though she was wise enough not to speak the words aloud.

Vane whirled her around until she was facing him. "I've had dozens of Delias in my bed," he growled, and Isabel winced as her thoughts wandered to those nameless women who once thought they had a claim on him. "I want you. How can I prove myself to you?"

She shook her head. Despite his notoriety, Vane was an honorable man. She believed him. He was unfailingly, often brutally honest. She was the one who was the liar. How many times had she lied to him and herself?

Isabel could give him what they both desired, even if it was just this one night. "Show me."

His eyes flared at her simple request. Reaching around her, he set the glass of brandy down on the nearest table. "Are you positive?"

"Teach me how to be daring." Her voice wavered, but she refused to give in to her fears. "Show me how to please you."

Chapter Twenty-one

Her quiet request almost shattered his hard-won control.

Vane wanted this first time with Isabel to be special—for both of them. In the past he had enjoyed countless couplings, mindless, frantic fucks where carnal needs were sated, but the heart was left aching. Isabel deserved more from him, and he intended to prove something to her and himself, if she would let him.

Vane gently swept her dark tangled tresses until the heavy length flowed over her shoulder, exposing the nape of her neck. "Have I told you how much I adore your neck," he said, kissing the delicate swells of bone. "It should be adorned with gold, silver, and jewels. Do you have a favorite stone? Diamonds, perhaps?" He methodically began to unfasten the buttons at the back of her dress.

"I-I have not given it much thought." She trembled at his light touch.

"A favorite color, then."

"Blue. No green," she hastily amended, glancing over

her shoulder. "Like your eyes. Both cool and hot. Though I doubt such a stone exists."

Pleased that she would prefer a gem the exact color of his eyes, Vane vowed to pester every jeweler in London until he found such a stone. "If one does, it will be yours."

The bodice of her dress fell away, and minutes later her stays and petticoat. Wearing only her linen chemise and drawers, she sat down on the mattress at Vane's silent urging. He knelt in front of her and removed her evening slippers. Her flight into the stormy night had ruined them beyond repair.

"Pray do not feel obliged to buy me jewelry, my lord."

Frowning slightly at her formality, Vane slowly followed the subtle curves of her calf, reaching higher until his fingers brushed against a garter. "Why would I deny myself the pleasure?" He had always been generous with his lovers. The expense meant little to him. Early on, he had discovered that a lady's appreciation had its own rewards.

Vane untied the garter. Attempting not to heighten Isabel's fears, he forced his hands to move slowly as he stripped the stocking from her right leg. Then her left. He noticed that her nipples were erect, a hint of pink offering him an enticing glimpse of the delectable flesh still hidden from his eager gaze.

"A gentleman buys jewelry for his mistress," Isabel blurted out. "No woman should sell herself so cheaply. I will not be anyone's kept woman. Not even yours."

Vane lowered his gaze, struggling not to feel defensive. Isabel did not understand the arrangement between a gentleman and his mistress. Such affairs could be rather cold-blooded, and had nothing to do with his feelings for the lady sitting on his bed.

The storm raging outside seemed to match his inner turmoil.

"I would not be so arrogant as to believe that I can keep you, Isabel. You are free to leave or stay. The decision has always been yours." Vane stared at her bare feet and waited for her response. Like her neck, her feet were perfection. They were small, slender, and delicately boned. He wondered how she would react if he licked the arches.

He stifled the urge to snort. Knowing Isabel, she would probably panic and kick him in the head.

"I do not want to leave."

Vane's head snapped up at her admission.

His fingers tightened around her ankle. "Be certain, Isabel," he entreated softly.

Outdoors, the winds from the escalating storm moaned and wailed.

"I only have so much restraint. I do not—" It was clearly a difficult admission for him to make to her.

Isabel held out her hand. "Come to bed."

Vane tensed. Unblinking he stared at her, his eyes taking on an almost feral glint in the candlelight. For a second Isabel thought he was going to leap upon her like a large wolf taking down its prey.

Instead, he released her ankle and used the edge of the mattress to stand. "For your sake, I will extinguish the candles."

Isabel blinked as lightning brightened the interior of the room. When Vane stood she saw the proudly displayed evidence of his desire, which his trousers could not conceal. Perhaps he thought her nerves were so fragile that she would faint at the sight of his manhood.

"Leave one candle lit, my lord." She wrapped her arms around her body at his questioning glance. "I would not have you stumble and bump your head. What would Cheswick think if you ruined your shirt for the sake of my modesty?"

Vane chuckled, and blew out several candles before bringing the half-lit candelabra closer. He set it down on the side table. "God created you to bedevil me, did he not?" He untied his cravat.

"Then I would not want to disappoint him."

If he was adept at undressing a lady, Vane was doubly impressive when it came to shedding his own garments. Bare-chested he was an impressive specimen, all muscled flesh with a dark patch of short coarse hair across his chest that revealed he was a male in his prime. He hesitated and looked down at the blatant mound at the apex of his trousers.

"You are unused to viewing a man's body. I will not be offended if you wish to avert your eyes while I finish undressing."

Isabel felt treasured that Vane wanted to protect her, even from himself. However, a coward would not have walked into his house. She slowly slid off the mattress and stood. Ignoring his guarded expression, she unfastened the buttons at his waist.

"It seems only fair," she teased, peeling back the

flap on the front of his trousers. She discovered that the line of hair on his flat abdomen expanded to a nest of crisp masculine hair between his legs.

"Isabel, you are playing with fire," he growled as she reached out to touch the swollen flesh still tucked within his trousers.

"A true philosopher embraces all new discoveries," she said, marveling at the size of his manhood. The small glimpse revealed that every aspect of the gentleman was generous.

"Remove your chemise," he said hoarsely.

Her pulse quickened at his request. Isabel could see that her body was responding to his proximity. Her nipples had hardened at his first kiss. The sensitive tips were chafing against her chemise. She longed to bring her hands to her breasts and rub away the ache.

"If it will not offend."

"Never," he said, visibly straining to keep himself from closing the space between them. "Let me see all of you."

Taking a fortifying breath, Isabel tugged her chemise over her head and let the undergarment fall to her bare feet. Her first instinct was to cover her breasts. A wave of heat suffused her face and chest as Vane stared hungrily at her.

"Christ, Isabel, you are so beautiful," he said, taking the final steps to her.

He lowered his head until it rested lightly against hers. Wordlessly, his fingers sought the ties for her drawers. A firm tug, and the garment glided down her legs.

Isabel shivered, the reaction having nothing to do

with being chilled. Awkwardly she placed her hands on his hips. It helped to steady her, because she could not seem to stop trembling. Vane captured her lips when she lifted her face to his.

The kiss was tender and hesitant. She parted her lips, knowing he would not be satisfied with just a taste. Vane groaned as he crushed her body against his. Fierce and commanding, he turned his head, his mouth grinding against hers. Her breasts tingled, and the marvelous sensation drifted lower, making her aware that the hard flesh between his hips was pressing against hers.

A daring lady might have pushed Vane's trousers lower, freeing his manhood from its confines. Isabel gripped his hips tighter, but she could not bring herself to take the next step.

Her indecision ended when Vane took charge of the situation. As if an invisible tether had severed within him, he swept her up into his arms and carried her to the bed. With a farewell kiss to her lips, he lowered her onto the bed.

Wordlessly, he shoved his trousers over his narrow hips and stripped the fabric from his each leg. Isabel turned her head to the side and watched him undress. Her eyes widened as Vane's manhood jutted out from his hips. Amazingly thick and rigid, the lengthy staff seemed to swell before her eyes now that it was free from the tight confines of his clothing.

Vane had twisted, offering her his profile. She doubted he was motivated by any modesty. Instead, his economical movements revealed that he probably did not want her to dwell too much on what was to come.

Isabel squinted at the sudden bright flashes of lightning, followed by the rumbling growl of thunder.

"A hellish night to be out," he murmured, pausing to glance at the windows. "No one will be eager to rush to their carriages and coaches."

His face cast in shadows, Vane climbed onto the bed. As he crawled up her body, Isabel was acutely aware of the hot velvet staff brushing against her inner thigh.

With his arms braced on each side of her head, he said, "The night is ours, Isabel."

And you are mine!

Vane did not utter the words aloud. By morning, Isabel would be aware of his physical claim. Every movement would remind her of what they had done during the long hours of the night. She would taste him on her lips, smell his scent on her flesh, and when she closed her eyes all she would see was him.

He dipped his head and captured her left nipple with his tongue. Isabel squirmed underneath him as he suckled the sensitive pink nubbin.

"Such sweet breasts." Vane nipped the soft curve of her right breast, and then laved her nipple. "I shall enjoy discovering all your secrets."

Isabel made a tight dismissive noise. "I have no secrets, Vane."

"No?" He smiled against her belly. "Care to wager on it?"

She sucked in her breath when his fingers trailed down to the small thatch of hair between her legs. "Wager?"

"I was born with a gambler's heart, love." Vane traced the seam of her womanly folds, pleased by the dampness collecting as her body prepared for his cock.

"Ha! Only a fool would wager with a self-professed gambler."

"Money is not what I'm after." *Not with you.* Vane deepened his caress, the pad of his thumb circling the knot of flesh within. "Take a chance, Isabel. If you win, I will allow you to name your reward. Your heart's desire."

"And if I lose?" she asked, sounding skeptical.

Isabel was too distracted to notice that she had been relaxing and opening herself up to him.

"Then you will allow me to win *again.*"

Her body started shaking, before she burst into a fit of uncontrolled giggles. "Oh, Vane," she gasped as she tried to sober, the corners of her eyes glittering with moisture. "It sounds like I win either way."

"Only a fool would refuse me," he said, pressing his advantage by sliding his fingers into her dewy sheath. "And you proved on the day we first met that you were no man's fool."

Vane did not give her a chance to form a clever retort. With his forearm braced against the mattress, he overwhelmed her with pleasure. He teased the circumference of her womanly sheath. Circling and tormenting her with swift shallow thrusts that were meant to excite and stretch her for his impatient cock.

His other hand stroked her hair and teased the curvature of her ear, while his mouth leisurely nibbled on her lips moving downward, laving and tickling her throat with his nimble tongue, and finally feasting on her beautiful breasts. He returned to her well-kissed lips, happy to retrace his sensual journey over and over until her need was as great as his own.

Vane had never hungered for a woman as he did for Isabel.

Her innocence should have dissuaded him from the course he had chosen this evening. There was no sport in despoiling a virgin, particularly when the fertile nymph usually had a murderous father who would present the unhappy gent with the option of marriage to his ruined daughter or a festering bullet wound in the body part of his choosing.

A wiser man would seek his pleasures elsewhere. Places like Madame Venna's Golden Pearl provided virgins for male clientele, though he suspected these women lost their innocence countless times each week.

His cock should have shriveled at the mere thought of claiming Isabel's maidenhead, but it hung between his legs like a heavy club. The damn thing throbbed, and touching her was only heightening his agony. As his fingers became drenched with her arousal, the scent of her desire was making his head spin.

Outdoors the wind was keening and shaking the windowpanes as the rain battered the old town house. The wild, stormy night had seeped into his blood, and it called to him. It called to Isabel as well. Her head came off the mattress and she cried out. Ruthlessly he drove his fingers into her wet sheath over and over, wringing out of her body her first pleasurable release while he struggled for control over his own unruly body.

He hooted with laughter at her wondrously bemused expression, and leaned forward to give her a rough kiss on the mouth.

"A woman's pleasure is a potent aphrodisiac," he said, bringing his damp fingers to his lips and licked them. "If this is a potent spell, my Circe, then I do not wish to recover my senses."

Chapter Twenty-two

The man had robbed her of all reason. And voice, Isabel thought as she struggled to catch her breath. With her back pressing into the mattress, she felt too weak to lift her limbs even if her life depended on it. So she did not protest when Vane rose up and positioned himself between her parted thighs. His handsome face hovered inches from her. He looked very pleased with her current condition—as well he might, considering he was responsible.

She should have been mortified that he had managed to make her shriek with pleasure simply by using his hands. But she could not work up any genuine outrage about it. All she could do was gaze up at him and silently wonder if he planned to gloat about his victory.

The realization that she could feel such bliss had been a secret her body had even kept from her.

"You win," she rasped, willing to bow to his expertise.

"Not yet." Vane lowered his head and kissed her. His tongue glided against hers, and she sighed against his lips. He shifted, allowing her to feel the weight of his manhood against her womanly folds. "I pride myself on being a thorough lover."

Was he testing her resolve? Or his? Did he truly have the strength to leave her with her innocence intact when his body was demanding that he complete the seduction?

Her body, still warm from the fire Vane had created within her, welcomed him. A graceful wiggle of his hips, and Isabel was wholly aware of his rigid staff as it pushed against the soft, damp flesh between her legs. His thrusts were shallow, a gentle albeit persistent exploration to see if her body could accommodate his claim.

Isabel flinched, feeling impossibly stretched. "I think you have reached your limits. We do not seem to good fit," she said, feeling as if she had failed him.

"Patience, love." Vane murmured wordless soothing sounds as her face crumpled and she struggled not to cry. His hands seem to be caressing her everywhere: her hair, her breasts, down the side of her waist, over her thighs. The touch was reverent and arousing, and she arched against it, allowing his manhood to slip deeper.

The ache he was creating within her was torturous. Apparently Vane felt the same way. Groaning, he tore his mouth from hers and slid his hands down her back until he cupped her buttocks. After a slight retreat, he thrust his manhood wholly into her sheath.

Isabel did not expect the sharp pain, but it faded when Vane stilled. "Is it supposed to hurt?"

"Only this first time, I'm told," he said apologetically, giving her time to accept his full measure, the weight of his body against her pelvis driving him deeper still. "Can you bear it?"

She nodded.

The tension in his face eased. "Brave, sweet lady. You humble me."

Before she could question him further, Vane began to slowly withdraw his manhood, which eased her discomfort until he surged forward again. His expression tightened as he moved his hips. Advance and retreat, her sheath bathing his rigid flesh with the honeyed moisture of her body until they moved together with a fluidness that left both of them breathless.

One of his hands found its way back up to her face. His fingers encircled the nape of her neck in a possessive fashion. Vane sealed his mouth over hers and his tongue licked and thrust, allowing the memory of her initial discomfort to fade from her mind.

All Isabel could think about was Vane. She suckled his tongue and her fingers tried to grasp his thrusting hips. Sweat coated his body as his tempo quickened. Pounding into the very heart of her, the broad head of his manhood created a new kind of ache within her. She wiggled her hips experimentally, and Vane's response was enthusiastic.

Any sense of control seemed to abandon him. As her nipples scraped against the coarse hairs of his chest, Isabel felt her womb flutter and then clench with some yet-to-be-discovered anticipation. Vane seemed to sense it, too. His eyes shut, he groped blindly for her, his heavy, hard-muscled body melding into hers.

A white bright light akin to lightning filled her vision. Isabel thrashed her head from side to side as her womb pulsed, sending wave after wave of pleasure rippling through her body and into Vane.

His body bucked and his left fist slammed into the pillow above her head. Isabel felt his breath, warm against her cheek as his hips frantically pumped against her and then stilled. Her sheath clenched around Vane's manhood as he shuddered and the buried flesh pulsed. His hot seed filled her and a tranquility she had never experienced settled over her as she tenderly held the man who had become her lover in her arms.

Vane became slowly aware that his cheek was pressed against Isabel's breast. As the lust faded from his loins, he realized that she was valiantly bearing the burden of his body. "I am crushing you."

"Not at all," she murmured sleepily. "You are rather nice to cuddle with."

He snorted in disbelief, and reached for the sheet that had been kicked to the end of his bed. Pulling it over them, he settled down on his side. Isabel sighed and moved closer, wiggling her sweet buttocks against his turgid cock, still damp with her arousal. Vane tucked the sheet around her and wrapped his arm around her waist.

His cock thumped against her. The damn thing should have been sated. All he could think about was how long he had to wait before Isabel would allow him to touch her again.

What if I've frightened her with my lust? he thought,

his mind vehemently rejecting such a notion. *What if she does not want me touching her again?*

"I could bring you some brandy?" he blurted. "To calm you. Ease your aches."

Her neck stiffened at the concern she heard in his voice. "I do not require brandy. Though . . ." She slowly rubbed her leg against his as she took a silent inventory of her body. "I do have a few aches. What about you? Do you need some brandy?"

If he had been alone, he would have poured himself a glass. It was not every day that a virgin could teach him a thing or two about lovemaking. "Not if it requires me leaving the bed. Will you stay the night?"

Vane could not decide who was more startled by the question, Isabel or him. He seemed to be breaking all of his personal rules this evening. First, he brought a lady to his private residence. Second, his rule about deflowering virgins was abandoned, though technically Isabel no longer qualified as one; and third, and most telling, he wanted her to stay with him. The notion of waking up and finding her curled against him held a certain appeal. He absently wondered if she snored.

Isabel stirred and made an attempt to rise. He touched her shoulder and nudged her to settle back against him. "I cannot. Delia would worry if I did not return home."

Vane did not argue with her.

"If I remained, your staff would know. Not to mention your sister. Do you want her telling your mother that you seduced me?"

Vane winced. "Christ, no!" If his mother learned that

he had bedded Isabel, she might spread the news herself if she thought it would get her only son leg-shackled.

Isabel sat up, her hand clasping the sheet to her breasts. "Well, you do not have to worry about Lord Botly. He is not likely to work up any righteous anger over a granddaughter he does not acknowledge." She would have left the bed if he had not captured her wrist to prevent her from fleeing.

Belatedly he realized that his enthusiastic denial had hurt her feelings. As if he could sooth away the insult, he rubbed her back. "I spoke thoughtlessly."

She shook her head, brushing aside his apology. "What we've done—I would not want anyone to use it against you. This was my choice and I do not regret it. You did not lure me into bed with flattery and false promises. If you ever decide to marry, it will not be someone like me."

It was on the tip of his tongue to demand an explanation from Isabel. *What the devil is wrong with marrying you?* he wondered, and then saw the delicate trap he had created for himself. Or had that been her intention all along?

"I have been thinking."

Warily, his brows lifted as his finger explored the small dent at the base of her spine. "A dangerous occupation to be certain."

Isabel wrinkled her nose. "Well, it concerns our wager."

Intrigued, he said, "You are referring to the wager that you lost? You are not crying off?"

"Now you are being insulting."

She turned and smiled at him. The impact of it made his head swim. Any suspicion that she might be playing games with him vanished. Isabel did not have a deceitful bone in her body.

"No, I was pondering the terms. For winning, I am to allow you to win again." She looked awfully delectable sitting on his bed with a sheet wrapped primly around her body. "I have not had the opportunity to study the practical applications of the male body—"

Vane let out a throaty chuckle at her lecturing tone. "So you have a question?"

Isabel beamed at him. "Precisely! I would like to know when you will be capable of winning . . . *again*."

She shrieked with laughter as Vane dragged her down until she was under him and proceeded to prove that he was a man of his word. A Lord of Vice considered all wagers a serious affair.

Chapter Twenty-three

"You disappeared early? Where did you go?"

Isabel's hand shook slightly as she raised the teacup to her lips. Her gaze had not strayed from the book of poetry since she had sat down with Delia in the tiny morning room. She made a soft inquiring noise to buy herself a little time.

After all, what was she to confess to Delia?

Forgive me, sister. While you supped at Lord and Lady Fiddick's, I was in a compromising position with the very man Lady Netherley hopes you will marry. Worse still, I enjoyed it! Well, most of it anyway, she silently amended.

She grimaced as she swallowed the tepid tea. "My apologies for abandoning you, Delia," she said, lowering her teacup into its saucer. "My departure was sudden and unexpected. I would have preferred speaking with you directly, but with so many masked guests filling every crevice of the Fiddicks' residence, it was impossible to find anyone last evening." Isabel gave her sister an apologetic smile. "The footman did convey my regrets, did he not?"

"Yes, I received your message," Delia said crossly. "However, it is unlike you to simply vanish without any explanation."

Her actions had been highly emotional and uncharacteristically selfish. Even if Isabel was willing to confess the truth, she doubted her sister would believe her outlandish tale.

So Isabel lied.

"I suffered from a nasty bout of dizziness before a megrim struck without warning," she confessed, mentally grasping for a plausible reason for her odd behavior. As excuses went, it was an atrocious one—Isabel rarely suffered from illness.

"Oh, you poor dear!" Delia leaned over and placed her palm on Isabel's forehead. "You do feel a bit feverish. Perhaps you should go back to bed."

The suggestion sounded so heavenly, Isabel almost whimpered. She grimaced and shook her head. "No, I have too many tasks that I need to address." With a sigh, she closed her book of poetry. "Later I plan to visit the shoemaker at Great Surry Street. I ruined my evening slippers, and I warrant you could use a new pair, too."

Delia pushed her food around on her plate. "I thought you left Lord and Lady Fiddick's ball before the rain?"

Blast it all! Leave it to her sister to pick up on her small slip. "I was caught in the middle of the storm," Isabel smoothly replied. "When I stepped down from the coach, I unintentionally stepped into the mud. It was most unfortunate since the slippers were my favorite."

"A pity," Delia agreed. "I fear you will have to run your errands alone. I was invited to Lady Harper's literary salon by Miss Tyne and her friend." She paused for a moment. "Oh, the lady's name escapes me. Perhaps you should put off your tasks for another day and join me. While I enjoy reading, I do not feel the need to unstitch each sentence to find hidden meanings as so many people do. What say you?"

"A tempting offer." Isabel tried to recall Miss Tyne. "Is she the petite blonde who recently became betrothed?"

"Yes." Her sister gestured with her fork. "Oh, you remember, the marchioness introduced us to her. She is one of Lady Pashley's dearest friends."

"Lady Pashley . . . Regan." Family ties and connections shifted like puzzle pieces in Isabel's head. Regan had married last season, and was the sister of Lord Chillingsworth. Frost, the ladies called him, and one of the more notorious members of Nox. "Good grief." He was likely one of Vane's closest friends.

"Something wrong?"

"Not at all," Isabel said crisply. "I just recalled something else I must do. I will have to decline your invitation."

"It is just as well." Delia picked up her cup of hot chocolate. "I daresay it will be a dull afternoon."

"Really, Delia. Show some respect," she scolded. "Lady Netherley has gone to great lengths to introduce us to many members of the *ton*. That cannot be said for our own flesh and blood."

Her sister scowled. "You speak of our illustrious

grandfather. Were you aware that he attended the Fiddicks' masquerade last evening?"

Isabel froze. "Did he approach you?"

"That old judgmental prude? Ha!" Delia set her cup down with a sharp *clink*. "That man would drink a pot of rancid vinegar before he'd hold his nose and speak to the likes of us."

Before last evening, Isabel would have agreed. She could not fathom why the elderly viscount had approached her. Nor was she certain that she should mention the encounter to her sister.

Mrs. Allen entered the room. "Miss Thorne . . . Miss Delia, there is a persistent gentleman caller in the front hall. I have already told him that it is too early for visitors, however, he claims to be a *good* friend."

It was clear what the housekeeper thought of such a claim.

Without the luxury of a footman to assist her, Isabel pushed back her chair. "Did this gentleman give you his name?"

"Mr. Ruddel."

Delia also stood, her demeanor brightening at the gentleman's name. "Malcolm is here in London? How wonderful!" She clapped her hands and bounced on her heels with excitement. "Isabel, were you aware of this?"

Isabel's heart had sunk. "No, I was unaware of his plans."

After their awkward parting, she had not expected to see Mr. Ruddel again. The shock of finding him and her sister in an ardent embrace had passed, as well as her initial hurt. What concerned her now was his presence in London. She had confessed to Vane that she was almost betrothed to Mr. Ruddel as a means to gain his trust. What if Mr. Ruddel learned of their fictitious betrothal?

And what of Vane? Last evening, he had not seemed particularly concerned about her absent future husband. In fact, Isabel had forgotten all about the man. Good grief! She could not even contemplate what Vane thought of her wicked behavior. On second thought, she knew firsthand that he thoroughly enjoyed himself. She covered her face with her hands and groaned.

"Isabel?" Delia asked, confused by her sister's sudden distress.

Mrs. Allen eyed both sisters. She was likely wondering if she was working for two courtesans. "What should I tell, Mr. Ruddel?"

Dragging her hands from her face, Isabel tried to compose her rattled nerves. "Show him to the drawing room, Mrs. Allen. My sister and I will join him shortly."

"Humph" was all the housekeeper said before she left the morning room to deal with their unexpected visitor.

Isabel nudged Delia toward the door. "Go wash your face and tidy your hair. Mr. Ruddel can wait."

Delia turned back and said, "But—"

"Go."

Satisfied that her sister was too vain not to comply with her orders, Isabel dug her fists into her hips and scowled at the empty table. How was she going to convince Mr. Ruddel to leave London?

Chapter Twenty-four

Mr. Ruddel stood as soon as Isabel entered the drawing room. She was relieved to see that her sister was still upstairs. It would give her a chance to talk to the gentleman in private.

"Isabel, town life suits you," he said, giving her an appraising look. "It has put color in your cheeks."

If there was color in her cheeks, she blamed her unwelcome visitor. "The heightened color is annoyance, Mr. Ruddel. How did you find us?"

He made an expansive gesture with his hands. "It was simple enough when you have the right connections."

Isabel stared, patiently waiting for him to recall that she was no longer impressed with his knowledge or his connections.

Mr. Ruddel sighed. "Mr. Fawson mentioned that he had paid you a visit."

"Ah."

She motioned for him to sit, and then deliberately selected the chair farthest from him.

"Fawson also said that he made a generous offer on your father's journals."

"My father's journals are not for sale," she said in a clipped voice. "We have discussed this in the past, and I have not changed my mind on the matter."

"Be reasonable, Isabel. Those old books are merely collecting dust sitting on a shelf. Fawson's offer was fair. Your family could use the money."

"Why do you care if I accept Mr. Fawson's offer or not?"

His somber eyes conveyed his disappointment in her. "There was a time when you called me Malcolm."

"That was before I caught you kissing my sister."

"So you were jealous!" Mr. Ruddel glanced at the open doorway to ensure no one was listening. "Isabel, what you saw . . . it was regrettable. I can assure you that it will never happen again. Let us put this behind us and be friends again. I miss our discussions."

"I miss our conversations, too, Mr. Ruddel. Nevertheless, it does not alter my decision about selling my father's journals to Mr. Fawson."

"Then forget Fawson!" he said fervently. "Sell them, keep them . . . I was only concerned about your welfare, Isabel."

A soft sound at the doorway had both of them glancing up.

"Forgive me for interrupting," Mrs. Allen said, entering the room carrying a small basket. "There was a delivery at the back door for you, Miss Thorne."

"What is it?"

"More like who, I'd say," she muttered as she placed the basket on the table.

Warily, Isabel untied the ribbons used to secure the cloth covering. Mrs. Allen was correct. Whatever was beneath the cloth was moving. She peeled back the cloth and let out a soft gasp. Within the basket an orange tabby kitten stared up at her with large opaque green eyes.

"Well, well . . . look at you," Isabel cooed as she picked up the kitten. "Goodness, aren't you a darling?"

"Who would send you a kitten?" Mr. Ruddel demanded.

Rubbing her chin against the animal's head, Isabel noticed the calling card at the bottom of the basket.

Vane.

Turning it over, she read aloud, "Not quite bluegreen, but it will suffice for when—uh . . ." She glanced uncomfortably at Mr. Ruddel, refusing to read the rest. *For when I cannot cuddle you properly* was too intimate to be shared with anyone else.

Isabel could not help herself; she suddenly grinned. She had told Vane that blue-green was her favorite color. He had promised to find her a jewel that matched the color of his eyes, but she preferred a kitten to jewelry.

"Let me see that calling card," Mr. Ruddel said, plucking it from her fingers before she could stop him. "Lord Vanewright. Arrogant scoundrel, thinking he has the right to send you gifts. Do you want me to have a word with him, Isabel?"

Isabel stopped smiling. A meeting between Vane and Mr. Ruddel would be disastrous. "Mrs. Allen, could you

take the kitten to the kitchen and give him some cream."
She handed the kitten to the housekeeper and turned to
Mr. Ruddel. "We must talk."

Delia walked into the room, wearing one of her favorite morning dresses. "What have I missed?"

"Mr. Ruddel," Isabel replied. "He is leaving."

The afternoon did not improve Isabel's disposition.
Lady Netherley paid her an unexpected visit. She had
learned that her son had left Lord and Lady Fiddick's
masquerade early, and there were rumors circulating
that he had not left the house alone.

After her encounter with Mr. Ruddel, Isabel had little
strength to engage the elderly marchioness. Delia sat
between the two ladies with an uncharacteristic owlish
expression pasted on her face until an annoyed Isabel
ordered her sister to retire to her bedchamber. Once her
sister had gone upstairs, she tried to comfort Lady
Netherley by denouncing the lady's suggestion that her
son had taken up with his mistress again. If Lord Vanewright had left the ball early, Isabel speculated, he had
departed with his friends.

By the time Isabel had said her farewells to the marchioness, she had developed a terrible megrim in her
right eye. Mrs. Allen added a medicinal tonic to Isabel's
tea, and urged her to drink it. The scent reminded her of
her mother, and she dumped the contents out the nearest
window.

The notion of spending a quiet evening at home
sounded appealing, but she and Delia had promised

Lady Netherley that they would join her in her private box at the theater. Isabel assumed Vane would drop by to pay his respects.

The gentleman rarely disappointed her.

Vane entered his mother's private theater box, his gaze immediately settling on Isabel. She and Delia had their heads together as they shared a private conversation. Both his sisters had joined his mother—and apparently Susan's husband had been forgiven, for he was also present with two male companions.

His father was noticeably absent. For once, he was relieved. With his father's threats dangling over Vane's head like a hangman's noose, he wasn't in the mood to quarrel with the man or yield to his dictates.

Vane's gaze settled on his mother.

"Christopher." She motioned him to her side, patting the side of his face as he bussed her cheek. "You have been spoiling, of late. If this persists, you will have me believe you are a reformed rake."

Vane cast a side glance in Isabel's direction. She had yet to acknowledge him, but he was not discouraged by her coyness. He knew how to break down the barriers she erected to keep everyone at a distance. "Then I will have to do something truly wicked and depraved to convince you otherwise." He straightened and bowed to his brother-in-law and companions. "Pypart. I see your wife has accepted your apology."

"Leave him alone, brother," Susan scolded. He noticed that his sibling had an expensive new bauble adorning her neck. "Pypart is striving to get back into my good graces, and it shall prove more entertaining than what is transpiring below on the stage."

Ellen touched him on the wrist. "Are you joining us, Vane?"

His smile had a trace of regret. "No, I've come to steal away one of your charming companions. Isabel, the Moirae desire an audience." At her blank expression, he swiftly explained, "Lady Rainecourt, Lady Sinclair, and Lady Pashley hope you will join them in their box. Lady Pashley, in particular, missed your entrance at the masquerade and she wanted to hear the tale from your lips since she believes Saint and Frost are exaggerating."

The look Isabel sent his mother was apologetic. "I will accept only with Lady Netherley's permission."

It was on the tip of his tongue to brusquely remind his interfering family that Isabel was not bound by their dictates unless she chose to be, but the marchioness was already waving Isabel off.

"Go. We will look after your sister," his mother assured her. "It is good that you are making friends, my dear."

Delia stirred in her seat. The look she gave Vane was withering. "And what about me? Do I not deserve to make new friends?"

Isabel hesitated, conflicted about leaving her younger sibling.

Vane, on the other hand, had no such compunction. Delia was a spoiled young lady who got her way much too often. He extended his arm to Isabel as he managed to keep her sister from rising with a menacing glance.

"Behave yourself, Delia. Else I'll send Frost over to keep you from getting lonely," he said over his shoulder as he stole Isabel away from his family's watchful gazes.

Vane did not seem to notice the curious stares as they strode down yet another one of the numerous dim, narrow corridors that split off into the private theater boxes of the *ton*.

"Vane," Isabel whispered, making a soft hissing sound when she realized he had no intention of slowing down or releasing her. "Delia should have joined us. It must have seemed peculiar to your mother that you only invited me—"

"Not at all. In fact, I am certain my mother is giddy with relief that I am paying attention to you since she and my father have decided that I will select a bride this season or—" Vane abruptly halted in front of one of the curtained doorways.

"Or what?"

He focused on her face. Some of the bleak anger faded from his expression as his hand slid down her arm and captured her palm. "Or nothing. It is not important. Let me look at you, Isabel."

She blushed at his brazen stare. There was an intimacy that had not been there before. It was as if he could peer beneath her flesh and see the secrets she kept hidden in her heart.

"By God, you are beautiful." Vane stepped closer, breathing in the scent she had dabbed at her throat. He nuzzled her ear. "I have thought of nothing but you, sweet Isabel, since our parting. Our night together haunts me.

When I close my eyes, I can summon the sensation of your skin as it rubs seductively against mine, the subtle musk of your desire . . . your soft cries of pleasure when I fill you."

Isabel pressed her gloved fingers to his mouth.

"You cannot speak of it," she cautioned, stunned that her body was warming to his words alone. "Your mother would never speak to me if she learned that I left the Fiddicks' masquerade with you."

Annoyance crept into his gaze. "Do not concern yourself with my mother's opinion."

"But I must," Isabel countered, unaware that she was caressing his hand. "My sister and I do not really belong here."

"What utter rot!" he began.

"I have no reason to lie," she said, silencing him. "We do not possess the wealth or family to weather a scandal. We both know that your mother hopes you will find a bride this season."

"Do not fret about my mother," Vane said dismissively. "She is acquainted with disappointment and tolerates it admirably."

"We both know that a casual dalliance is not what your mother is asking of you."

"At the moment, I do not care what Lady Netherley wants, Isabel, so neither should you."

"You should." Isabel angled her chin as her gaze hardened. "And I should as well. I do not want to be just another silly miss who allows you a little playful tickling behind a drawn curtain."

It was difficult to tell for certain in the gloomy corridor, but Vane's cheekbones darkened at the reminder of what he and his female companion had been doing behind the curtain at the dressmaker's shop.

"What are you asking of me, Isabel?" Furious and defiant, Vane seized her by the shoulders and shook her. "Marriage?"

"If I said *yes,* it would undeniably solve your dilemma of finding a bride." Isabel's smile was insincere, but Vane was too panicked by the notion that she might have bedded him to gain an offer of marriage to notice. "However, you will understand if I ignore your insulting unspoken accusation. I have no desire to be forced into marriage any more than you, Lord Vanewright."

Vane gave her an unfathomable look as Isabel braced for his angry retort. He surprised her by saying, "Perhaps it would be prudent to reserve this discussion for another time."

"Shall we reserve it for before or after you find your bride?"

Any response Vane might have made was quelled when Lord Sainthill parted the curtain and stuck his head through the opening.

"Thought I might find you out in the corridor with Miss Thorne," the marquess said, noting the placement of Vane's hands. "Stealing a few kisses, eh? Well, now, there's no time for that. Dare is threatening to toss Frost out of the box. Headfirst if he gets his way."

Vane's grip on her arms relaxed, and then his hands slid away. "No one will take your wager?" He stepped away and Isabel was grateful for the reprieve.

"Hunter isn't here," Lord Sainthill said simply,

opening the curtain for them. "Regan is counting on Miss Thorne to add a little respectability to our box."

He smiled at Isabel, and she shyly returned his friendly overture.

"Your charm is wasted on Miss Thorne," Vane said, glaring at his friend. "The lady claims to be almost betrothed."

Isabel glowered at Vane. "How convenient of you to recall that bit of information *now.*"

He tried to place her hand on his arm, but she resisted. "It seemed appropriate that one of us should, Miss Thorne."

"Oh, really?" Lord Sainthill glanced curiously from Vane to Isabel. "Who is the lucky gent? Anyone I know?"

"Well, it certainly is not Lord Vanewright!" she snapped before she marched through the parted curtains.

Chapter Twenty-five

Although Isabel was being polite about it, Vane knew when a lady was vexed at him. She was now seated at the front of the private box with Regan to her left and Juliana and Sophia to her right; his friends' wives had taken her under their collective wing and banished him to the back of the box with Reign, Sin, Dare, and Saint. Frost had been present when he and Isabel had entered the box. It wasn't long before the earl pronounced the gathering too domesticated for his tastes, however, and wandered off in search of Hunter. Half an hour later, Saint also excused himself claiming that he was too restless to remain.

Last spring, Vane would have happily joined Saint and Frost as they prowled the theater looking for a willing lady or mischief. It surprised him how content he was now to merely observe Isabel as she watched the play and quietly shared her observations with her new friends. He had not really understood that bringing her had been an unspoken challenge, both for Isabel and for him.

He suspected she would be startled if she were aware of his thoughts.

"You could do worse for a bride," Reign said, his gaze resting thoughtfully on Isabel.

Dare snorted in disbelief. "I cannot believe you would accept any lady handpicked by your mother."

"Lady Netherley believes Miss Thorne's sister would be a suitable bride for me." Vane did not add that Isabel was his choice. Her presence this evening conveyed his unspoken feelings about the lady in question to his friends, even if he had no intention of keeping her. "Regardless, someone else has already claimed Miss Thorne's hand and affection."

But not all of her, Vane thought with grim satisfaction.

Isabel had willingly shared a part of herself with him. Her innocence and first passion were his alone. Vane had given her something of himself, though it was not as simple to define as a lady's virginity. He doubted Isabel had noticed, but when she took another lover, she would be able to compare . . .

Vane grimaced at the thought of another man bedding Isabel.

Perhaps they had more in common than the lady was willing to admit. She had claimed that she did not wish to be forced into a marriage, but she seemed resigned to marry her mysterious betrothed. Vane suspected the gent was the reason why Isabel had fled the country and brought her sister to London.

She was shirking her responsibilities, too.

Isabel leaned closer to Regan, and nodded as Dare's

wife whispered something in her ear. Sensing she was being watched, Isabel glanced back and their gazes collided. For a few precious seconds, the world fell away and all he saw was Isabel. Vane grinned at her, and Isabel returned one of her own before she realized that Sin, Dare, and Reign were also observing the exchange. Her entire face reddened before she turned away.

"Do you think it is wise to seduce another man's bride?" Sin asked.

Vane detected concern more than disappointment in his friend's question. He shrugged. "I have never been particularly wise when it comes to women. There seems little point to starting now." He rose from his chair, unwilling to listen to his friends' reasons why he should leave Isabel alone.

He had enough of his own, but it did not prevent him from approaching her chair. From leaning over and brushing his lips against her ear as he whispered, "I should return you to Lady Netherley's box before she accuses me of kidnapping."

Isabel said farewell to the ladies. Vane waited impatiently as Juliana invited Isabel to an afternoon gathering the women had planned next week. He would find out the details from Sin later. If gents were included, he would make certain that he received an invitation. Vane gritted his teeth while Isabel moved on to paying her respects to his friends. He had to remind himself that all three gentlemen were happily married. Their smiles and courtly manners were not meant to provoke him.

Vane realized that he was jealous.

It was an irrational emotion. All he wanted to do

was plant his fist in Sin's face and drag Isabel out of the box.

Vane managed to avoid committing violence, but his firm grip on Isabel's elbow appeared possessive to any onlooker. When he held open the curtain for her, she used his divided attention to break free.

"What is wrong with you?" Isabel asked as she whirled around to confront him.

"This!"

Before she could protest his mouth slanted over hers as he pushed her back up against the closest wall.

"Mmph!"

She thumped her fist against his upper arm twice in a halfhearted protest before she sighed and allowed her body to melt against his. Kissing Isabel was more satisfying that taking his frustrations out on his friends' faces. Vane used his hips to hold her in place while his fingers idly explored the contours of her jaw and neck. Their tongues tangled and teased in a silent, desperate dance that caused his cock to swell, reminding him that the open corridor was no place for a tryst.

With regret, he ended the kiss. Both of them were breathless.

"Isabel, I—"

A firm hand clapped his shoulder. Vane turned to snarl a reprimand at one of his friends, but the unknown gentleman had him swallowing the oath that bubbled to escape.

"You might want to remove that hand, gent," he said crisply. "Otherwise, I will view your oversight as an invitation to see to the task myself."

The man immediately released Vane, but he did not scurry away as most men would have. He took a nervous step forward, then belatedly comprehended that his actions could be misconstrued as another invitation so he hastily retreated. "Do what you will with me, but I must insist that you unhand Miss Thorne at once!"

"Mr. Ruddel?" Isabel squeaked, peeking around Vane in utter dismay. "What are you doing here?"

Suddenly recalling his manners, the gentleman bowed. "Forgive me for intruding on your evening. I—I saw Delia in one of the private boxes and came upstairs to pay my respects. I had expected to find you at your sister's side, but the kind owner of the box directed me to your whereabouts." From his expression, Vane could tell the man had not been pleased with the company Isabel had been keeping. "I offered my services and told your companions that I would escort you back to their private box. I was concerned for your well-being, so you can imagine my shock to discover that this brute had shoved you against the wall and was pawing you without regard to your reputation."

Vane glanced down at Isabel. She was still clutching his arm as she gaped at the gentleman. "Isabel, who is this arse?"

The insult stiffened the man's spine. "I will have you know that I am a very good friend of the family. Is that not correct, Isabel?"

Isabel sighed. She released Vane's arm and stepped away from him. "Mr. Ruddel, may I present Lord Vanewright. My lord, may I present Mr. Ruddel."

If Isabel thought he would be satisfied with a vague

introduction, she was mistaken. "Is he . . . damn me, is Ruddel your betrothed?"

Isabel glanced helplessly from Vane to Ruddel. "I— I—"

"Yes," Ruddel said, cutting off Isabel. "Yes, the lady is my betrothed . . . and—and I would appreciate it if you would not kiss my lady again!"

Chapter Twenty-six

"How could you?" Isabel railed at Mr. Ruddel the next afternoon when she was able to discuss the matter with him in private. "You had no right to tell Lord Vanewright that we are betrothed."

Isabel had seen the frozen fury on Vane's face. The unspoken denial as he glared at her, silently demanding that she disavow Mr. Ruddel's arrogant claim. Oh, how she had wanted to do that very thing, but she was soundly caught in her own lies.

Mr. Ruddel seemed unmoved by her accusation. He stretched out his legs as if he were sitting in his own drawing room. "You should be grateful I was nearby to rescue you from the clutches of that blackguard. I have done some checking on this Lord Vanewright. Do you know he belongs to some notorious club? That he and his fellow band of miscreants have been dubbed by the *ton* as the Lords of Vice?"

Isabel crossed her arms over her chest, wondering what she ever saw in the arrogant prig. If Vane had not been so stunned by Mr. Ruddel's claim, he would have broken the man in half on principle. Instead, to Isabel's chagrin, Vane had apologized and abandoned her. Not that she could blame him. After all, she had warned him that she was almost betrothed.

Ugh, I was a fool to spin such a ridiculous lie!

Isabel gave her unwanted betrothed a measured look. "Lord Vanewright and the Lords of Vice are not to be trifled with, Mr. Ruddel. Notorious miscreants or not, they are part of the *ton,* whereas you and I are not. You insult them at your peril."

He flicked his wrist in a dismissive gesture. "Bah, they do not frighten me."

"Then you are the arse Lord Vanewright accused you of being," she said, ignoring his dismay over her crude language. "You just do not understand what you have done."

"Isabel." He moved from the chair and knelt at her feet. "My sweet, do not cry." He reached into his coat and produced a linen handkerchief.

Isabel accepted it and wiped her eyes.

"I think I know why you are upset," he said, not unkindly. "You are humiliated that you have been caught in a lie."

Isabel sniffed into the handkerchief. "That is part of it." She hardly could admit her bargain with Lady Netherley. Mr. Ruddel was smitten with Delia. He might ruin everything by blurting out the entire sordid ordeal to her sister.

"You never expected me to discover your little ruse, did you?"

Isabel thought about the day she had caught him

kissing Delia in a manner that she had never inspired in him. *"Never."*

He patted the top of her hand affectionately. "Well, you will discover that I can be quite reasonable when it comes to these delicate matters. Last evening, when I found you in the arms of Lord Vanewright, it was painfully apparent why you of all people had to resort to such desperate measures. The bounder was intent on ravishing you."

Isabel brought the handkerchief to her face.

"There, there . . . my girl. Hold steady. We will muddle through this."

Before she realized what he planned to do, he leaned forward and kissed her on the mouth.

"Mr. Ruddel!"

"Everyone believes I am your betrothed, Isabel," he reminded her. "A stolen kiss or two would be expected."

"No, it certainly will not be expected or required." Isabel stumbled from the chair as she attempted to distance herself from her unwanted suitor. "We"— she pointed at him and then to herself—"are not getting married."

Mr. Ruddel slowly climbed to his feet and followed her to the other side of the drawing room. "Everyone believes we are betrothed. Why not allow the lie to stand? I am willing if you are."

The man was deliberately being obtuse. "No one was supposed to meet you. Ever. Once I had returned to Cotersage, no one in London would have given me another thought—or my imaginary betrothed. Now you have ruined *everything!*"

Mr. Ruddel's expression hardened at her accusation. "Exactly what have I ruined, Isabel? My appearance should lend credence to your story." He gently tugged on her fingers until Isabel lowered her hands from her face. "You know I have feelings for you."

"Oh, Malcolm," she said, feeling worse, because she did not want to hurt him even if he deserved it. "Do you think I have forgotten about you and Delia?"

He gave her an impatient shake. "That kiss meant nothing. I told you that before and have already apologized. I swear on my honor, it will never happen again. Do you believe me?"

Isabel nodded.

"Good. Then it is settled."

He tried to kiss her again, but she was prepared for it this time. She placed her palms on his chest to prevent him and lightly pushed him away.

"I might have lied to half of London about my betrothal, but I have grown weary of the ruse. I will never marry you, Malcolm."

Mr. Ruddel flinched as if she had slapped him. "Your casual dismissal of our friendship makes me wonder if I misunderstood what I witnessed last evening. Did you welcome Vanewright's advances, Isabel?"

Isabel bowed her head, fearing her face would give her away. "Either way, it does not really matter. Lord Vanewright was never meant to be mine."

Astounded, Mr. Ruddel stared at her as if he were seeing her for the first time. "Is your family aware of your mischief?"

Isabel's gaze narrowed on Mr. Ruddel's pinched features. "The answer to that question has not been your concern since the day I caught you kissing and fondling my sister. Good day to you, sir!"

Vane's sour disposition had not improved since he had come face-to-face with the gentleman who claimed to be Isabel's betrothed. It had taken all of his restraint to resist punching the gent and flattening his nose. He waited for Isabel to deny the man's claim. After all, she had seemed as befuddled by Ruddel's appearance as Vane was.

Even so, Isabel never denounced the irritating man and Vane had left her in the capable hands of her lover. No, wait. *He* was her damn lover. Isabel had surrendered her innocence to him, not Ruddel.

By the next day, Vane was seething. During the long sleepless night, he had decided the lady owed him a few answers and he intended to collect them. When Mrs. Allen opened the door, she told him that Isabel and her sister were not at home.

Before he could accuse the housekeeper of lying, the servant assured him that forcing his way into the house would not gain him the answers he craved: It was Lady Netherley who had invited the sisters for some shopping. Mrs. Allen bade him to glower elsewhere and rudely shut the door in his face.

By God, the women in his life gave him no quarter.

Nor his father, Vane grimly reminded himself.

He avoided his parents' town house. When he thought his temper had been pushed behind repair, it was his sister Ellen who innocently told him that their mother was planning to attend Lord and Lady Mainstone's ball. Since his mother seemed determined to toss Delia in his path, the Thorne sisters would likely be in attendance as well.

Vane did not care if he had to confront her in the middle of the Mainstones' ballroom with her simpering fiancé at her side—Isabel would answer his questions, and then he was getting the hell out of her life.

Admittance to Lord and Lady Mainstone's ball was simple enough. It was rare for anyone to refuse the man who would one day inherit the Marquess of Netherley title.

Vane quickly paid his respects to his host and hostess and went directly to the ballroom. Along the way, he acknowledged friends and acquaintances with a nod as he searched the ballroom for Isabel. He had made it halfway around the large room when he spotted her. She was standing close to his mother, which came as no surprise. His mother was not about to let two unmarried ladies slip away when she had a son who required a bride. Isabel might not be Lady Netherley's choice for her son, but even from a distance it was apparent that his mother doted on the young woman.

"Mother," Vane said, kissing his mother's cheek. "What providence to encounter you this evening."

Lady Netherley patted both of his cheeks. Isabel had not moved an inch since his arrival. "Christopher," his mother said, her pleasure in stark contrast with her companion's silence. "No one told me that you were attending this evening."

"It is an unplanned stop, I must confess," he admitted cheerfully. "However, I could not resist dropping by and showing my appreciation for all your efforts. If I must be beggared, let it not be said that I was cut off because I refused to inspect every toothsome miss and wallflower you have cajoled on my behalf."

The joy in his mother's wrinkled face dimmed. "You are still cross with your father."

"Your intuition never ceases to amaze me, my dear mother."

His sarcasm made both women wince.

"My lord, have you been drinking?" Isabel said, frowning at him.

"Nothing worth bragging about. Although I do plan to make up for my shortfall once I attend to a few unpleasant matters." Before Isabel could respond, he turned his back on her and smiled appreciatively at Delia, who was approaching them. "Miss Delia, you look enchanting this evening. Would you honor me with a dance?"

Delia's eyes widened with surprise. "I would be delighted, Lord Vanewright!"

He glanced at Isabel. The hurt in her liquid brown gaze only spurred him to say, "My lovely girl, I told you when we first met that all of my *good* friends call me Vane."

Oblivious to the undercurrents of tension around her, Delia gave him a smile that lacked the coyness he found so beguiling in Isabel.

Delia placed her hand on his arm. "Then I have no choice but to yield to your wishes, Vane."

He covered her hand with his. "Ah, there is nothing as tempting as a biddable young lady," he said, causing Delia to giggle. "I will have to compile a list of requests while we dance, and we'll see if I can coax you to agree to them all."

Without a backward glance, he and Delia strolled off.

Isabel heard a soft cracking sound and lowered her gaze to her hand. She had been clutching her closed fan so tightly, she had snapped one of the wooden blades.

"Lady Netherley, you must be pleased that your son has finally turned his attentions to my sister."

Isabel glanced up at the marchioness when she did not reply.

"Not particularly," Lady Netherley replied, her answer startling Isabel. "It might be prudent to keep an eye on your sister. Christopher is in a rather odd mood this evening, and there is no telling what mischief he is prepared to indulge in."

Mrs. Allen had told Isabel that Vane had come to the house, demanding to see her. Isabel had braced herself for a confrontation, but she had not expected him to take his revenge by flirting with her sister. She should be thrilled that she had driven him into Delia's arms. It had been the plan all along, and she had almost ruined everything by allowing him to slip through the barriers she had erected around her heart.

But Isabel had not prepared herself for the pain. She was losing him, the man who was never meant to be hers. "Lady Netherley, you do not believe—" She gasped. "No, it cannot be possible." She started for the door.

The marchioness grasped her arm before Isabel could leave. "Isabel, what troubles you? Is something amiss?"

Her lips moved as she tried to warn Lady Netherley of the disaster that loomed before them. Vane was the least of her concerns now. "It is my mother. Somehow she has escaped her keeper and found us."

Isabel barely recalled her hasty apology to Lady Netherley as she crossed the ballroom to confront her mother. Sybil's face brightened with recognition and relief at her daughter's approach, but any joyful reunion was quelled by Isabel's angry words.

"Is it your intention to ruin everything?"

Taking her mother by the arm, Isabel was prepared to drag Sybil out of the ballroom if she proved to be stubborn.

"Isabel," the older woman said, sounding exasperated. "A measured pace would be prudent if you do not wish to draw everyone's attention."

Isabel gritted her teeth at the notion that her mother dared to censure *her* actions. Even so, she deliberately slowed their retreat from the ballroom. The last thing she wanted was for Vane or anyone else to become curious about her new companion.

A minute later, any hope of leaving the ballroom unnoticed proved to be futile when the gentleman the *ton* called Frost approached them.

"Miss Thorne, this is an unexpected pleasure!" Lord Chillingsworth said, his speculative gaze shifting from her to her mother. "These days, it is rare for me to encounter you without Vane at your side, baring his teeth at any gent who deigns to speak with you. I hope his absence does not suggest that you will be leaving?"

"Who is Vane? Why does he feel he has the right to make such a claim on you?" Sybil glared at her daughter. "What scandalous mischief have you been engaging in?"

"Knowing Vane, her sins are likely too numerous to recount," the viscount said, earning a basilisk stare from Isabel.

The man pointedly ignored her. If anyone deserved a sound thrashing for his meddling, it was Lord Chillingsworth. Isabel attempted to walk by him, but the man was not quite through assuaging his curiosity.

"And you are?" he asked her mother.

Sybil was very flattered by the handsome viscount's interest. "Mrs. Thorne. And you are—"

"Delighted to meet you. I'm Frost." Lord Chillingsworth bowed, and her mother reciprocated with a curtsy. To Isabel, he said, "So why have you been hiding this treasure from us, Miss Thorne? Has Vane had the pleasure of an introduction?"

"No, I . . ." Isabel trailed off as she noted with mounting dread that Lord Botly was staring in their direction. From his cold expression, it was apparent that he was not longing for a tender reunion with Sybil.

It was time for them to leave.

She tightened her grip on her mother's arm and gave Lord Chillingsworth an enthralling smile. He seemed startled by her rushed attempt to charm him, which should have come as no surprise to her. Until now, she had little incentive to flirt with the man.

"We were just on our way to meet Vane." She cast a wary glance at Lord Botly. Good grief, could this evening get any worse? Lord Botly was moving toward them.

"I wish you a good evening, my lord."

Her mother's lips parted as she noticed her father's approach. One look at her expression, and Isabel deduced that Sybil was as dismayed by his unanticipated appearance as Isabel.

"Come, Mother," she said, her eyes frantically searching for the nearest door.

Lord Chillingsworth called out to them. "If you are looking for Vane, you are heading in the wrong direction."

Good, Isabel thought with grim determination. If she had her way, Sybil and Vane would never meet.

Chapter Twenty-seven

From the window of her bedchamber, Isabel watched with almost detached interest the arrival of a familiar coach. She'd known when she accepted Lady Netherley's invitation to London that she was gambling with her reputation and her family's future. She just hadn't anticipated how quickly the delicate tapestry woven by her half-truths and brazen lies would collapse.

If one knew which thread to pluck, the rest unraveled with appalling swiftness and ease.

Mr. Ruddel had been the first sign of trouble. No—that was not quite true, she silently amended. Lord Botly approaching her at Lord Fiddick's masquerade had been the first indication the chimera that was her and Delia's life in London was about to come to an end.

Her mother's arrival in town just proved to be the death knell.

Isabel stepped away from the window at the sound of a pounding first against the door. Her eyelids closed as she attempted to decipher the angry conversation below. She could identify Mrs. Allen's brisk tone as she told Vane that the Thorne women were not receiving visitors this afternoon. The housekeeper had been forced to turn a dozen callers away. Some names on the cards she recognized; others she did not. Of course, none of it mattered anymore.

Her chin lifted at the soft knock at her door.

"Miss Thorne." Mrs. Allen waited patiently on the other side of the door.

It was tempting to ignore the summons. The house-keeper would have respected Isabel's need for solace, and her desire to lick her wounded pride. The gentle-man waiting downstairs, however, was impatient and angry.

"Yes." To her dismay, her voice wavered as she strug-gled not to cry.

"You have a visitor in the study. Lord Vanewright," she added gratuitously. "I told him that you were not receiving visitors today, but he insists on seeing you anyway."

Yes, Isabel was certain that nothing would prevent him from confronting her this afternoon.

Mrs. Allen listened for Isabel's reply. When none came, she continued, "Mrs. Thorne has expressed a de-sire to speak with the earl. So far, I have managed to talk her out of it, and she remains in her room."

Good grief, the notion of Sybil explaining anything to Vane froze the blood in Isabel's veins. Coming to a decision, she strode toward the door.

Unaware of her mistress's actions, Mrs. Allen spoke with a sense of urgency, "Nevertheless, that angry young man pacing the threadbare rug in the study will not leave the house until he sees you. If you refuse, he is likely—"

When Isabel opened the door, the housekeeper sagged with relief. "This house has turned into bedlam since your mother's arrival. You need to put things in order, Miss Thorne."

Mrs. Allen's scolding was exactly what Isabel needed to coax her out of the bedchamber and down the stairs. "Make certain my mother remains in her room. Ply her with one of your special teas if you must."

"Very good, Miss Thorne."

Isabel halted at the entrance of the study, allowing her greedy gaze to commit every detail and line to memory. Vane still wore his evening clothes, and it appeared sleep had eluded him, too. He looked dreadful, but also wonderful. When he realized he was being observed, he froze and slowly turned around to confront her.

"I wondered if you'd have the courage to see me."

His cutting remark struck with impressive accuracy. Since she deserved it, Isabel ignored his baiting and sat down on the settee. She did not invite him to join her, doubting he planned to remain in the same room any longer than it took him to rid himself of the vitriol burning in his stomach.

"Have you nothing to say?" he said thickly.

"My lord, I am so sorry—"

He silenced her with a gesture. "Spare me your regrets. You have been thoroughly caught, Miss Thorne, and I demand an explanation."

"What is the point, my lord? Last evening, you judged me and found me guilty."

"You lied to me." Frustrated, he speared his fingers through his uncombed hair. "Our first meeting was even a lie!"

"Yes." Isabel saw no reason to hide anything from him. "Your mother told me where you and your—your mistress would be that afternoon. She trusted me to arrange an introduction with my sister that would not make you suspicious."

"And the pickpocket?"

"One of Mrs. Allen's nephews." She clasped and unclasped her hands. "I intended to feign an injury to gain your sympathy. However, the boy panicked and I truly twisted my ankle when I fell."

Isabel cried out in fear as Vane dropped to his knees in front of her and seized her hands. "Tell me, Isabel. Was everything a sham? Did you accept my offer of friendship because you were counting on me to choose your sister over you?"

She had ruined everything. Unable to meet his furious gaze, she concentrated on his fingers. He was gripping her hands so fiercely, she would have bruises by morning.

"Yes. It was simple enough to include Delia, and your mother was pleased that you had taken an interest in her."

He released her with a curse on his lips. "Damn it, Isabel, I took an interest in *you*. From the very beginning, it was you, and you betrayed me. Every smile and timid glance, the honeyed lies that dripped from your tongue each time you spoke."

His thunderous expression revealed just how close

he was to losing his temper. He stared down at her as if he hated her.

"And what of your innocence? Was that feigned, too?"

It was a vile taunt. Isabel thought he was beneath such calculating cruelty. Then again, perhaps they did not truly know each other.

She deliberately met his harsh gaze. "No, my lord. You took my innocence."

Vane pointed his finger at her. "By God, you will not lay ravishment at my feet. You gave yourself freely."

"Yes."

Her quiet acquiescence only seemed to enrage him. "It was not enough to have me merrily dancing on your strings. You had to ensnare me further, using your virginal body to bind me to you."

"It was nothing like that," she snapped, her composure crumbling with his horrid accusations. "Do not sully what we shared."

"No, Miss Thorne, you already did that with your deceit," he shouted back at her. "What were your intentions? Did you think I would be so smitten that I would marry Delia?"

Her tears coursed down her cheeks. "I do not know what I was thinking! Your mother kept insisting that Delia was perfect for you. I did not want to disappoint her, and yet the more time I spent with you, the more conflicted I became."

Vane remained unmoved by her tears or her rambling explanation. "And what of Ruddel?"

Isabel sniffed. "Once he learned of my ruse, he offered

to make the betrothal genuine, but I do not plan to accept."

"I paid a visit to Lord Botly," he said, abruptly changing the subject.

Anger unfurled in her chest for the first time since she'd entered the study. She rose from the settee. "What gave you the right to speak to him?" she demanded, thoroughly incensed that he had gone behind her back.

"You did." He lowered his chin so they were almost nose-to-nose. "The night you surrendered your innocence and became my lover, you became *mine*. Botly was behaving like an arse. I thought I might be able to reason with him, and if that didn't work, then I was willing to settle for straightforward threats."

Isabel's eyes widened as her fingers dug into her temples. "I cannot believe you threatened that old man!"

"What makes you think reasoning didn't work?"

She gave him a scathing look. "Because that unreasonable old man turned away his own daughter when she needed her family. He has never acknowledged that he even has granddaughters . . . as far as Lord Botly is concerned, we might as well be baseborn." The sound she made was a mix of bewilderment and outrage. "Just when I thought things could not get worse. You had to meddle in my business."

His mocking bow had her grinding her molars. "Forgive me, Miss Thorne. I see that I have overstayed my welcome." He headed for the door.

"You ruined everything!" she shouted at his back, knowing as the accusation escaped her parted lips that she was being unfair.

Vane paused, and glanced over his shoulder. "No, Isabel. You did. I fell in love with you."

He left her standing alone in the middle of the study.

"Now who is the liar!" she cried at the sound of the door slamming shut.

The man who had just claimed he loved her had walked out of her life.

Sobbing, she crawled onto the settee and buried her face against the padded armrest. Isabel felt Mrs. Allen's strong arms encircle her as she was pulled into a comforting embrace.

"He hates me!"

"Hush, now, child," she crooned, rocking her. "Your earl will be back."

Isabel shook her head. Mrs. Allen was wrong. Vane would never forgive her for her lies and conspiring with his mother.

"No, he's right. I have ruined everything!"

Chapter Twenty-eight

"I never thought I would see the day when my own mother would betray me."

His mother peered up from her embroidery. "Really, Christopher, that is being a tad dramatic, do you not think? I merely provided you with the opportunity to meet two ladies you would never have encountered on your own. Admit it. You would have given me a dozen excuses if I had asked you to meet the Thorne sisters."

Vane saw no point in refuting his mother's claims. He *had* been avoiding her attempts at matchmaking. Too restless to stand still, he paced in front of the sofa and concentrated on his bitterness.

"And Isabel. She had me completely fooled. I never met a more skillful liar, and having known Frost for fifteen years that is quite an achievement."

"Pish! Isabel is no more a liar than you."

Vane did not know how to respond. He rubbed the back of his neck. Since he had walked out of the Thorne residence, the knotted muscles were giving him a nasty headache. "If I am a liar, then I learned from the best."

"And who is that, dear?"

"You!"

Unperturbed, the marchioness put aside her embroidery. "And exactly how did I lie to you, Christopher," she asked, removing the spectacles she wore for close work. She placed them on the table.

"You never mentioned meeting Isabel and Delia at Cotersage. Hell, you did not mention traveling to the village at all."

"And why would I?" she asked in reasonable tones that made him feel like a brute. "Do you regale me with every aspect of your life? No. Nevertheless, if you had inquired about my little trip to Cotersage, I would have told you the truth. I was visiting a cousin of mine. It was she who introduced me to Mrs. Thorne and her daughters."

"Do not play games, Mother. I am aware that you invited Isabel to London," he said scathingly, his ire renewed as he recalled what he had learned the previous evening and his recent confrontation with Isabel.

"And so I did. Thanks to their neglectful mother, Isabel and Delia were withering in Cotersage. I thought a visit to London might improve their spirits."

Vane groaned, fighting the urge not to throttle his own mother. "How far do you want to push me? I know of the proposition you made to Isabel. I am also aware that the day I met Isabel and Delia in the dressmaker's shop, the meeting was orchestrated by you and Isabel."

His mother looked warily at him before she opened her mouth.

Vane ruthlessly cut into her next words. "Do not bother denying it. Isabel admitted that much to me."

"I had no intention of denying it, dear boy. It is true that I sent Isabel to the shop. I knew you would be there with that greedy creature, Miss Corsar."

"And how did you learn that salient fact. Do you have spies in my household?" he said, aghast that someone had been reporting the details of his life back to his mother. "Who?" If necessary, he would fire his entire staff.

"Really, Christopher. You have a suspicious nature. No one told me that you were going to be at the dressmaker's shop. It was I who suggested it to Miss Corsar when I chatted with her."

His mother had paid a visit to his mistress. Vane covered his face with his hand and collapsed into a chair. "Have you no shame?"

"I could ask the same of you. Miss Corsar was entirely unsuitable. I'll wager she was rather disappointing as a mistress."

Vane opened his mouth, and then quickly shut it. He refused to discuss his former mistress with his mother. *Ever.* In an attempt to change the subject, he said, "So you ordered Isabel to find a way to introduce herself to me."

"The shop seemed like a less threatening way to meet her and her sister. My word, you've become positively skittish when I try to introduce respectable young ladies to you. A more inventive approach was called for."

Vane let his hand fall away from his face. "Because you've got some maggoty notion that I should marry Delia," he sneered.

Isabel had offered him friendship, and he had been

relieved that she had sought nothing more from him. Even when she had surrendered to passion and given him her innocence, she had asked nothing from him. It had been trickery to lower his guard and gain his trust. The silly fool had sacrificed everything for her ungrateful sister.

"Wrong! I never wanted you to marry Delia."

His gaze shot up and locked onto his mother's. "There is no reason to deny it. Isabel told me everything."

"Isabel only told you the part of my plan that I revealed to her."

Vane gave a humorless snort. "Isabel Thorne does not warrant your protection, Mother. She willingly participated in your schemes, and was prepared to sacrifice everything in your name. You should be proud."

"No!" Showing the first signs of agitation, his mother braced her hand on the armrest and leaned forward. "Oh, you've got it all wrong. Isabel *was* my plan. I brought her to London for you, you ungrateful child!"

The lack of sleep was making his head spin. "Perhaps you should start from the beginning," he said gruffly, feeling like a bounder when the marchioness retrieved a handkerchief from her embroidery basket.

"I was not lying about how we met. I did travel to Cotersage to visit my cousin, and it was through her that I met the Thornes." She sniffed and dabbed at her eyes. "It took only minutes for me to realize she was perfect for you!"

She glared at Vane, silently accusing him for not coming to the same conclusion.

He straightened in his chair as he recalled one of

their earlier conversations about Isabel. "You told me that Isabel was all wrong for me—that you would be disappointed if I pursued such a spiritless young lady."

"All lies. I *adore* Isabel, but if I said as much, you would have avoided her without a second glance."

It did not set well with him knowing that she spoke the truth.

"Isabel believes you wanted me to marry Delia."

For the first time, his mother had the grace to look uncomfortable. "A small ruse, I must confess. Believe it or not, Isabel can be rather prickly about certain things, and I sensed straightaway that she would never agree to meet you if I told her the truth about my little match-making scheme."

"Why the hell not?" he asked before he realized his angry question revealed more than he liked.

His mother looked startled by his outburst, and then gave him a very catlike smile that had him silently cursing. "First of all, there were her responsibilities to her family. She would not have dashed off to London and abandoned them. Then there was that Mr. Ruddel. Isabel seemed quite fond of the gentleman last summer," she said as if the news still did not sit well with her.

Vane was not fond of the bastard, either.

"It became apparent that if I desired Isabel's cooperation, a little subterfuge was necessary. I told her to bring Delia to London, and I would arrange an introduction. Isabel had doubts about the whole thing but I brushed them aside, telling her that spending the season in London would allow her to find the proper business contacts for her father's papers."

"You knew she was selling her father's work?" It was one thing for his mother to meddle in his life, but she had been playing with Isabel's as well. "Are you aware how much it hurt her to part with those papers? To watch other men claim her father's inventions for their own?"

"What was I supposed to do? I offered to pay all her expenses, but the stubborn girl refused. She said that we were not family yet so it was improper to accept my generous offer. I helped when I could, even going so far as to inform Lord Botly that his granddaughters were in town."

The pressure behind Vane's eyes increased with that bit of news. "You were the one who warned Botly? Do you know what trouble you caused with that bit of mischief?"

"Christopher, it was not my intention to hurt Isabel and Delia. I thought that once Lord Botly learned his granddaughters were right under his nose, he might see past his pride and anger. Those girls should not have to pay for their mother's sins. How was I supposed to know that Isabel inherited her obstinacy from her unpleasant grandfather? I feel just awful about everything!"

"As well as you should," Vane said sternly. If his mother was looking for a sympathetic ear, she would have to ring for one of his sisters. "I have often found your meddling rather endearing, but this time you have gone too far."

"I know," the marchioness said miserably.

Vane pushed out of the chair and resumed his pacing. "I cannot fathom why you thought Isabel had the makings of a decent wife. In truth, Delia and I had more in common."

Vane thought of the masquerade, when Delia had wrapped herself about him and kissed him. Although the kiss had been mildly pleasant, it paled in comparison with those he'd shared with Isabel against the side of his coach. He had been so crazed to have her that he had taken her back to his town house, where he had claimed her innocence and spent the rest of the night making wild, passionate love to the reckless woman.

Later, he thought the sadness he occasionally glimpsed in Isabel's brown eyes was her unspoken regret for giving her innocence to a man who had no interest in marriage. He had been wrong. It was not regret that had been eating away at Isabel's happiness, but guilt. She saw him as Delia's future husband and felt she had betrayed Lady Netherley's trust. *Deceitful, stubborn, and selfless to a fault,* Vane silently raged. Not once had Isabel thought to keep him for herself. The insight put him in a nasty mood. He furiously wondered: If he had married Delia, would Isabel have continued to welcome him into her bed? If so, perhaps marrying into the Thorne family would bring its own rewards.

"Marrying Delia would have been a disastrous choice," his mother said, blithely unaware of his dark thoughts.

"How so?" he asked silkily.

"You are too much alike in temperament. I doubt the bliss of your union would have lasted a fortnight." His mother dismissed his fictitious marriage to Delia with a wave of her hand. "Isabel, on the other hand . . ." She left the sentence unfinished and gave him a shrewd look.

"She has been lying to me since the first day I met her," he said, trying not to think of her shy smiles or her unfeigned responses when he coaxed her into his bed. It was probably the only time she had ever been honest with him. "And because of you, she still seems to have her heart set on me marrying her annoying sister."

His mother's frown deepened at the bitterness in his voice. "So I was wrong about Isabel, after all." She bowed her head and sighed. "Forgive me, Christopher, I only wanted you to be happy. I would never have meddled if I did not think Isabel was perfect for you."

Vane dropped to his knees and clasped both of the marchioness's hands. "It was wrong to manipulate me and Isabel, especially when hearts are involved."

His mother shuddered as tears slipped down her cheeks. "I know, son. Never again. I have learned my lesson."

Vane nodded and inhaled deeply. He slowly exhaled. "You weren't, however, wrong about Isabel. About her being the perfect woman for me. Before I learned about your damn scheme and Isabel's part in it, I was working up the courage to ask her to marry me."

The marchioness's face creased as she fought back her tears. "Oh . . . oh, Christopher!" She brought his hands to her lips and kissed his knuckles.

He gave her a stern look. "This does not mean that you are forgiven so quickly for your mischief," he warned.

"No, no . . . of course not."

The discord with his father remained, but he did not want to upset his mother further by mentioning it. Vane leaned closer so his mother could wrap her arms around him. He hugged her tightly to his chest when her sobs racked her body.

"There, there," he said, rubbing her back to comfort her. "Forget what I said. You are forgiven." Vane kissed the top of her head. He would never have met Isabel if not for his mother. "Besides, I may need your help if things get sticky."

"Anything," she said, drawing back and giving him a watery smile. "What do you need from me?"

He returned her smile. "Advice. How do I convince Isabel that I am the perfect man for her?"

Three hours later, a tight-lipped and very frustrated Vane stormed into his empty town house. Apparently Isabel had not been languishing in her rented house, waiting for him to forgive her. Without a word to anyone, she had packed up her family and departed London.

Chapter Twenty-nine

Disembarking from the stagecoach with the kitten Vane had given her curled up against her chest, Isabel smiled as she spotted their housekeeper near the side of the cottage. Mrs. Dalman was carrying a wicker basket of wet linen against her ample hip. As soon as she noticed the stage, she dropped the basket and rushed toward them.

It seemed as if nothing had changed in their absence.

"Gracious, I was not expecting you for another day!" The housekeeper hugged Isabel, and then Delia. Mrs. Dalman scowled when their mother poked her head through the open door of the coach. "I don't care if this gets me sacked, I must have my say, Mrs. Thorne. Shame on you for locking me in the cellar and running off to London. If not for Mrs. Willow, I might have been trapped in my dank prison for days."

"Fear not, Mrs. Dalman. I have been severely chastised by Isabel and half of London for my recklessness," Sybil said, her exaggerated manner causing both Delia and Isabel to roll their eyes. The journey home had not been too taxing, since their mother had spent long stretches of the drive sleeping. Isabel had suspected her mother had gotten her hands on another bottle of laudanum at the coaching inn, but she had been too lost in her own thoughts to press the issue.

Sybil slipped past her daughters, still irked that no amount of arguing had persuaded her daughters to remain in London. To the housekeeper, she said, "If you do not mind, Mrs. Dalman, I will be taking my tea upstairs."

"Make sure it is just tea," Isabel murmured to the housekeeper.

"Yes, Miss Thorne." Mrs. Dalman picked up one of the thick canvas satchels and hurried after Sybil.

Isabel nodded to the coachman and the postboy as they removed the family's trunks from the coach. "I hope you are willing to grab one of the ends of that large trunk, because the days of having footmen waiting on us hand and foot have ended."

Delia giggled as she sat down on one end of the trunk. "I do not recall us ever having a single footman, dear sister."

"Well, you would have if you had married Lord Vanewright," Isabel said teasingly, though her heart was breaking.

"An entire staff to fulfill my every wish," her sister said wistfully. "It might have been worth putting up with a man who could barely tolerate me."

Isabel sat down on the opposite end of the trunk. She leaned over and released her little tabby cat. It plopped down on its back and rolled from side to side.

"Vane—uh, Lord Vanewright liked you." Well enough that he did not prevent Delia from kissing him, Isabel glumly thought, thinking of the night of the masquerade. "Lady Netherley had a high opinion of you, too."

Delia shook her head. "The earl never really looked at me. Not the way he looked at you." Her sister raised her hand as the coachman touched the brim of his hat and said farewell. "Perhaps you should have stayed. Once Lord Vanewright's anger cooled—"

"No," Isabel said decisively. "It would have never worked. Lady Netherley wanted you for her son, and Vane . . . well, he will never forgive me for my part in his mother's ruse. Besides, I have missed Cotersage. This is where we belong."

"Not me." Her sister stared at the cloud of dust left behind by the stagecoach. "You might be content to bury yourself in the country, but I plan to return to London. Your earl was not the only unmarried gentleman in town."

"He is not *my* earl," Isabel protested. *Oh, what is the use arguing?* She sighed and stood. "Come on. Mrs. Dalman is busy with Sybil and these trunks need to be brought into the house before it gets dark."

By ten o'clock that evening the household was silent. Once she and Mrs. Dalman had unpacked the trunks, it amazed Isabel how quickly she fell back into her old routine. She helped the housekeeper set the table for the evening meal, and to Isabel's relief Sybil requested that a tray be brought to her bedchamber. She was still sulking, but Isabel was too upset about her own woes to feel guilty about her mother's bruised feelings.

After supper, Isabel played piquet with Delia. Neither of them seemed very interested in the game, so by nine o'clock they had decided to retire for the evening.

Unfortunately, Isabel could not sleep. The kitten she had dubbed Christopher had curled himself into a little orange ball and buried his nose near her right ear. She absently reached up and stroked his soft fur, and was rewarded with a low purr.

"Oh, Christopher," she murmured to her pet. "I have made a fine mess of my life."

It was early for London revelers, and Isabel felt restless. When she closed her eyes, all she saw was Vane's handsome face, the corners of his mouth curled with revulsion. His parting words had been spoken in anger, and while her heart craved his forgiveness, Isabel knew she did not deserve it. So she had departed London without sending him a final note.

"Perhaps it was cowardly, but I could not face him again." She blinked away the sharp sting of tears. "He was just so furious."

By now Vane had likely resumed his debauched life of gambling and mistresses. His friends the Lords of Vice would help him forget her, and mayhap he would look upon their time together as an aberration because of Lady Netherley's meddling. Oh, Isabel had no doubt that the earl would come to forgive the dear lady. After all, his mother had acted out of love, while Isabel had been motivated by less noble purposes.

Giving up her pretense of sleeping, she kissed the kitten and gently pulled her braid free from his tiny coiled body. She threw back the sheet and climbed down from her bed. Dressed in her nightgown, she tugged the cap off her head and tossed it aside because she felt overly warm. She was about to open the window when a soft shuffling noise outside her door caused her to halt.

Everyone was in bed. Isabel's eyes rounded in trepidation when she heard a low, very male voice curse. Without hesitation, she grabbed the first thing that was within reach and crossed the room in her bare feet to the door.

As the latch on the door moved, Isabel bit her lower lip to keep from screaming. She raised her makeshift weapon above her head, prepared to teach this would-be housebreaker a harsh lesson for preying on helpless women.

A dark head appeared as the door opened, and Isabel struck with ruthless intent. Metal collided with flesh, and the thief was brought to his knees with her unexpected attack.

"Devil take it, it's me!" a familiar angry male voice raged at her as he turned his head to glare at her.

"Vane!" Isabel gasped, his presence shocking her into silence.

He climbed onto his feet and snatched the handle from her loose grasp. "A bed warmer," he said, shaking his head with disgust. "Why am I not surprised?"

"W-what are you doing here?" she asked, suddenly finding her voice when he shut the door and locked it. The key disappeared into a waistcoat pocket as he stalked away from her and set down the bed warmer. "Who let you into the house?"

Vane gave her a guarded look. "Delia. It appears that she is having trouble sleeping, too, and was helping herself to the port when she heard my knock."

"And she just let you upstairs?" Isabel said, aghast at her sister's impropriety.

"Well, she might have had a few glasses before my arrival," he said with a careless shrug.

Delia was *drunk*. "I need to go downstairs and have a chat with my little sister."

Vane cut off her escape by wrapping his arm around her waist. "Let her be. You can always lecture her tomorrow when she has a sore head and weak stomach."

He stilled, suddenly aware that she was dressed only in her nightgown. Wary, she stood there rigidly with his arm around her and listened to his breathing.

"Vane." She swallowed, realizing she had no right to claim such familiarity. "Pardon me, Lord Vanewright, what are you doing here in Cotersage?"

"You had it right the first time, Isabel." Sensing her discomfort, he gave her a slow grin that bordered on lecherous. "As for why I am here, I think that is obvious."

Isabel brushed aside his arm and stepped out of reach. "You did not have to leave London to find *that*."

Vane laughed. "My, my . . . sweet Isabel, does your mother know you have such wicked thoughts? Not that I mind and I am willing to accommodate you, but first things first." He pointed to the chair. "Sit."

Isabel stared at him, wondering if she could reach the copper bed warmer before Vane. A few more bashes to the head might make him more reasonable.

As if reading her thoughts, Vane glanced at the bed

warmer. "If you want me to put my hands on you, Isabel, all you have to do is ask."

Her eyes narrowed. "You would not dare!"

"Sit!" he said in a thunderous voice.

Isabel sat, but she took her time about it. "Fine. As you can see, my lord, I am sitting as you have requested. Why have you come?"

There was a swagger in his gait that had her chin lifting and her upper lip curling. *Arrogant swine,* she thought uncharitably when he stopped in front of her, his fists planted on his hips.

"I've come for my apology."

Isabel's eyes were dark unfathomable brown pools as she stared up at him. Her lips parted in surprise at his demand. "You journeyed all this way and charmed your way past my sister so I might beg your forgiveness?"

His cocky grin faded. *Well, when she put it like that—*

Isabel rose up from the chair, her slender body rigid with feminine outrage. "You had my apology, you pompous rogue, and you tossed it at my feet." She shook her fist at him, and he wondered if she was planning to plant it in his face.

Not that I don't deserve it.

Instead she pounded it against her breast. "I cried that day, and every day since because I knew that you despised me for helping your mother with her crazy scheme."

"You cried over me."

It pleased him that Isabel had shed a few tears at their angry parting. As he followed her back to Cotersage,

Vane had had a few bad days wondering if Isabel had left London because her hopes of making Delia his countess had been ruined.

Misconstruing his joyful expression, Isabel flew at him with her fists raised. Vane caught her wrists, but she still managed to clip him on the chin.

"Heartless, jaded, conceited arse!" she shouted, her struggles causing him to stagger backward.

"Isabel, listen to me."

"Never!" Isabel snarled, her long hair spilling out from her loose braid.

She gave his chest a hard shove while he was fighting to keep his balance, probably hoping he'd fall and crack his already bruised skull on a heavy piece of furniture. It would save her from grabbing the copper bed warmer and finishing the deed herself.

Vane's spine collided with one of the ornate posts of her four-poster bed. "Damn it, woman, are you trying to kill me?"

"Yes," she hissed, charging at him.

In his short life, Vane had tangled with numerous angry ladies intent on castrating him. Saint once told him that he had a talent for causing trouble, and perhaps his friend was right.

In a practiced motion, Vane caught Isabel in his arms and spun them about so he was on top of her when her lovely backside bounced on the mattress. The tiny orange tabby he had given her jumped straight into the air before darting off the mattress.

"Don't hurt Christopher!"

Vane peered over the edge of the mattress, but the

kitten had disappeared. He gave her an inscrutable look. "You named your cat after me?"

"If I were naming the cat after the conceited scoundrel who gave him to me, I would have called him *Vane*," she said defensively. "Christopher just happens to be a name I favor. I know several gentlemen who bear the name whom I respect and admire."

"Hmmm."

"Let me up," she said, the slender body he had come to know so well arched against his.

Perhaps it was rather arrogant of him, but he was feeling aroused and triumphant when he pinned her wrists above her head. "Struggle all you want. I promise to relish every delicious rub."

Impotent and soundly caught, she glared up at him with defiance. "I hate you!"

Vane calmly studied her flushed face and glittering angry eyes. "No, my dear, in fact you are in love with me."

Isabel stopped struggling and gaped at him. Her lower lip quivered mutinously before she burst into tears.

"Isabel . . . Isabel," he crooned as he released her wrists. "There, there, darling . . . don't cry."

Taking advantage of her limited freedom, she covered her face with one hand and tried to push him away with the other. "Oh, you horrible man. Have you come just to torment me? Why must you take everything from me?"

She rolled, burying her face into the nearest pillow and beginning to cry in earnest.

Her misery cut him to the quick. Vane felt helpless, and it unmanned him that he was responsible for her tears.

"Isabel, look at me." He tenderly peeled her hands from her face. "Hush, love, no more games. I've come to give you something."

Isabel hiccuped. "What?" she asked warily.

Wet strands of hair were clinging to her cheeks. His fingers brushed them from her face. "Everything. I have already given you my friendship and body. It seems appropriate that you claim my love and name as well. Isabel Thorne, will you do me the honor of marrying me?"

"W-what?" Stunned, she tried to push herself up on her elbows. Her forehead connected with his chin. Groaning, she slapped her palm over her bruised brow and stared at him with a dazed expression. "What did you say?"

Uncertainty crawled up his spine until he felt the tension in his neck. "I am asking you to marry me."

Instead of the enthusiastic assent he was expecting, Isabel's expression crumbled as her eyes gleamed with unshed tears.

In his entire life, Vane had never felt the slightest desire to offer marriage to a lady. He had always assumed that when he got around to it, the lady would be *happy* about it.

"Have I mistaken your feelings, Isabel?" Vane asked, lowering his head and kissing her cheek. "I am not a bad gent. My looks are passable, I have all my teeth, and I can make you a countess."

She choked back what could have been a sob or a giggle and turned her face away, giving him access to the side of her neck. Perhaps it was ruthless of him, but he was going to gain her consent even if he had to seduce her. His cock throbbed in agreement. He had been hard and ready for her the moment they had landed on the mattress.

Isabel shuddered as his tongue licked her earlobe. She turned her head to halt his sensual ministrations, and to his relief and amazement she was laughing. "Stop. Passable looks and strong teeth are no reason to marry a man."

"Do not forget that you will be my countess," he teased, and was rewarded with a watery smile from her.

"Vane, your mother—" Isabel sighed when he nibbled her neck.

"This is not the moment to bring up my mother," he said, letting his body press against hers so she could feel his arousal.

"But . . . Delia?"

Vane cupped her chin. "If you must know, *you* were my mother's choice all along. Delia was merely a ruse to keep us from figuring out her true intentions. She's a wily old woman, I grant you, but she managed to pick the perfect bride for me. Marry me, Isabel."

"I—"

The look he gave her was positively mischievous. "So you want to be convinced."

"No, I . . ."

He lowered his head and put his mouth over her right breast, suckling her nipple through the thin linen fabric of her nightgown.

"Ah, yessss," Isabel drawled until her breath hissed through her teeth. Her legs moved restlessly against the mattress.

"Like that, do you?" he murmured, his hands sliding possessively over the soft mounds until his fingers grasped the lacy collar of her nightgown. Without warning, he tore the thin fabric down the front, exposing her form. "Lovely." He took a few seconds to admire her bared breasts. "And mine to lick and fondle, are they not?"

Isabel responded by cupping his testicles through his trousers. Solid instincts made the flesh between his legs retract and tighten. The snug garment offered little protection if she planned to maim him. He shuddered as she caressed him.

"Only if I can make the same claim. Is this mine?" she purred. The sound had his cock straining for release.

"Christ, yes," he said hoarsely. "Everything. It is yours."

"Prove it." She lightly squeezed his testicles, and his body reacted as if she'd wedged a bit in his mouth. He gave way, allowing their positions to reverse.

"I was lying the day that we argued." With a hooded gaze he watched as she unfastened his trousers and tugged at the fabric until she had freed his cock. Vane was fully aroused, a condition that seemed to occur whenever she was close. "What we had—it was more than fucking. I always wanted more, long before I could admit it to myself."

Isabel leaned over him, her breasts spilling out of her torn nightgown. "I know." She offered him the top of her head as her tongue tentatively licked the spot just beneath the head of his cock. "Nevertheless, I knew from the beginning you could not be mine."

Vane blindly gripped the sheets; his spine felt like it was about to break as he strained against her gentle, exploratory onslaught. He had not bothered to undress, but Isabel did not seem to mind since she was wholly focused on the thick length of flesh between his legs.

"Wrong. I'm yours. Please!" he begged, his mind clouding as her front teeth grazed his sensitive flesh.

Vane had tasted her arousal, but he had never invited Isabel to do the same: He had not wanted to frighten her with his carnal appetites. In truth, he loved the feel of a woman's lips and tongue close around his cock, the gentle thrusting that coaxed her to take as much of him as she could handle. The heady thrill as his seed burst out of him while his lover's throat worked to swallow every salty drop. How many nameless, faceless females had pleasured him in that manner? Even in the beginning, Isabel had meant more to him, so he had denied himself the indulgence out of respect for the woman he had fallen in love with.

"Isabel, you do not have to. You have nothing to prove."

"Hush." She shifted the position of her body so she could do more than impress him with her tongue.

Vane gasped and his buttocks tightened as the head of his cock brushed over her lips, over the teasing scrape of her teeth, and then deeper still until he was cradled by her tongue.

"Show mercy, Isabel!" He moaned as her inexperience proved to be more arousing than a courtesan's skillful hand. "I am not made of stone."

He almost whimpered when she released him. Giving him a saucy look, she said huskily, "Feels a bit like hot marble to me." Isabel circled her fingers around the base of his rigid staff and squeezed. "I am not certain what to do. Should I suckle you, much as you do my breasts?"

His hips came off the mattress as her lips settled over the head and suckled him with enough pressure to make his eyes cross.

"Yes."

Isabel's fingers slid lower as she learned the shape and texture of him. More to herself, she said, "I like it when you stroke me with your tongue." To prove her point, she teased the tip of his cock with a tantalizing flick. "Mmm, exotic and bitter. I've never tasted a man's seed."

"You will if you persist," he gritted out as she tried to nibble down from the throbbing length to his hard testicles. Her hand moved lower, curious about what must have felt like marbles shifting within the hairy sac. Bemused by her discovery, she giggled softly, making every fine hair on his body prickle. Her breasts brushed against his outer thigh, when her tongue wiggled experimentally over the wrinkled flesh.

Vane seemed to have limited control when it came to Isabel, and the minx had provoked him to the point of madness. "Enough," he said, roughly pulling her up until she covered him, and then rolling her onto her back. He removed his frock coat and sent it sailing over the side of the bed.

There was laughter and a smidgeon of smugness in her eyes until he forgot about undressing and instead hastily sheathed himself in her slick channel. They both groaned as he filled her.

"Temptress," he muttered, kissing her and tasting himself on her tongue. His need to claim her with his body bordered on madness, but this was nothing new for either of them. Pulling him closer, Isabel bit the side of his jaw, and dragged his mouth to her neck. Her hips arched against his as he madly pounded his cock into her, each enthusiastic stroke drawing him deeper.

Vane was out of his depth when it came to this woman, but he no longer cared. Seizing her by the hips, he surrendered himself completely to her. Isabel sobbed his name and clung to him as his hips gave one frenzied thrust. He buried his face against the side of her neck. The head of his cock seemed to explode as the constricting muscles of her sheath milked him for his seed.

Vane held nothing back. His body spoke with an eloquence his tongue often lacked when he was around Isabel. She muddled his brain and left him crazed with lust. He wanted to spend the rest of his life pleasuring her in and out of bed.

Still buried inside her, he cupped her face with his hand. "Marry me, Isabel."

His heart fluttered with panic when she sighed. "Why?"

"Because I love you," he said without hesitation. "Don't think me honorable, my motives are selfish in nature. I cannot go a single day without you. I want to see you at my table in the morning and my bed each night. When our gazes meet across a crowded ballroom, everyone will know that you are mine. This is not about my mother or my duty to my family. This is about me . . . and you. About the life we can build together. What say you, Isabel? Are you daring enough to gamble with a Lord of Vice?"

His heart almost stopped when she shook her head.

"No, but I'll take that risk with you." She gave him a tremulous smile. "Yes, I'll marry you. I have loved you for so long, but it seemed hopeless. I have been miserable for weeks because Delia was fated to be your countess."

Vane swallowed his anger. His mother had much to answer for—her good intentions had almost cost him Isabel. "No chance of that," he said, kissing her nose. "Since my heart was already ensnared by a brown-eyed temptress."

To demonstrate the power she had over him, Vane moved his hips against hers, a gentle reminder that he was far from finished with his lady.

From the corner of his eye, Vane noticed that his furry namesake was clawing his way back onto the mattress. Large green eyes regarded him somberly as the kitten tried to use Isabel's long hair for bedding.

She laughed and extended her arm upward to pet the creature. "There, there, sweetheart, you will have to learn to share."

It was on the tip of his tongue to ask if she was speaking to him or the cat. "I cannot believe you gave the beast my name," he grumbled, eyeing the sharp claws warily. For once, he was grateful most of his flesh was covered.

"Somehow it seemed appropriate." She grinned up at him and wiggled her hips, which got his attention.

A new wave of desire washed over him. The mischievous girl was playing with fire. "Perhaps you should give him another name."

His friends were never going to let him hear the end of it when they learned Isabel had named her cat after him. He could just imagine Frost's raunchy jokes about Isabel's partiality to *little Christopher.*

"But I *love* Christopher," she protested.

So changing the name of the kitten could wait. Vane had more important tasks that deserved his attention. He reached for the nearest pillow. "And so you shall, my lady. Often and most thoroughly, if I have anything to say about it."

With her warm laughter filling the bedchamber, the pillow was the first to hit the floor with a soft *plop.* A very disgruntled cat landed on top of the feathered mound. Stepping off the pillow, the beast sat on the rug and began the meticulous task of cleaning himself.

More than an hour would pass before it was safe to climb onto the bed again.

Chapter Thirty

"There is no sign that your sister slept in her bed."

Mrs. Dalman made the announcement in the calm, seemingly unflappable manner that the Thorne family had come to rely on over the years.

Any other morning, Isabel would have been scandalized to be sharing an intimate breakfast with her lover. However, Delia always had a way of becoming the center of attention even when she wasn't in the room.

"Are you certain?"

"There is no reason for her to be hiding," the housekeeper said, worry adding lines to her face. "You haven't had time to write up your instructions for the day."

Mrs. Dalman was correct. Something was amiss. Isabel stood, but Vane caught her hand before she could leave his side. "Have you checked the parlor?" he asked the older woman. "She might have fallen asleep in one of the chairs."

Vane winked at Isabel.

As far as Mrs. Dalman was concerned, Lord Vane-wright had arrived at the Thornes' cottage before dawn.

Isabel saw no reason to correct the housekeeper. As it was, she could barely look her in the eye when she dwelled on how she and Vane had passed the long hours of the night. Jubilant and possessing unflagging vigor, the earl had made love to her with enthusiastic abandonment that left her aching and breathless. Then he stripped off the rest of his clothes. Isabel's face warmed at the memory. Vane had left no inch of her flesh unexplored. The man was turning her into a wanton slave to his lust.

Her telling blush revealed the direction of her thoughts. Vane gave her a smug smile and brought her hand to his lips. "Do not fret, love. We will find your sister."

Isabel nodded absently as her thoughts switched to her absent sibling. Delia tended to slip away when it suited her, but usually it was to avoid some unpleasant task. "Mrs. Dalman, could you check the back gardens and orchard? Vane—ah, Lord Vanewright and I will search the house again."

The housekeeper pretended not to notice the intimacy between her lady and the earl. "Yes, Miss Thorne."

When Mrs. Dalman left them, Isabel glanced at Vane. "Are you certain Delia returned to the parlor after she let you into the house?"

Vane pushed away from the table and stood. "As I told you last night, she had been drinking when I pounded on your door. Delia invited me in and asked me to join her for a drink. I was anxious to see you so I politely declined. She directed me to the stairs and told me where to find you. Once she set me on my course, she returned to the parlor."

With Vane trailing after her, Isabel went up the

stairs and checked the parlor. Nothing seemed out of place until she saw the bottle of port and two half-filled glasses. "I thought you declined the drink."

He peered over her shoulder and scowled. "I did."

"Vane, you were not the only visitor last evening," Isabel said, rushing to the door. "Delia!" she yelled into the stairwell.

"It's too early to be shouting, Isabel," her mother said sleepily from the landing above. "I have a terrible megrim and did not get a wink of sleep."

Isabel had trouble believing this: Sybil usually had a bottle of laudanum or brandy hidden away in her bedchamber for restless nights. "Perhaps you should go back to bed," Isabel said, motioning with her hand for Vane to remain out of sight.

"It was that bothersome cat. All that caterwauling. How could you even sleep in the same room with that beast?"

Utterly mortified that her mother could have overheard her and Vane, Isabel was speechless. Vane, the scoundrel, threw his head back and started laughing.

"Isabel, who is down there with you?" her mother asked, her voice sharpening.

Ignoring Isabel's silent plea, Vane stepped forward so Sybil could see him. "Good morning, Mrs. Thorne."

"Lord Vanewright! Good heavens, no one told me that you were here." Realizing she was not dressed for visitors, her hand unconsciously checked to make certain her hair looked tidy under her lace cap. "Isabel, did you have Mrs. Dalman fix our guest a hearty breakfast?"

"Yes, Mother. I have not been shirking my responsibilities," she said, a slight edge to her tone.

Only belatedly did Isabel notice that Vane's appearance gave the impression he was the master of the house instead of a visitor. At her urging, he had donned his waistcoat and retied his cravat—though upon closer scrutiny, his shirt was wrinkled and the basic knot he had employed did not match the crisp folds his valet had pressed into the starched fabric. His hat, gloves, and frock coat were missing. Delia must have taken his hat and gloves when he had arrived, and Isabel suspected Vane's coat was currently being used as a soft bed by her cat.

"Forgive my early arrival, Mrs. Thorne," Vane entreated, managing to appear humble and apologetic. "Nevertheless, your daughter has been an amiable and capable hostess."

The outrageous man then had the audacity to stroke Isabel's backside.

Fortunately, Sybil did not notice the shameless caress. "I shall come down and join you," her mother announced, stepping out of view.

"No!" When her mother returned and peered over the railing, Isabel explained, "What I meant to say is that there is no need to hurry. Lord Vanewright has finished his breakfast." Feigning a calmness that seemed to be eluding her this morning, she continued, "Actually, we are looking for Delia. Have you seen her?"

Her mother stifled a yawn with her hand. "No. Perhaps the cat's cries kept her awake all night, too."

"Not a single word from you," Isabel muttered under

her breath as she stepped in front of Vane. To her mother, she said, "I am certain we will find her. Do you want to help us search the upstairs?" She knew her mother would decline.

Sybil's next words confirmed it. "You two can carry on without me. I think I will take your suggestion to heart, my dear, and return to my bed."

Isabel inclined her head. "Very well."

"By the by," her mother called, halting Isabel and Vane before they could continue down the stairs. "Lord Vanewright, you never explained why you have come to Cotersage."

With his hand braced on the banister, Vane grinned at Sybil. "I thought that was obvious. I've come for Isabel. We'll be marrying as swiftly as my mother can arrange it." To Isabel, he said, "Do not be surprised if she has everything planned before our return." He stared up at his future mother-in-law, who was beginning to look a little too pale for his liking. "If you behave yourself, we'll even let you attend the wedding in London."

Her mother's eyes rolled back into her head and she dropped like a stone.

"Mother!" Isabel dashed up the stairs. "Good grief, Vane, did you have to be so blunt? If the news hasn't killed her, the bump on her head might finish her off."

Downstairs, the housekeeper was calling her name. Isabel stuck her head over the side of the banister and shouted, "Mrs. Dalman, bring your vinaigrette. Mother has fainted."

She continued up the stairs, acutely aware that Vane had not abandoned her.

As Isabel reached her unconscious mother and knelt at her side, she glanced up at Vane and was strangely comforted by his concerned expression. After years of looking after her family, she no longer had to shoulder the burden alone.

The smelling salts revived Isabel's mother. Or perhaps it was the news that her eldest daughter was marrying well and she no longer needed Botly's blessing and wealth to return to London. Calling for some tea, Mrs. Thorne returned to her bedchamber, most likely to repack her trunks. Vane did not mind as long as he did not have to ride in the same coach as his future in-laws.

After Mrs. Dalman had assured Isabel that her mother was unhurt, Isabel resumed her frantic search for Delia. Vane knew what his lady was thinking. Isabel feared that her sister had lied about her feelings toward him and had run off when she realized that she could never have the man she loved. He snorted at the absurdity, but he suspected Isabel believed it. Mrs. Thorne and her daughter were used to having Isabel at their beck and call. Although it had not occurred to Isabel, Vane was certain Delia knew that her days of badgering and bullying her sister were numbered. If her bride did not have the heart to stand up to her family, then Vane was prepared to be the villain. No one was going to prevent him from marrying the woman he loved, and that included Isabel.

To expedite the hunt, he had agreed to check the rooms upstairs while Isabel searched the downstairs. When Vane was finished, he found Isabel in her father's study. She was sitting in one of the chairs with a paper in her hand. At her feet was his furry namesake. The kitten was stretched out on his back, batting at dust motes.

"Delia isn't here."

Since they had searched the house from top to bottom, and Mrs. Dalman had done the same outdoors, the news hardly came as a surprise to him.

Vane strode into the study, and gestured at the paper. "She left you a note?"

She blinked and glanced down at the paper, startled to see it in her hand. Isabel was beginning to worry him. Her customary exuberance had evaporated in his absence. Whatever Delia had written had shaken Isabel.

Vane crouched down beside her, and caressed her arm. "Tell me."

Wordlessly she offered him the letter. It only took him seconds to read the short note Delia had hastily written to her sister. Vane stood and crumbled it with a curse. "Foolish little girl! How could she run off with that bounder Ruddel?"

"I daresay she loves him," Isabel said simply, the corners of her mouth twisting upward into a sad smile. "And perhaps, he loves her as well. I caught them together more than once. His affection for Delia appeared to be genuine."

Unlike the pretty lies he had whispered in Isabel's ear to win her trust and friendship.

For his deception and casual cruelty, Vane wanted to beat the man senseless for bruising Isabel's heart. "Listen to me, Isabel." He grasped her by the upper arms and pulled her onto her feet. "It will take them time to travel to Scotland. I'll get some men and we will ride after them. We can stop the marriage from—"

"No."

His brows furrowed at his disbelief. "Are you telling me you want Delia bound to that cheating speculator? What do you think your mother will have to say about all this?"

"She might surprise you and approve of the match. Mother was rather fond of Mr. Ruddel. You see, there was something about him that reminded her of my father."

Isabel looked away. She did not have to explain that she had felt the same about the man, and the ruthless bastard exploited a young woman's loneliness so he could steal her father's work.

Her father's work.

Vane tightened his grip on her arms, but she did not seem to notice. "Your father's journals," he said, already knowing the answer. "Where are they?"

Isabel closed her eyes and shook her head.

He dragged her into his arms, and she buried her face into his chest. Ruddel had not only run off with Delia but also stolen Thorne's legacy to his children. When he could not charm the journals from Isabel, he'd decided to claim them as her sister's dowry.

"I'll get them back," Vane vowed with deadly purpose in his blue-green eyes. "He will rot in prison for his crimes."

Isabel hugged him as a soft sob caught in her throat. She turned her face upward, and once again Vane was spellbound by her beauty. "A lovely thought," she said, leaning forward to press a kiss to his chin. "However, if my sister truly loves Mr. Ruddel, she would suffer, too."

She pulled away, moving out of his embrace. "My father's words. It was all I had left of him, and I died a little each time I had to sell his wonderful work." Isabel held out her hand, and Vane closed the space between them. "Those journals belong to me, but they also belong to my mother and Delia. My sister has a right to them." She blinked rapidly to stop from crying. "I may not agree with Mr. Ruddel's methods, but if he treats Delia kindly, then he is welcome to them."

Vane vehemently disagreed, but he remained silent. This was not the time to argue. Whether she admitted it or not, Isabel was hurting. It did not escape Vane's notice that Delia had used him as well.

Last night, she had shared a glass of port with someone in the parlor. Had Isabel's sister been waiting for Ruddel when Vane surprised her by arriving first? The clever girl had recovered quickly. Instead of waking Isabel, Delia had sent Vane upstairs because she knew his unexpected arrival would provide the distraction she needed to slip out of the house unnoticed.

If he did not already have reason to despise Ruddel, Vane could have pitied the man. Marriage to Delia might be punishment enough.

"How quickly can you pack for London?"

Isabel glanced at her father's study as if the room held the answer to his question. "A few days. Why?"

Vane needed to talk to the Runner he had hired to look

into Ruddel's affairs. If there was a chance to recover her father's journals without hurting her sister, he intended to give them to Isabel as a wedding present.

"I told my mother that I was returning to London with my future bride at my side, and she would be sorely disappointed if that lady wasn't you."

"Oh." The shy smile he loved surfaced, warming him from the inside out. "A touching tale. Truly. However, I thought she was so desperate to see you wed that any lady would have sufficed."

"How fortunate then that my beloved mother found you."

Isabel gasped in surprise as he tugged her back against his chest and slanted his mouth over hers for a smoldering kiss. "How very fortunate," she concurred after the kiss ended.

He rubbed his cheek against hers. "You know this isn't the end."

"About Delia and Ruddel? No, I suppose you are correct. If possible, we should rescue my sister before she marries him."

The kitten dashed by them and disappeared under the desk.

"That, too." Vane shook his head. They *were* changing the cat's name. He did not care what it cost him. "However, I was speaking of my mother."

"Lady Netherley?" She walked over to the desk and bent over, giving him the opportunity to admire her backside. "With you settled, what else could she possible want?"

"More grandchildren."

Vane grinned at her startled expression. "My mother is relentless when it comes to getting what she wants."

Isabel turned her head and looked over her shoulder. "Reminds me of someone else I know." She murmured to the kitten, attempting to coax him out from his hiding place.

The large desk and her nicely rounded backside were giving him a few wicked ideas, but he would save them for his library in London. Vane curled his arms around Isabel's waist and nuzzled her neck.

"I think we should slip upstairs and work on that grandchild she will undoubtedly want from us," he murmured against her skin as his hand slid up the front of her bodice to her breasts. "Then she will have more time to pester my sister Ellen."

Isabel leaned against him. "So you think this will work?"

"At keeping my mother from meddling?" he asked, hoping they could avoid Mrs. Thorne and Mrs. Dalman as they made their way up to Isabel's room. His desire for her was evident. "It is a worthy goal."

In truth, he doubted his mother could resist meddling any more than he could stop wanting Isabel. He clasped his lady's wrist and headed for the door.

Marriage. A life with Isabel. Children.

Who could believe such a fate was for him?

Hand in hand, Vane and Isabel raced up the stairs.

For the second time this month, he was going to follow his mother's sage advice.

DAMON KAPPELL/STUDIO 16

An unrepentant Anglophile, **ALEXANDRA HAWKINS** discovered romance novels as a teenager and knew that one day she would be writing her own stories. Alexandra has combined her love of English history, mythology, and romance to create sensual character-driven stories that she hopes will touch readers' hearts.

Alexandra lives in Georgia with her husband and three children. You can contact her through her website at www.alexandrahawkins.com or by mail at: P.O. Box 2192, Woodstock, GA 30188.

ISBN 978-1-250-00136-8

*Dashing, decadent, and deliciously seductive,
the notorious Lords of Vice indulge their every desire—
from dusk until dawn...*

FOREVER THE BACHELOR

Christopher Courtland, Earl of Vanewright—
known around London as "Vane"—is the very
picture of a rich, handsome ladies' man. Why
shackle himself to just one lady when he's
free to sample them all? In spite of his own
mother's attempts at matchmaking, Vane has
sworn to stay single. Until he has a chance
run-in with Miss Isabel Thorne...

NEVER IN LOVE—UNTIL NOW...

A modest and refined beauty, Isabel is a lot more brazen than
she appears. When a pickpocket tries to make away with Vane's
bejeweled snuffbox, Isabel attempts to thwart his escape...and
manages to steal Vane's heart. But the harder he tries to seduce
the sharp-tongued, strong-willed Isabel, the more she resists.
Now it's up to this tried-and-true bachelor to find a new way
to play the game...or risk losing the one woman who's ever
captured his heart.

"Romantic and erotic...the Lords of Vice series
is hot enough to curl your toes!" —Celeste Bradley,
New York Times bestselling author

"Sizzling, smart, and sophisticated."—Gaelen Foley,
New York Times bestselling author

ISBN 978-1-250-00136-8
50799

COVER ILLUSTRATION BY
JIM GRIFFIN

HAND LETTERING BY
DAVID GATTI

U.S. $7.99
CAN. $9.99

9 781250 001368